A DEAL WITH HER REBEL VIKING

Michelle Styles

MILLS & BOON

First Published in Great Britain 2019
by Mills & Boon, an imprint of HarperCollins*Publishers*
1 London Bridge Street, London, SE1 9GF

© 2019 Michelle Styles

ISBN: 978-0-263-26949-9

MIX
Paper from
responsible sources
FSC® C007454

This book is produced from independently certified FSC™ paper
to ensure responsible forest management.
For more information visit www.harpercollins.co.uk/green.

Printed and bound in Spain
by CPI, Barcelona

Born and raised near San Francisco, California, **Michelle Styles** currently lives near Hadrian's Wall with her husband and a menagerie of pets in an Edwardian bungalow with a large and somewhat overgrown garden. An avid reader, she became hooked on historical romances after discovering Georgette Heyer, Anya Seton and Victoria Holt. Her website is michellestyles.co.uk and she's on Twitter and Facebook.

For my niece Elizabeth

Chapter One

***

Late June AD 873—Manor of Baelle Heale, Forest of Arden, West Mercia, now modern-day Balsall Common, near Birmingham, England

A late-morning heat haze shimmered on the water meadow, where a cloud of blue butterflies rose in the slight breeze. Peace personified. Ansithe, middle daughter of the *ealdorman* Wulfgar, whose manor lands included the meadow, breathed in deeply and made a memory before adjusting the quiver of arrows she'd slung over her back.

The water meadow in bloom with yellow, pink and blue wildflowers had to be one of her favourite places in the whole world. No one bothered her here, or complained that she was weaving a cloth of dreams instead of a woolen one. Her eldest sister's jibe earlier that day about Ansithe's housekeeping standards and how no one decent would want a widow whose weaving threads always tangled rankled. She had run the household capably before Cynehild and her young son had arrived, fleeing the Mycel Haethen or the Great Heathen Horde of Danes' inexorable advance in East Mercia. And she did her best thinking outdoors, always had.

Someone had to work out a way to save their father and Cynehild's beloved husband who had both been taken prisoner. They could be freed, according to the message from the Danish warlord who held them, for a price, gold that they didn't have. He had sent the severed finger of Cynehild's husband to back up his demand. If Ansithe could engineer a way to free them, then maybe her father would understand she was indispensable to the smooth running of the estate and any talk of her entering into a new betrothal would cease. One unhappy marriage was enough for a lifetime.

She withdrew an arrow from her quiver, imagining the tree knot was the commander's head, but the sound of tramping feet made her freeze.

Ansithe retreated to the shade of the great oak which stood at the edge of the meadow. She concentrated on forcing air into her lungs. It would be nothing—a deer if she was lucky, or a wolf if she wasn't.

She turned slightly. Her heart skipped a beat. The Heathen Horde, here in Baelle Heale rather than where they should be—fifty miles to the east in the conquered lands. Openly. And not skulking in the shadows or keeping to Watling Street, the Roman road which ran a few miles from Baelle Heale.

Ansithe flattened herself against the oak and watched their progress as the group of warriors emerged from the woods. They seemed in no hurry and in no mood to conceal themselves.

The lead warrior, a tall blond man with broad shoulders, put his hands on his hips and examined the water meadow as though he owned it. She admired his chiselled cheekbones, and tapered waist for a long heartbeat until she noticed the large sword hanging from his belt alongside the iron helm. Her blood ran cold.

She wanted to scream that it wasn't his land, that the people here were not weak and lily-livered like the Eastern Mercians, giving in without a fight, but managed to choke the words back.

Shouting at a warrior was likely to get her killed. Despite the sentiment her older sister had recently voiced about her reckless, mannish ways, Ansithe knew she possessed some modicum of self-preservation. She concentrated on keeping still and silently willing the warriors to move on.

The warlord turned his head as if he'd sensed her unspoken defiance, gazed straight towards where she stood and took a half-step towards her, saying something to the others with a slight smile on his lips.

With trembling fingers, she notched her arrow in the bowstring and muttered a prayer to all the saints and angels. Just when she thought she would be forced to loose the arrow and fight to her death, a wood pigeon arched up into the sky, launching itself from a branch above her with a loud clap of its wings.

Another man pointed to it, giving a harsh laugh and saying something that Ansithe didn't quite catch. Her warrior nodded, but gave one last searching look at the oak before striding in the direction of the river.

Ansithe lowered her bow and drew further back before his ice-blue eyes spied her again.

She knelt on the ground, grabbed a handful of dirt and raised it.

'I will defend this land or die,' she vowed.

The manor-house yard appeared unnaturally still in the late afternoon shadows when Moir

Mimirson entered it, following in the wake of his younger charge and his four companions.

A rundown air clung to the once substantial hall. The barns needed fixing and the stone walls had tumbled down in three places. Even though this area of Mercia had not witnessed a battle, Moir was willing to wager that the war had irrevocably altered this place, taking the able-bodied to fight and leaving only the weak, infirm and the women to defend it. Easy pickings for a raid, but such a thing would be a violation of the treaty his *jaarl* sought to sign with the Mercians.

The sheer stillness of the place made his skin prickle, just as it did before a battle was due to start. Instinctively his hand went to the amber bead he wore about his neck, the one which had belonged to his mother. Before any battle, he touched it and remembered his final vow to her—to be better than his father. Always.

'There's nothing here,' Moir called in a low voice. 'They have departed. I can't even spy a hen or a pig for supper. We should move on, discover the way to Watling Street and return to your father—something which would have been easier if you had not tangled with our guide and made him abandon us.'

His wayward charge halted. His face contorted as it always did when Bjartr was forbidden anything. 'Why was it my fault that the guide ran off? Or that we got lost trying to discover where he'd gone?'

'Men tend to dislike having swords held at their throat when they quite rightly suggest that looting and raiding is not what one does when trying to negotiate a peace treaty.'

Bjartr's mouth turned down in a petulant pout. 'You should have stopped him. You are supposed to be my steward. And you should have provided us with proper food. My belly is rumbling. My father, your sworn *jaarl*, assigned you this task. Or are you like your father—given to disloyalty?'

Moir struggled to control his temper. Bjartr had not been alive when the tragedy with his parents had occurred. Bjartr's recollection bore passing little to the truth of why Moir had been sent on this fool's errand of a mission and was now having to play nursemaid to a group of barely blooded warriors rather than providing protection for his *jaarl* at the delicate negotiations with the Mercians and the other warlords.

'I swear I heard bells earlier and that means an abbey,' another warrior said, winking broadly at Moir. 'There is always gold for the taking at a place like that. Here? Even the chickens have flown.'

'Asking for hospitality remains the custom in the North. I suspect they follow similar customs here.' Moir tried one last time. His sense of looming disaster rather than victory increased with every breath. 'It is why we set out with gifts for those who favoured us. We can still ask for food to ease our starving bellies.'

Was this the meaning of his vision of a Valkyrie earlier? To be wary of this place?

'Instead of being the rock who held the shield wall together, you have become my father's craven hound,' Bjartr jeered. 'My father will be beyond proud when I return laden with gold and hostages—no matter what he told you about keeping the peace.'

Moir firmed his mouth. Any treasure to be found was probably safely buried long ago. Hostages simply caused unforeseen problems. And he was loyal to Bjartr's father, Andvarr, the man who had taken a chance on him a long time ago. 'You think seven warriors are enough for an all-out attack? How are you going to deploy them?'

'Are you coming, Moir?' one of Bjartr's more obnoxious companions called. 'Or does blood run true? Will you be as craven as your father was?'

'No man calls me a coward and lives,' Moir retorted, drawing his sword. 'I challenge you. Here and now.'

'Leave it, Moir,' Bjartr shrieked. 'As leader of

this *felag* I command you. We attack this manor house.'

Without waiting to hear Moir's explanation of why it was a poor idea and why they should instead just ask for help in finding the Roman road, Bjartr charged, screaming his battle cry, and the other younger warriors followed in his wake.

A heavy axe hit the barred doors to the hall. Ansithe's stomach knotted. Twenty arrows in her quiver. Twenty arrows to save her family from the Heathen Horde.

She regarded the various bee skeps, mantraps and other devices scattered at strategic points in the hall. They were all designed to stop the invaders in their tracks.

'Are you ready?' she called to her sisters. Each gave a nod and held up their sealed skeps. On her signal they had agreed to unblock the entrance ways and toss them at the invaders. The bees would do the rest of the work.

Ansithe adjusted her veil, fixed her first arrow and began to count.

The door crashed open and the first warrior blundered in, missing the skep she'd set up at the entrance entirely. Ansithe swore under her breath.

He turned towards her older sister with his

sword raised, ready to cut her throat or worse. She panicked and tossed the skep at him without removing the straw. It fell harmlessly to the floor. The bees remained imprisoned. Disaster loomed.

Ansithe loosed her arrow. It arched and connected with his throat. He stumbled over the skep, releasing the bees from their prison and they began to swarm over him and his companions. Her younger sister removed the entrance block and tossed her skep. It landed at the feet of a warrior and the battle cries soon became shrieks of pain.

Ansithe unleashed her second arrow.

Somewhere, a lone dog began to howl, sounding like one of Hel's when she sucked out the souls of unworthy men. Bjartr's battle cry turned into an agonising scream for help, swiftly followed by the others' cries of anguish. Moir's muscles coiled. He drew his sword and raced around to the back of the building.

He slammed the small back door open, rushing forward with his drawn sword. A precariously balanced basket toppled down on top of him, temporarily blinding him. Sticky honey flowed down his face as he fought to remove it. The sound of angry bees filled his ears swiftly followed by sharp stings.

Bees slithered down his tunic, seeking the warmth and the dark. He flailed about with his arms, trying to remove the skep, to avoid more stings and to fight whatever danger lurked in the darkness. He took a step backwards and tumbled over a log, falling with a crash, letting go of his sword as he fell.

Before he could remove the skep, someone stamped on his sword arm, and grabbed his axe from his belt. He pulled the skep from his head. The sound of angry buzzing in his ears was almost unbearable.

'Stay completely still, Dane, if you want to live,' a woman's clear precise voice said, cutting through the incessant buzzing of the bees. 'You are our prisoners. Surrender.'

Ansithe concentrated on the warrior before her and not on her rapidly dwindling supply of arrows. Unlike the others who had burst into the hall through the front doors, this warrior did not cower when the skep had hit him, but instead seemed impervious to the bee stings. Her younger sister's quick thinking had relieved him of his sword and axe, but he remained the most dangerous.

Her heart thundered and her fingers trembled on the bow. Any mistake and this fragile victory would vanish like a puff of smoke.

She pulled back further on the bowstring and

tried to get the right angle for her shot. 'Surrender, Dane.'

'I am no Dane, but a Northman!'

Ansithe wet her lips and started to count to ten. The action steadied her. 'Whoever you are, you have no choice.'

'I beg to differ. There is always a choice.' The warrior heaved the skep away from him and towards her. Ansithe jumped to one side. It landed with a thump and rolled harmlessly away, but he dodged the arrow she loosened.

She frantically snatched another arrow out of her quiver and set it to the bow. Five arrows remained from the originally twenty.

'You missed,' Ansithe said, fixing her gaze on the final skep balanced on the rafter just over him. She breathed easier. She had a better target than his throat. 'Do not make me angry.'

'Should I fear your anger?'

'Yes.' Ansithe restarted her counting and tried to steady her arm. She had one chance to get the ransom money she required and this warrior was not going to take it from her. 'Surrender and I will endeavour to keep you and your companions alive.'

'I've heard that lie before.'

'The truth.'

Moir rubbed an arm across his eyes, clearing the bees and the honey from his sight. The bee stings were sheer agony, far worse in ways than a sword cut. He groaned. His throw of the skep had fallen far short of his intended target. And his charges remained in danger. A lone woman with dark auburn hair faced him, seemingly oblivious to the angry bees flying around, with a quivering arrow notched in her bow. The air seemed tinged with magic and enchantment. Could she truly bend bees to her will?

Moir squinted in the gloom. His adversary wore some sort of netting over her face, obscuring her features and making his shot difficult. No witchcraft, but foresight. She was a formidable, if an unconventional, foe, but human.

Someone else would have plotted this plan of attack. Some man must have tracked their movements. Saxon, particularly Mercian, women were unskilled in the arts of war. The back of his neck tensed. Had Guthmann Bloodaxe, a leading Danish *jaarl* and his sworn enemy, discovered him? He dismissed the notion as pure fancy.

'Where are your warriors? I will speak with them. Arrange terms,' he offered.

She gave a contemptuous wave of her hand. 'I have no need of warriors. See, I conquered your comrades.'

His fingers inched towards where his dagger lay concealed in his boot. He hated harming a woman, but she'd left him no choice. His duty was to keep Bjartr alive and return him to his father. If there were no warriors here, then he could still win.

'Don't make me kill you. Remain alive.'

He inwardly smiled. This would-be Valkyrie didn't have the stomach for killing. Her bravado was smoke and mirrors like the soothsayer had used back when he was a young boy. He breathed easier.

He palmed the dagger, and took a step forward, towards her. He could end this fight and provide Bjartr with a victory. Then they could return to the camp and he could finally gain his promised lands. All he had to do was reach the Valkyrie, wrestle that bow from her hands, then...

An arrow whizzed past his left ear, so close it ruffled his hair and landed with a thud in the back wall, knocking another bee skep to the floor which rolled to come to rest against his shin.

'Ha—you missed.' He gave the skep a contemptuous kick.

'I beg to differ. I would keep still and drop that knife if I were you.'

Bees crawled up his legs, getting into his boots and the bare skin under his trousers. Several landed on his wrist, stinging him fiercely, making it difficult to hang on to the dagger. He tossed the knife, but it landed to the right of the Valkyrie.

'Quite an amusing game we are playing, isn't it?' she remarked. 'My turn again? Or are you willing to accept defeat?'

A bitter laugh escaped his throat. The Valkyrie was a better shot than he had imagined. And her planning had been exceptional. She'd known precisely where the arrow would land. A worthy foe indeed.

She jerked her head towards a bulky shape on the ground. 'You don't want to end up like that one. Do you still consider I need warriors to hide behind?'

A corpse with an arrow protruding from its throat lay on the floor a few feet from him. Moir whispered a prayer to the gods that it was not Bjartr. He'd given his oath to Bjartr's father to protect him and, unlike Moir's father, Moir kept such oaths. 'You have convinced me. A woman like you has no need of warriors to guide her hand.'

'Sense from a heathen. Will wonders never cease?' She muttered something else, something he failed to catch.

'Who?' he asked in a hoarse whisper towards the jumble of bodies when the silence except for the buzzing of the bees became oppressive. 'Who died? Can anyone tell me?'

Bjartr called out the man's name from where he lay somewhere to Moir's right. Moir breathed easier. Bjartr remained alive. He could still keep his promise to Andvarr.

The dead man was the one who had consistently undermined Moir's counsel and had encouraged Bjartr in his more reckless acts, the one who had called Moir a coward earlier.

'Drop all your remaining weapons.' The Valkyrie's ice-cold voice echoed around the hall. 'You have more. I can see them.'

Moir pulled his eating knife from his belt and dropped it to the floor. 'Will you kill us in cold blood? You have already captured all of us.'

'You have surrendered. That is possibly enough for now.' She nodded.

At her signal, someone brought in a smouldering torch. The light cast shadows over the tapestries which lined the walls.

He groaned. They were surrounded by a group of women, old men and young boys armed with swords, sticks and bows, not warriors. They all wore some sort of netting or thin cloth over their faces. One of the boys gathered up the discarded weapons. The torch was tossed on the fire, creating a thick smoke to subdue the bees.

He sank to the ground and tried to plan a way to escape. He might have surrendered for now, but not for ever. He would return his *jaarl*'s only son safe and sound. In doing so, he would finally erase the stain from his family's name and regain the honour his father had casually thrown away.

'You are our prisoners,' the woman with the auburn hair said and her voice echoed ominously above the buzzing. 'Keep your hands where I can see them, ready for binding. Unless you would prefer an early date of reckoning with your heathen gods like your friend here.' She gestured to a couple of the boys, who came towards them with lengths of rope.

Moir and the others did as she asked.

'Who is the leader here?' she called out. 'I will parley with him and him alone.'

'I… I…' Bjartr's face was streaked with tears. He cradled his arm as if it were broken. He made no move to resist the ropes which were being placed around his wrists. 'Moir Mimirson speaks for us, Lady Valkyrie.'

'Do you intend on killing us eventually?' Moir pressed, grinding his teeth. And he would remind Bjartr of his words later. Bjartr had issued his last command. Moir had no intention of releasing the responsibility Bjartr had ceded to him lightly. 'Or merely torturing us?'

'Interesting question.' Her teeth shone white in the light. 'I shall have to ponder it.'

'Answer now,' he insisted. 'We deserve to know our fate. What are you going to do to us?'

The woman tilted her head to one side as if she was listening for something. Satisfied the bees were calm, she removed the cloth from her face. Her features were strong but regular. There was something in the way her jaw was set. If the Mercian army had had warriors like her, the Great Horde would never have won any land.

'At the moment you and your companions have some worth to me—alive.' Her lips curved in a predatory smile. 'I have, however, been known to change my mind.'

'Who are you? My friend swears you belong to the handmaidens of Odin, the ones who pluck worthy warriors from the battlefields.'

Shocked laughter from her helpers rippled around the room.

The Valkyrie moved her chin upwards in a gesture of defiance. Her eyes were almost catlike and an unusual greenish-brown. She might not be conventionally pretty, but she was striking, the sort of a woman who would haunt a man's passionate dreams if he were given to dreaming.

'Ansithe, second daughter of Wulfgar, the *ealdorman* of Baelle Heale manor where you have trespassed. And you are, Dane?'

'Moir, son of Mimir. We are from the North country, not from Denmark, Lady Ansithe.'

There was no need to explain about Bjartr or his parentage, not until Moir was certain he could keep his foolish charge safe. Far worse enemies than the Mercian woman who stood before them lurked, waiting to pounce. This woman clearly sought to keep them alive…for now.

'What are your plans for us?' he asked, trying to wipe the remaining bees from his face with his shoulder. 'Can you share them in more detail?'

She coughed, pointedly. 'We intend to trade you to the commander of the Danes, Guthmann Ulfson.'

The helpers who had bound them stamped their feet in approval.

Moir's heart sunk. Guthmann Ulfson, better known and feared as Guthmann Bloodaxe. After Moir's interference in Guthmann's 'sport with the ladies' as he termed it, Guthmann had demanded Moir's head. Bjartr's father, Moir's overlord, had sought to diffuse the situation by sending him to act as steward to his only child as he toured the lands of Mercia to find the correct spot for the hall Andvarr planned to build, predicting Guthmann would have forgotten about their altercation by the time Moir returned. Privately, Moir had his doubts that Guthmann would forget the fierce slash to his face any time soon.

If he was going to get Andvarr's son back unscathed, he was going to have to disappoint this Valkyrie made flesh. There would be no meeting with Guthmann Bloodaxe. No prisoner exchange. No wholesale torture followed by an agonisingly slow death.

He willed Bjartr to keep his fool mouth shut about his importance as a hostage. If this woman considered them unimportant to Guthmann, matters would be far easier.

'What do you think you will get in return for us? What can this Dane, this Guthmann, give you?' he asked, feigning ignorance of his arch-enemy. 'Danes dislike parting with gold for no good reason.'

'My father. My sister's husband. They are being held hostage by him.'

A knife twisted in Moir's gut. His fabled luck had finally run out. The Valkyrie had every reason to trade them to the Danish commander and Guthmann had every reason to end their lives or at least torture them until they were little better than dead men walking. Moir's promise to Andvarr that he'd ensure his son became a leader was little more than a hollow boast.

He should have listened to his instinct, rather than permitting a few jibes about his courage and relationship to his *jaarl* to goad him into inaction. He should have forced Bjartr to relinquish the command of the *felag* to him days ago when the guide vanished and they'd become lost in the woods.

He clenched his fists and the ropes dug into his wrist. He could not undo the past, no matter how much he might wish to. He had learnt that lesson well years ago.

'Are you certain you will get them back?'

Her eyes flashed green fire. 'For a sum, they have been promised. Word arrived two days ago.'

Moir concentrated on keeping his face carefully blank. He pitied her father and brother-in-law. Few emerged from Guthmann's care intact. But that was not his concern.

'Are you truly that naïve? Guthmann will eat you alive.'

Chapter Two

❦

Ansithe struggled to keep her bow steady.

Even with honey dripping down his face, the tall warlord was far too handsome and confident for her liking. It was as if he expected to get his way simply by speaking in that deep rich voice. Maybe women melted before him, but not her. The Danish warlord eat her alive? She had stopped listening to tales told around the hearth years ago.

'Issuing orders already, Northman? From where I stand, I have an arrow trained at your throat and you have what? Your silver tongue?'

'I use what I can.'

'I can think of other uses for your tongue.'

His mouth quirked upwards into a half-smile. 'Can you, Valkyrie? I generally like to know a woman for longer before putting my tongue to alternative uses, but for you I am prepared to make an exception.'

Ansithe's cheeks heated at his heavy-lidded glance. There was no mistaking his double meaning. And he was doing it deliberately to make her squirm. She knew what she looked like in this old gown which she'd chosen for the freedom of movement it gave her rather than because it enhanced any of her meagre charms. 'I am warning you, Northman. I am not in the mood to banter.'

'Pity. We could have fun.' He made an expansive gesture with his arm. 'Put your bow away. The Danes will not pay any gold for our corpses.'

'Why do you fear Guthmann Bloodaxe?' Ansithe asked, keeping her bow steady and the arrow still trained at his throat.

'I don't fear him any more than I fear you.'

She kept her face impassive. The man was trying to save his skin. But she'd spotted his startled reaction to Guthmann's name. Good. It meant she might get more for him from the *jaarl*. 'I'm pleased you have sense enough to fear me.'

In the faint light, she slowly counted again. Six men alive and one dead. Despite her older sister Cynehild's warnings of total disaster, she had managed to best them, even though she had had to destroy most of her beehives to do it.

She had done more than just drive them off; she had captured them all. None had escaped to raise the alarm with any waiting band of marauding warriors. How many warriors had accomplished such a feat? Her father would surely have to admit that she was as good as any son when he returned.

'You have achieved a victory, true,' he said in a gentle voice as if he were soothing a fractious horse. 'But victories have a way of slipping through fingers and vanishing to nothing if proper precautions are not taken. This is doubly true in this case when the inexperienced lead.'

'You lie. The victory is mine and will remain such until the end of time. You are my prisoners to do with as I will,' Ansithe said in a voice that carried to all parts of the hall.

'Only as long as we remain under your control and alive.'

Her temper rose. Was this man implying that she was less than honourable? It would be a Northern trick to slaughter prisoners, not a Mercian one. 'I will keep you alive to exchange for my father and brother-in-law. I give you my word.'

'You are personally acquainted with the Danish commander, then?' he asked. 'Do you know what he is like? How many men he has killed? How many women?'

'I have not had the misfortune to meet him.' A prickle ran down her back. She had heard the whispers about how he'd emptied villages and abused women. But she had to believe he'd treat her father and brother-in-law like the valuable prisoners they were…except he had already sent Leofwine's finger back to them, adorned with his signet ring. Cynehild had taken it very badly. 'However, Guthmann Bloodaxe must know Mercians do not part with gold for corpses either.'

'Guthmann is an untrustworthy snake,' the Northman said patiently. 'He will cheat you and then he will punish you for being arrogant. You don't want that, Lady… Ansithe.' His mouth twisted. 'I have seen what he does to women and the pleasure he takes in his sport.'

There was something in his voice which gave her pause. If Guthmann's reputation was far from savoury in the North, it was not her concern. 'Tell me something new.'

'Guthmann doesn't expect you to raise the ransom,' the Northman continued. 'He seeks to use your failure as an excuse to attack you and gain these lands. You will not recover your father by sending my men to him. You will lose everything when you seek to parley with him.'

Ansithe drew herself up to her full height and met his ice-blue gaze without permitting her own to blink. 'That is my decision to make, not yours, Northman who speaks my language better than I'd have credited.'

'Other ways exist, other opportunities to do

what you want without endangering all you hold dear. Listen to me. Trust me.' His voice lowered to a whisper, one which made her think of soft fur piled high and velvet darkness. His gaze lingered on her body. 'You are not naturally a warrior. Mercian women, particularly women as stunning as you, are not trained in the arts of war. You are used as prizes to be won. I've learnt that much in my time on this fair island.'

She ground her teeth. As if flattery could make her change her mind. She knew her defects. No one would ever think her stunning. 'I'm not most women.'

'Something we can agree on. I have never encountered a Mercian woman like you before.'

Never encountered a woman like her before.

She knew that damning phrase from her father. Normally said with a curl of his lip after she had done something he found particularly trying. Ansithe concentrated on the rushes and filled her lungs with air, trying to rid herself of the familiar sense of complete inadequacy.

Everything had worked out beautifully. Even Cynehild, who had watched from the shadows, was going to have to admit that Ansithe had accomplished something beyond all imagining and prediction. She was the heroine. Finally, she was the saviour of her family instead of the near destroyer.

The knots in her stomach eased. 'You have little idea what I am.'

'Perhaps I should like to learn.'

His gaze raked her form again, but this time she remembered her height, gangly arms and less-than-well-endowed chest. She'd spent years waiting for the luscious curves her sisters and mother enjoyed to appear, but they remained conspicuous by their absence. Then, one day, she'd decided that they should not matter. Curves would not help her scrub floors, keep bees or do any of the myriad other tasks she needed to do after her mother's death. She would be practical and capable, instead of waiting to be rescued by some handsome kind-hearted warrior.

'I know what is best for my family, for my people, for these lands,' she said and concentrated on standing erect. 'I defended them well today.'

'Don't be too proud to consider alternatives— that was one of the first lessons my *jaarl* taught me,' the Northman continued in that soft persuasive voice of his. 'Ways which will be more beneficial to you and these lands are available.'

Ansithe curled her fists and ignored his rich tones. 'Six Northern warriors must surely equal two Mercians. And I am sure he will take some interest in you. You know his name.'

'It is possible to know a name and not know

the person,' he continued with a faint smile playing on his lips. 'What is going to stop him from simply attacking your estates? He will see you are a company of women rather than trained warriors capable of a fight.'

'I presume you are trained, and yet we defeated you.'

The Northern warlord winced. He slowly looked around the hall, in search of more malleable prey. 'Do you make the final decision?'

Ansithe kept her gaze away from Cynehild and her disapproving frown. No doubt her younger sister, Elene, also watched the exchange with round eyes from her vantage point. 'From where I stand, I have earned that right.'

'Then I will have to try harder to persuade you that you are making a mistake, before you compound your error and lose everything while gaining little.' Moir's mouth quirked upwards as if he was anticipating the task of persuading her. 'I come from the North. I do not bow to the Danish King. Return us to the Northmen. You will get a better price for us if you deal with *jaarls* from the North than the Danes.'

'But Guthmann holds my family. All I care about is their freedom.'

The annoying man gave a pointed cough. 'The *jaarl* Andvarr comes from the North. Send word to him. Send me.'

Send him? As if he'd return. He would leave his men behind and free himself. He had not led from the front, but had entered after the battle had begun.

Giving in to her anger, she marched up to him and put the point of her arrow against his throat. Although she was tall, she still only reached his nose. 'What would you have me do? Let you go on the whisper of a promise?'

He did not even flinch, but stared at her with those icy eyes of his, which seemed to peer deep down in her soul and ferret out all her secrets. 'It would be a start. I give my word to return. I do not abandon my men.'

The man's insolence took her breath away. He had lost. She'd won. Now he expected her to simply let him and his men walk away as if nothing had happened.

'Forgive me if I distrust your word.'

'A pity. My suggestion is the best way out of this impasse.'

'Stop trying me. If you continue to badger me, I will simply shoot you and stop your mouth that way.'

His amused laugh rang out. 'There are other ways to stop mouths, Valkyrie. More pleasurable ways for the both of us, particularly if they involve tongues.'

Ansithe stared at him in astonishment. The

infuriating man was flirting with her. Flirting when she had just made him a prisoner and threatened to kill him. As if she was some feather-brained woman who would melt after receiving a little masculine praise.

'Ansithe.' Cynehild's voice resounded in the hall. 'The Northman knows he is our prisoner. Do not undo the good work you have done today by losing your temper and shooting the leader. And, Northman, cease your twisting of words, or else my sister will shoot you. She killed one of your men today. Don't make it two.'

The Northman glanced between Ansithe and her sister. His mouth became a thin white line. 'I take your advice, Lady, and will speak no more of it.'

Ansithe reluctantly lowered her bow and collected her wits. As much as she would have liked to despatch the arrogant Northman, she had to keep her mind on the ultimate prize—the safe return of her father and brother-in-law.

She signalled to Owain the Plough to escort the prisoners to the byre and to keep a watch over them. The lad practically grew three inches as he ordered the stable lads and the swineherd about.

'A pleasure to encounter you, Lady Valkyrie.' Moir looked her up and down, making her aware of how much her filthy gown with its new tears revealed of her limbs. Her hands itched to straighten her skirts and scrub the soot marks from her face. His slow smile transformed him. 'I look forward to our next meeting with eager anticipation.'

Ansithe deliberately turned away. His insolent look was designed to make her uncomfortable. Her grandmother had told her often enough that it was a good thing she was clever because she'd never be pretty. And Eadweard, her late husband, had confirmed it on his deathbed—he'd married her for her skill at household management and dower lands, and not for her appearance.

'I look forward to seeing my father's face again.'

Ansithe stood by the door of the makeshift prison, the tumbled-down byre where they kept cows in the winter, carrying a tallow lamp, bandages and ignoring the great crows of doubt fluttering in her stomach.

She'd changed into her new dark blue woollen gown, fastening the woven belt shot with gold that Eadweard had given her the only Eastertide they had shared. It was an ensemble which proclaimed her status as a daughter of an *ealdorman*, rather than some raggedy beggar who could be cajoled into letting the prisoners go free for the price of a kiss.

Father Oswald, the priest, had reached for his rosary beads and flatly refused to tend to the heathens, claiming they had murdered far too many of his brothers when she confronted him with the situation. Ansithe wanted to ask if it was a very Christian thing to do—refusing to treat the wounded. But for now, she would do what she could and worry about enlisting his help later. Honey, not vinegar, would have to be used if she needed it. Any hint of a raised voice from her always made him click his beads louder and mutter audible prayers for forbearance.

'We treat them with honour, Elene. As the byre is secure, we can loosen their bonds, tend their wounds and ensure they are adequately fed. We keep them alive until we can trade them for Father and Leofwine,' Ansithe said before Elene refused to enter the byre. She drew a deep breath. 'We treat them like we hope Father is being treated.'

The words were said more to settle Elene than because she believed it. A man who was willing to sever a finger was more than capable of doing far worse to his hostages. Ansithe straightened her back. Then they had to be better than him.

'Father will be well, won't he?' Elene asked, clinging tighter to the loaves of bread she carried. 'We will get him back, I mean.'

'I am doing everything in my power to get

him back and if that means tending these men to the best of my ability, I will do it.'

Elene's face paled even further. For a breath, Ansithe feared her sister would faint, but she rallied. Her fingers clenched white around the loaves. 'I understand, Ansithe. We pretend they are honourable men like we know Father to be. I wish I were as brave as you.'

'Not brave,' Ansithe whispered and peered into the gloom of the byre where the Northmen sat with their ankles and hands bound. 'Too scared of the consequences if I fail.'

A few of the warriors groaned, cradling vicious-looking bee stings. The warlord she'd clashed with earlier, Moir, looked up from where he sat next to the warrior whose leg had been caught in the wild-boar trap. His eyes blazed cold fury before he concealed his feelings beneath a bland smile.

At Ansithe's gesture, Elene put the bread down and backed away. Several of the men fell on the loaves like starving animals, ripping it apart with their teeth. Moir and the warrior with the injured leg remained where they were seated.

Ansithe lifted her tallow lamp. The light made strange shifting shadows on the stone walls of the byre and highlighted the chiselled planes of Moir's face.

Moir put his hand to his eyes, shielding them

against the light from her lamp. 'Why have you come here? To gloat? We are defeated men and cannot harm you or your people. Grant us dignity if nothing else, Lady Valkyrie.'

'The name is Lady Ansithe.'

'The question remains the same whatever the name used.'

His voice held more than a hint of tiredness. He appeared far older than this morning when she had seen him trampling on the edge of the water meadow. With an effort, he rose and positioned himself so that he was a barrier in front of his cowering men as if he wanted to protect them from more pain or hurt.

'You have wounded. They need attending to and you obviously require food,' she said, using the sort of voice she'd used when she had had to cajole her late husband into taking the medicine he'd usually just rejected.

'You are the main cause of the wounds.'

'Guthmann will not release my father and brother-in-law if I bring him corpses.' Ansithe gave a tight smile as she remembered the uncomfortable conversation she'd had with Cynehild about it. 'One should treat prisoners with honour and respect. That is the Mercian way.' She lifted the lamp higher. The shadows danced on the walls. 'We are not animals or torturers.

We leave murdering in cold blood to the Heathen Horde.'

'Not only beautiful, but with a kind and generous heart. Truly a formidable combination.'

'Luckily I don't have to worry about other people's opinions.' Ansithe forced a laugh. Knowing her flaws and limitations had saved her when she first married. Several of her husband's retainers had started paying her extravagant compliments and waylaying her in corridors. Later she'd learnt that they had acted at her stepson's instigation as he'd wanted to show his father how untrustworthy she was. 'Yours or anyone else's.'

He gave a crooked smile, softening the hard planes of his face. He was the sort of man who would have maidens stammering and blushing if he as much as glanced in their direction. She blinked and concentrated. He was her captive and the means by which she'd free her father.

'You dislike me speaking the truth. I wonder why you seek refuge in denying it,' he said with a lilting laugh in his voice. His accent, while distinctive, was not hard on her ears.

She gave a ticking noise in the back of her throat and made a show of looking over the prisoners, making a great sweeping motion with her lamp. 'Your days of preying on innocent Mercians are over. That is a truth we can both agree on.'

His eyes became piercing slits of ice. 'Have I ever preyed on innocents?'

'What do you call what happened today? A friendly gesture?'

'I went to save my comrades. They were starving as you can see.'

There was something in his voice which made her pause. He had come in last, after the fighting was nearly done. To save his comrades or ensure that they succeeded in their attack?

'My home was attacked without warning. You claim leadership of the very warband who attacked it. And we Mercians have a reputation of giving hospitality towards strangers, but a ferocity towards those who would harm us.'

She firmed her mouth. It was something she needed to remember, instead of being lulled into doing something she'd regret by the silky soft sound of his voice.

'Release us from the ropes which bind us.' He held up his hands. 'I pledge my word. We surrendered. We will not attack you again. What more do you require besides my word? My word is a sacred oath. Why would I wish to break that?'

'The word of a pagan warrior is reliable? I learn something new each day.' She forced a smile and ignored the sweat dripping down her back. Could Northmen smell fear like wolves could? 'I have yet to see any reason why I should trust a Northman.'

'Not just any man, but me.'

'Ansithe,' Elene whispered. 'Maybe he speaks the truth. You never waited to hear what they wanted. You simply fired your arrows.'

'There, you see, your sister speaks the truth.'

Again, the smile to make silly women melt combined with the intimate note in his voice which caused a warm pulse to go down the back of her spine.

'The man I shot knocked down the door with an axe and attacked my sister.'

'And he was punished for it. But I am not that man. I did not break down your door, even though I, too, was starving.'

Ansithe tapped her foot on the ground. 'I'd sooner trust a hungry bear.'

'I didn't lead the raid,' he said in a voice which barely carried. 'And I counselled against it. My men now see the wisdom of obeying me and heeding my warnings.'

'Do you deny you lead this warband?'

'I lead it now.' He gave the cowering wretches a hard stare. 'I will lead it until we all are free. All of us, not just a favoured few.'

A sudden thrill of understanding went through her—Moir had seized power in the aftermath of the raid. And his words were directed at his men as much as at her.

'It is the present which concerns me, not reliving a past battle.' She knew that the reliving would happen when she closed her eyes and had to make the same choices again and again.

'Spoken like a true warrior, Valkyrie. Keep your mind in the present, so the past ceases to haunt you. It is what I try to do.'

Ansithe frowned. The infuriating warrior was far too perceptive. Whatever he wanted, he was not going to get it from her. Instead, he would learn an important lesson, a lesson to last a lifetime—Mercian women were strong and capable, not weak-willed creatures who could be easily fooled into permitting captives to escape.

'Ansithe,' Elene murmured. 'The golden-haired lad, the one younger than me, hasn't touched any bread. And it looks as though he might have been crying.'

'Pathetic considering the damage he has caused.'

'Will you have a look at him? His face is distorted something terrible.'

Ansithe knelt beside the youth. Elene had spoken true. His face was grossly swollen from the bee stings. Angry welts circled his throat like a collar.

Ansithe put her wrist against his forehead. It

was far hotter than it should have been, but it seemed to be coming from the stings rather than a more worrying fever.

She wished she could just leave him to his well-deserved agony from the bee stings, but she might need everyone healthy to ensure their value was equal to the ransom demanded for her father and Leofwine.

The youth, boy really, was dressed in fine wool with new leather boots. Everything about him screamed privilege and wealth. Given the state of his clothes, he was bound to command a higher fee. She sighed, rocked back on her heels and reached for the pot of Father Oswald's special paste.

Ansithe daubed the paste on the angriest of the welts. He winced, but allowed her to do it. She loosened the ropes and removed them from his wrists.

'That takes the pain away. More,' he whispered. His mouth turned up in a lopsided smile.

'Do you make demands here?'

The youth's cheeks flushed. 'Hard to talk. Please, pretty lady, heal me.'

Ansithe rolled her eyes. Everyone was obviously primed to make positive remarks about her appearance as if that would make her treat them differently. 'Then keep your mouth shut and save your breath for living.'

He gave a ghost of a laugh. 'You sound like Moir.'

She glanced towards where the large North warrior glowered at her and hurriedly back at the lad. 'I am nothing like him.'

'Even still.' He struggled to close his swollen eyelids. 'Should never have...'

'I agree with you—you should never have attacked us here. We were at peace. Your leaders are supposedly in talks with my King.'

He gave an indistinct groan which could have been an acceptance of the mistake he'd made.

'Are you hurting him, Valkyrie?' Moir asked in an abrupt voice. 'Can you not resist the temptation to torture us despite your earlier words about honour?'

Ansithe tucked a strand of hair behind her ear and gritted her teeth. 'He has many stings to his face and throat. These can sometimes be dangerous if they are not properly seen to. I've seen people die from such things.'

'You want to save his life, so you can throw it away again?' Moir's voice curled about her insides, making her thrum. 'Seems a waste of effort to me. Why not allow him to die with dignity?'

Her hands stilled. His words filled her with a nagging sense of disquiet. The Northman spoke a sort of truth—what precisely was gained in saving his life? Was she condemning him to face something worse? She pushed the thought away. Once she had delivered them to Guthmann and rescued her family, these men were no longer her responsibility, but until then she kept them alive. 'I gather you want him to live.'

'With dignity, not as a broken husk begging for death.'

'Get some cool cloths and more of the paste from Father Oswald,' Ansithe told Elene who stood wringing her hands and doing less than nothing. 'I will stay with him until you return. I am in no danger even with their hands unbound. Owain the Plough is looking for an excuse to practise with his bow. At this range, even he would be hard-pressed to miss.'

Elene nodded and scurried out of the room. Ansithe concentrated on examining the youth, rather than considering that she was alone with these fearsome Northmen, particularly Moir who watched her with an intent expression.

She left the youth as she could do no more until Elene returned. The grizzled warrior with the mangled leg appeared in the greatest need. She went over and knelt by his side. The leg was badly torn, but appeared unbroken.

'Will he live?' Moir asked, coming to stand close to her and making her aware of the strength he possessed in his bulging arm muscles.

'The bone remains whole and that is a start.' She rapidly rinsed the wound to keep the infection out and then packed it with honey-soaked bandages. It would have to do until she could convince Father Oswald to investigate the wound further. He was not an unkind man, just understandably wary. And he did have the reputation of saving many souls in his infirmary.

'Let me know the worst. Please. He is my friend. We have campaigned together for many years.'

Ansithe rocked back on her heels and looked up at Moir. His face was shadowed with concern. A seriousness had settled about him that had not been there when she first entered the byre.

'He'll live as long as the wound stays clean and uninfected.'

'You mouth fables to please children. Does he stand a chance? Will he keep his leg?'

'It is beyond my skill to decide who lives or dies. If he worsens or if you spot red streaks above the bandages, call for me. Someone will fetch me.' She dug half-moon shapes into her palms. If that happened, she'd force Father Oswald to assist. He'd cured Owain's father of infection after the plough broke his leg three years ago. 'Hopefully the next time, he will learn that barging into someone's house uninvited is not a good thing to do.'

'We are grateful that you are willing to bind wounds.' He nodded towards where the remains of the bread lay. 'And for the food. I don't know the last time we had our bellies full—before we left camp, probably.'

She assessed the warrior from under her lashes. The warrior was taller than her, but not overbearingly tall, and without an inch of spare flesh on his lean frame. A true warrior, rather than just playing at it like her stepson had been. Or a man more comfortable with his music than his sword as Leofwine was. Luck and the angels had truly been with her to be able to defeat him so easily.

'Someone has to.' She rose up from her crouched position.

'Still I am grateful.' He went over to the remaining loaf, broke it and took some to the youth and the injured warrior.

'Why break with Mercian custom instead of asking for bread and drink like any traveller?' she asked and instantly regretted it. She didn't want to know if they bore a grudge against her father or what their motive was. It should be enough that they'd attacked her and endangered her family, but she couldn't help wondering why. Curiosity—her biggest failing according to her late husband.

'Me personally? Or the group of us?'

'The group. You must have had a guide who knew Mercian customs.'

'The guide left us a week or so ago, after a disagreement with…with my bee-stung friend.' Moir rubbed the back of his neck. He winced. 'I cannot defend that choice. You will have to ask another, but I will say this—the one who pressed for the raid died today.'

Ansithe pressed her hands together to keep them from trembling. She'd killed the man who had brought this misfortune to her family, her true enemy.

Before she could reply, Elene bustled in, carrying a small jar.

'Cynehild says that you are to use as little as possible,' Elene proclaimed, holding the foul-smelling ointment out. 'We do not have many jars left. And Father Oswald refuses to speak to anyone. He is at prayer.'

'Since when have I ever taken any notice of Cynehild and her warnings? I will use what is required.'

Ansithe set to work, pointedly ignoring Moir and his penetrating gaze. Rudimentary healing like bandaging wounds or putting healing ointments on was well within her capabilities, but she had no real feel for it, not the way Father Oswald or Elene did. Most of the time it bored her. She lost count of the times she had wanted to shake Eadweard and tell him to stop despairing at each setback. She never had, but each time she had thought it, guilt rose in her because she believed she should be better than to resent people who were ill. So she renewed her promises and tried harder, but it never made it any easier. The resentment still clawed at her throat.

In the end, she'd sobbed when he died, not from grief, but from the relief of knowing that she'd never have to go back into that room and face his complaints again. She'd hated herself then and knew the insults her stepson had spouted about her were well-deserved.

Ansithe noticed Moir waited until everyone else was attended to, refusing Elene's offer of help.

'Are you suffering from the stings or are you miraculously immune to pain?' she asked. The welts on his face were large. 'My sister could have examined you.'

'No disrespect to your sister, but I prefer the Lady Valkyrie herself to give me her attention. However, it will take more than a few bee stings to harm my toughened hide.' He coughed. 'My pride is the most injured thing I have.'

'Losing to a woman.' She blew a breath out. 'I see where that might be tricky.'

'You were a worthy opponent. Never allow any to say differently.' He flexed his bee-stung fingers. 'My failure to convince the others it was a trap will haunt me for a long time. I'm no barely blooded warrior, but one who has campaigned for more than ten seasons. Your yard was far too quiet.'

She froze at the candid answer. Even though she'd sensed it, it gave her a shiver down her spine to realise exactly how experienced and dangerous a warrior he really was. But it didn't matter—he was the one she had to ensure understood that there would be no escaping, no easy way out. These men were going to provide the means to free her family.

'Keep an eye on your charges. Should they worsen, let the guard know and I will return to do what I can.'

Moir caught her hand in his as she was about to sweep past. His grip was firm, but warm. It was the sort of hand which made women feel safe. Ansithe stared at it for a heartbeat too long. 'Change your mind, Lady Ansithe. Change your course before you doom us all. Send word to my *jaarl*. Make the journey with me. What good is healing my friends if you only send us to die?'

She rapidly withdrew her hand. There was nothing safe about a Northman. He was her enemy. He had wanted her dead or, worse, a captive. He could never be her friend, let alone her ally. 'It is not pity, but practical necessity which drives me. You will be someone else's problem soon. I can give no guarantees for their behaviour.'

His soft mocking laughter followed her out of the byre. 'I look forward to our next encounter, Lady Ansithe the Valkyrie.'

Chapter Three

Moir flexed his stiff fingers and tried to get the blood back into them now that the ropes which had bound him were gone—a most unexpected gesture.

He stared up at the stars, faintly gleaming through the holes in the thatched roof while one hand curled about his mother's bead. *Be better than your father.* This was his chance to prove he could be better than a man whose main priority was to save his own misbegotten skin.

There had to be a way of convincing Lady Ansithe not to send word to Guthmann in the morning. Once he'd done that, then he'd stall things as best he could until everyone had recovered. He was not going to be his father and desert his injured men in their hour of need. They all escaped together. And he would ensure they all arrived back safely.

'My father will have me rot. This was my

final chance, Moir. I made a mess of it, listening to the wrong people,' Bjartr whispered, interrupting Moir's thoughts about when and how they could escape. He relaxed his hold on the bead. 'I would be better dead than facing my future.'

'Concentrate on breathing,' Moir said, rather than explaining that if they fell into Guthmann's clutches, he would in reality be better dead. 'Leave me to solve the other problems. I made a promise to your father, Bjartr. I intend to return you safely to him, even if you seem intent on throwing your life away.'

Bjartr's response was a barely audible moan.

Moir stood up and tried to stretch the aching muscles in his legs. Why was it that the aches and pains were far worse after a defeat than a victory?

'I could romance Lady Ansithe,' Bjartr said suddenly into the stillness. 'Women melt when I speak to them. You must have seen them. Last Jul?'

'Hey, Moir,' Palni whispered. 'Perhaps the boy is on to something. Perhaps I should try romancing the Valkyrie. She is the sort to stir the blood.'

'Would that you both looked in a still pond right now,' Moir said with a laugh, but his gut twisted. Neither of them would be romancing

Lady Ansithe. He had the first claim on her. The ferocity of the thought surprised him. Women for him were not something to be fought over. They were to be enjoyed for a brief but agreeable time before parting without regrets or recriminations.

Still his fingers throbbed where he'd touched her. In another life, one where he'd permit himself hopes and dreams, he and the very lovely Valkyrie made flesh might have had an agreeable time together.

He pressed his hands against his thighs. Dreams were for other men, men who hadn't had fathers who abandoned their comrades to die and then lied about it. Men who didn't need to keep proving their loyalty to their commander thanks to the reputation of their father.

He would focus on keeping his men alive and out of Guthmann's murderous clutches. If he achieved it, he would have fully removed his father's taint and fulfilled the vow he'd made on his mother's grave—he would be a better man than his father.

Lady Ansithe was the key to his achieving this—a counter to be used in his very real game of King's Table with Guthmann. 'Leave Lady Ansithe to me and me alone.'

Dawn had not yet arrived, but Ansithe had been unable to sleep for more than a few hours.

Her dreams had been full of buzzing insects, faceless warriors who escaped and someone with broad shoulders and golden hair who fought through everything to save her. She had woken covered in sweat and with a deep abiding sense that something was wrong. In her haste to get away from the blue-eyed Northman, had she forgotten to do something simple like lock the door of the byre? She hurriedly dressed and ran out into the yard.

A steel-grey light illuminated the yard with deep shadows and harsh planes. A rumbling snore resounded. She advanced towards the byre. The swineherd, the lad who had faithfully promised to keep watch over the prisoners, was sound asleep.

'What is this?' she asked putting her hands on her hips. 'Asleep? And here you promised that you could guard.'

The swineherd's eyes blinked open. He rapidly stood. 'My lady! Lady Ansithe!'

'Are they still in there?' she asked, tapping her foot on the ground. 'Or have they vanished in the night because you forgot how to stay awake?'

He tugged at his tunic. 'I haven't heard a sound. Honest. Not even a squeak louder than a hoglet.'

'It is amazing that anyone could hear anything

above that racket.' Moir's languid tones dripped from the byre.

The air rushed out of Ansithe's lungs. Moir. Her prisoners remained captive. Her dream of finding an empty byre and her best chance of proving her worth to her father gone had been nothing more than night-time imaginings.

'They are still here.'

'Where else would we be, Valkyrie?' Moir asked. 'Dining at Odin's table is a privilege saved for those who fall on the battlefield.'

'Are you all alive?'

'You did not make your promise lightly, Valkyrie. Good.' He pointedly coughed. 'We could do with breakfast. Our stomachs pang with hunger.'

'Her name is Lady Ansithe,' the swineherd said, his face contorting to a blotchy colour in the half-light. 'And you should be grateful that she brings you anything, not demanding food!'

'Rest easy. A Valkyrie is a woman warrior,' Moir retorted in a voice which was clearly designed to calm. 'Your lady Ansithe is the very definition of one. I seek to honour her, not mock her. And my men will be grateful for any food. Other than the bread, our bellies have been near enough to empty for many days.'

Honour her? She stared at the wall where

Moir's voice came from. He respected her ability as a warrior. She couldn't help smiling.

'It is all right, I will deal with him. You go and get breakfast before you take care of your normal charges—the pigs,' Ansithe told the swineherd.

'Valkyrie, are you going to answer me?' Moir asked again in a louder voice. 'Why are you here? The cockerel has not yet begun to crow. I thought ladies like you lay in bed until the sun had well risen.'

'You have no idea what women like me do.'

'I've met a few Mercian ladies, simpering giggling nonentities mostly, but none have been warriors until you.'

As if on cue, the cockerel began his morning crow. The sound echoed through the shadowed yard.

'Not so early,' she said, rubbing her hand against the back of her neck. The lock was there, but she hadn't removed the key. She carefully turned it and this time pocketed the key. 'And no one is in danger. Breakfast will happen once the chores are done. Starving you will not do anyone any good.'

'You have a good heart, Lady.'

'You have a glib tongue, Northman. Your compliments fall as easily as rain falling on the fields.'

'I do like a beautiful woman with wit.'

Again, the easy remarks about her beauty. He was flattering her now because he wanted something. She dredged her late husband's words from the depths of her memory—the ones he used to explain to his son why he had no fear of ever being made a cuckold by her—clever, capable but lacking in that certain something which made men's blood hot. It was why she had been the perfect wife for a man who was well past his prime and more in need of a nurse and housekeeper than a wife. She hated the tiny piece of her which still argued her late husband had been wrong about many things.

'Liking has nothing to do with anything.' She glared at the byre wall. Why did he persist in thinking that because she was a woman, she could be flattered and cajoled into doing anything she didn't want to?

His laugh resounded through the wall, rippling through her and reminding her of her dream about the golden-haired warrior. She wondered if his eyes crinkled when he laughed. 'You are the most interesting thing to happen to me in a long while.'

'I am not a thing. I am a person and I had fully intended on ensuring you were fed even before your pathetic attempt at flattery,' she said to the wall and imagined him standing facing her with his ice-blue eyes and a contemptuous expression on his face.

Silence from him. She breathed easier before she dusted down her gown, straightening the pleats. 'Dawn has broken on a new day. I trust it will be a less eventful one than yesterday.'

The yard rang to the sound of horses' hooves before she had gone five yards from the byre.

Ansithe's heart plummeted. Her neighbour, the *ealdorman* Cedric, with several of his warriors in battle dress trotted into the yard. She had sent word that they were under siege before the Northmen arrived, but there had been no offer of help, no explanation, just silence in return. Now this, bristling Mercian warriors ready to save the day, but many hours too late.

She had to wonder if it was deliberate and Cedric had been hoping to find them missing or dead or if he truly was all shiny sword and no action as her late husband had always claimed.

'Lady Ansithe,' Cedric said from his horse after they had exchanged pleasantries. 'I understand you experienced trouble yesterday. I was away hunting, but came as soon as it was practicable.'

Anger rose in her throat. Hunting? All day and night? She forced it back down.

'We did have some trouble, but we managed to cope perfectly well. We do not require your assistance now, Lord Cedric.' She gestured about the still yard. 'As you can see, everything is at peace.'

'A false alarm, then. Monks again? Like when you were a girl and were convinced Mercia was about to be overrun by Danes?' His high-pitched laugh grated. 'You cost your mother's life that day.'

'Not a false alarm, a plea borne of desperation.' Ansithe blew on her nails to show she wasn't intimidated, but the familiar claw of guilt twined about her entrails. Cedric did speak true—her excited warning about enemy Danes approaching who'd turned out to be monks had resulted in her very pregnant mother's death along with her father's much-desired son's. It was why this time she had to finally save the family instead of nearly destroying it. 'But I was wrong about one thing—no help or assistance was required. I…that is…we captured a number of Northern warriors.'

The man's complexion became a little more florid as the first pink rays of dawn appeared. 'You have captured some outlaws, you mean. There are no heathen warriors in Western Mercia, my dear lady Ansithe, whatever this scum may have proclaimed. The peace settlement ensures that.'

'I beg to differ. I have six Northern warriors

in my byre. Father Oswald buried the seventh whom I slew yesterday evening.'

'Whoever they are, I have come to take them off you.' Cedric patted a pouch that hung at his side.

Ansithe raised a brow. Cedric was notoriously tight-pursed and overly concerned about being robbed in the woods. 'You brought gold?'

Cedric drew his top lip over his teeth, making him resemble a startled rabbit. 'It seemed prudent after the rumours I heard.'

She firmed her mouth. 'Really?'

'Someone might have mentioned it.' His lip curled as he gave a withering glance to the byre.

That someone was most probably Ecgbert, the steward. She had longed suspected him of divulging their secrets to Cedric, but her father had refused to listen to any of her suspicions.

'The captured Northern warriors are nothing like outlaws and they fight with the Great Heathen Horde.' She gave a pointed cough. 'One is the son of an important Northern *jaarl*.'

His eyes became narrow slits and she thought naughtily that now he reminded her of a rather florid pig.

'Which *jaarl*? Do you have any proof?'

She opened her eyes wide and pretended that she had not exaggerated slightly. 'Is it necessary for you to know?'

The look Cedric gave her verged on pity. Ansithe took a deliberately steadying breath and hung on to her temper.

'You are far too gullible, my lady. If I might examine their brooches, I could tell in an instant.' Cedric held up the pouch and jangled it. She could tell from the sound that the purse contained some, but not a lot of, gold. 'Many will claim such a thing, my lady. However, you will find they are just miserable outlaws and thieves once you properly investigate the claim. First monks and then outlaws. Whatever next?'

His troop of men obligingly laughed.

Ansithe ground her teeth. Did the man think she was somehow mentally deficient? The swords she'd recovered were far finer than anything her father or brother-in-law possessed. Their axes alone would command a higher price than the gold Cedric currently held in front of her nose. 'I can assure you I know the difference. And they are my prisoners, not to be paraded in front of every fool who comes here proclaiming he knows best.'

He made a tutting noise. 'I meant no offence, my lady. I know from bitter experience that you can be overeager at times and more than willing to believe others' fantasies and fables.'

Ansithe crossed her arms. He made her sound like an impulsive puppy, rather than a grown woman. 'We are quite busy here as you might imagine. These Northern warriors will command a high ransom, once we send word to their *jaarl*.'

'Getting a ransom from a Northman can be worse than getting blood from a stone. I have had experience with this.' His smile increased in smugness as he jangled the tiny purse again. 'Go on. Take it. I would hardly like to think such lovely ladies as yourselves were being troubled with such ruffians. It should go some way towards getting your father released.'

'Unless it goes all the way.' She pushed the meagre purse away with impatient fingers. Cedric was the sort who'd sell his grandmother if he thought it would be worthwhile. 'Guthmann demands a steep price for my father and Leofwine's release and is not prepared to compromise.'

'I risk my men if I were to transport the prisoners to the summer gathering. There must be something in it for me and my men, *my lady*.'

Summer gathering. It was where any prisoners would be exchanged. If she could get the Northmen there herself, she could command a much better price for them. Ansithe clenched her fists. She should have considered it long before now. Her father and Leofwine were even likely to be there. It was the way to keep Guthmann and his men from Baelle Heale. All she had to do was work out a way to get there, without involving Cedric and without enabling any of the prisoners to find an escape route.

'Thank you for the suggestion, but everything is well in hand.'

Cedric's Adam's apple worked up and down. 'I was prepared to help. Out of friendship for Wulfgar, your father.'

'For a price…' Ansithe pasted on a smile. 'You do nothing for free, Lord Cedric. Forgive me if I think your charges are extortionate, but I respectfully decline.'

His florid complexion became that bit more like ox blood. 'Seeing as you are convinced you are capable, I will leave you to it. I hope it works well for you, my lady.'

His tone left her in little doubt that he didn't think it would.

'It will.' She gestured towards the gate. 'I look forward to welcoming you when we have the feast to celebrate my father's return. Unless you wish to take my prisoners by force?'

'That would be a Northman's trick, not mine, Lady Ansithe. I uphold the law.' Cedric turned his horse around and rode out of the yard, swiftly followed by his men.

'I heard everything from the hall. Are you sure you did the right thing? Leofwine needs to be rescued,' Cynehild said in an urgent undertone, coming to stand by her after the last horse departed. Her blonde hair was unbound and she'd wrapped a fur about her body.

'We agreed they were my prisoners and my responsibility,' Ansithe said. 'You've seen their collection of weapons. They are no outlaws, but warriors. Someone will pay gold for the weapons and for them. Far more than Cedric ever would. And his men would be spies, working against us. We'll take them to the summer gathering and sell them there. Father and Leofwine are bound to be there as well. It stands to reason.'

Cynehild thoughtfully regarded the byre. 'Without someone like Cedric's warriors to guard them, how will you be able to get them to the meeting place without them escaping? Owain the Plough is hopeless.'

Ansithe let out an exasperated huff. Cynehild made it seem as though she hadn't spent most of the night trying to work out a plan. 'We don't have to decide that yet, except it won't be Cedric or his warriors.'

Cynehild rolled her eyes. 'Have you ever thought that he might be doing it to impress you? He does want a betrothal with you, Ansithe.'

'It is my dower lands Cedric wants. The income is a decent one.'

'He swore it was you he wanted. People can

grow to care for each other like Leofwine and I did. Seeing his excellent qualities took me until little Wulfgar was born. You should give marriage with a younger man a chance.'

Ansithe stopped listening to the lecture. Cynehild currently possessed an overly romantic heart. Simply because Cynehild had fallen in love with her husband after she gave birth to little Wulfgar did not mean every woman did. Ansithe put her hand on her flat stomach. Not that her womb had ever shown any sign of quickening. Her husband's dying words about her shrivelled womb still hurt. And she could never confess the ache to Cynehild. The last time they had confided in each other was before their mother died.

'I need to guard these prisoners until Owain can relieve me…unless you care to do it.'

Cynehild blanched. 'You need to stop being so like a man, Ansithe. A woman's place is in the home with children about her feet. Think about that while you are guarding those brutes.'

Ansithe sniffed the air. 'Guarding beats burning the porridge.'

The door of the byre swung open, revealing Lady Ansithe carrying a large bowl of porridge. Moir's stomach obligingly rumbled. He had forgotten how good something simple like porridge could smell.

It had gone very quiet after the horses departed and Moir had begun to wonder what was happening. If Lady Ansithe had been persuaded to sell them to the nasal-voiced Mercian warrior after all…

'I have brought you and your men food.'

'It will be most welcome.' He took the bowl from her and passed it to the first of his men who drank some of the gruel before passing it on to the next man. 'Most unexpected, Lady Valkyrie.'

'I am not sure I like that name any more than I did a little while ago.'

'You should. Where I come from it is a high compliment.'

'Have you known other warrior women?'

Unbidden the memory of his mother teaching him how to hold a sword and swing properly rose to the forefront of his mind. 'Yes. My mother's skill with the sword took my breath away. More than equal to any man's.'

'What happened to her?'

Moir banished the unwanted memory. She had been a warrior until she met his father and had believed in his dreams, dreams which ultimately destroyed her. 'Unimportant. That is all in the past. I live in the present.'

'Living in the present sounds like something

which is easier to say than to do.' Lady Ansithe nodded, accepting his words. 'Who are Valkyries, precisely?'

'Odin's handmaidens. Brave and honourable, but fierce battle maidens. They choose the warriors who will grace his table. All men admire them and seek to win their favour.'

'And obtaining a seat at Odin's table is something warriors long for?'

'In my world, a seat at Odin's table is the highest honour any warrior can achieve. For when Ragnarok arrives, Odin's warriors will play their part in saving the world from total destruction.' He frowned. 'It is like achieving entry to heaven from what I know of the Mercian religion.'

'I see.'

'Some women from the North seek to emulate Odin's handmaidens. Yesterday, you achieved that status. A *skald* should compose a saga about your exploit.'

Lady Ansithe dipped her head so all he saw was the crown of auburn braids. 'You seek to flatter rather than to mock. My sister thought this, but I suspect an ulterior motive.'

He gritted his teeth. He left with everyone or not at all. He refused to betray his men like his father had done. Loyalty to the *felag* showed he was a different sort of man.

'I do nothing of the sort,' he said. 'I heard you

speaking to that Mercian, declining to sell us for what you implied was a paltry sum. I appreciate what you did for men you have every reason to hate and fear. We are in your debt. I firmly believe all of us wish we could turn the sands of time backwards. An impossibility, I know, but the desire is there.'

'You heard everything?'

'Enough to know you refused to sell us to a man with a nasal whine. He sounded the sort who will always seek to chisel and chip to get the most profit.'

'My neighbour is notoriously tight-fisted. He would not give me the best price for you. He declared you were outlaws, possibly even wolf-heads, rather than warriors who would command a decent price.'

'But you remain convinced we are who we say we are. Not a worthless band of outcasts fleeing from justice.' He leant his head back against the wall. A start, a glimmer of hope that there might be a way of convincing her to abandon her plan of sending them to Guthmann.

'Can you prove it?'

'Our swords and axes prove that we are who we say are, not some ragtag gang of outlaws.'

'Any man might pick up an abandoned sword and carry it.' Lady Ansithe tapped her fingers together. 'What else?'

'We have our brooches. My *jaarl* knows which ones are ours. More importantly, he knows me. If you'd grant me permission to take—'

Ansithe slammed her fists together. 'You go nowhere on your own until the ransom is paid. Until my father and brother-in-law have been freed.'

'Accompany me to where the two armies meet. My *jaarl* is there. You and I together in the wilderness. Alone together.'

Her tongue came out and wet her lips, turning them to a sunrise pink. The action made him ache to taste them. He ignored the sensation. He required a willing woman in his arms, not a Valkyrie.

'What say you?' he whispered. 'You and I out in the forest with the stars for our roof. The breeze at our back. A wood fire to guard against wolves when we stop.'

'Why…why should I do that?'

'It is the best way if you wish to get the full value for your prisoners. My *jaarl* is at the Mercian court. He will be there for the peace negotiations. It is where we were headed when we became…sidetracked.' He muttered a curse. 'The bee stings addled my brains yesterday. I should have thought of this. Explained it to you properly.'

A sudden great ache to see what was beyond

the Forest of Arden filled Ansithe, making her soul hurt. An adventure, finally. Something to prove she was more than a dried-up husk.

A noise made her turn and peer out into the yard. The assistant swineherd hummed as he returned from his breakfast and the maids poured out the slops. Peaceful people doing everyday things, not warriors or great lords, but people who depended on her.

Going with this Northman anywhere was an impossibility. She had a duty to these people. She had destroyed their certainty once through her thoughtless actions and she refused to do that again. She was no longer an overly excited girl, but a mature widow. She knew her actions always had consequences.

'You seek to spin fantasies to tempt me.'

A smile tugged at his mouth. 'I'd prefer to be in *your* dreams.'

Ansithe pressed her lips together. He could have no idea about her dreams last night. Or that having seen his compassion towards his men, she had started to like him, rather than fearing him. 'I rarely dream.'

She took a step backwards towards the clear blue light of morning instead of the gloom which could be night. Her feet tangled and tumbled over the doorframe and she landed on her bottom.

He reached out and put his strong fingers about hers, pulling her to standing. Their eyes locked. He was so close that she could see the beat of his heart in the hollow of his throat, the faint sprinkling of golden stubble on his jaw and the network of silver scars from previous battles. Her breath caught and she knew she should move away, but her feet appeared rooted to the spot.

'My lady,' the swineherd called, breaking the spell.

'I will leave you to your breakfast,' she said in a voice far too breathless for her liking. She curtsied, then pulled the door to and quickly locked it behind her with shaking hands. Then she whirled and ran as if a demon was chasing her.

Moir's voice floated after her through the door. 'Until we meet again, I will live in hope and anticipation of the day we do, Lady Ansithe.'

Chapter Four

'I have found a way,' Ansithe announced, hurrying into the hall. She had taken a few breaths to allow her heart to stop pounding and she hoped her cheeks were not as red as she feared they might be. She was simply unsettled and flushed with excitement at the prospect of obtaining her family's freedom.

Her sisters remained about the table, finishing their breakfast. Her father's wolfhounds sat under the table, looking hopefully for any scraps that might fall. Cynehild stopped spooning porridge into Wulfgar's mouth and frowned.

'Well, don't you want to hear what it is?' Ansithe asked.

'You are going to apologise to Cedric and accept his offer to take the prisoners?' Cynehild picked up a cloth to wipe the spilled porridge from Wulfgar's face. 'Ansithe, I knew you'd do the right and proper thing once you had time to consider.'

'Cedric was always intent on cheating us out of the full value of the ransom we would receive. I doubt that has changed.'

'You don't know that for sure,' Cynehild said. 'You only suspected. However, I'm willing to listen to your ideas and see if they are feasible. I know what you were like with the weaving rota before I changed it. You thought you had an excellent scheme, but it didn't work. My way was better.'

Ansithe ground her teeth. Cynehild seemed to positively delight in making things more difficult. And ever since her return, she had criticised Ansithe's household management. Never overtly, as that was not Cynehild's way, but she kept coming up with little ideas which she claimed would make things easier for everyone. Sometimes as with the weaving rota, if Ansithe was being honest, the ideas did work.

What Ansithe worried about was—what if Cynehild decided to stay, rather than Leofwine finding fresh lands as she'd promised would happen? Her father would not have any need for Ansithe's services then as he'd always said that Cynehild did things in a similar fashion to their late mother, which he would surely prefer.

'I'm hardly ignorant of the situation,' Ansithe

said when she knew she had her temper under control. 'All the prisoners made it through the night and they have had their gruel for breakfast. But they are not in a fit state to be moved yet. They need to regain their strength.'

'Do you think Guthmann will be doing that to Father and my Leofwine?'

'Let me see.' Ansithe pinched the bridge of her nose and closed her eyes, pretending to concentrate for a long heartbeat. Then she opened them wide. 'No idea, Cynehild. Nor do you.'

'If they escape from you, we will have gone through this for nothing. How are you going to contact Guthmann? Have you considered that?'

'Cynehild,' Elene said before Ansithe gave way to her growing ire. 'Ansithe said she had found a solution. Can we hear it before you find all the reasons it won't work? You thought she'd fail with using the bees as weapons as well.'

Ansithe reached down and gave the wolfhounds a pat while Cynehild did a good imitation of having encountered a particularly nasty odour.

'Of course I will listen, Elene. Our sister *sometimes* does have useful ideas.'

'They are wearing brooches which give a clue to their identity, particularly to their *jaarl*. Cedric mentioned this and Moir Mimirson confirmed it.'

'And?' Cynehild crossed her arms. 'How does that get us any closer to obtaining Leofwine's freedom?'

'The prisoners can't be moved yet without risking their health, but the brooches can go to the summer gathering where the Mercian nobles and the leaders of the Northmen are discussing the treaty. Our new King, once the nobles confirm who he is, can send a guard.'

'Our new King will send guards?'

After the Battle of Ashdown the old Mercian King had fled the country. Part of the gathering was to confirm who would rule in his stead— either a new king or perhaps merely a lord until the King and his family could return. 'Why not? Or we can hire them there, having taken his advice. Sell the prisoners' weapons.'

The silence which punctuated her announcement only ended when Wulfgar grabbed the bowl of porridge from Cynehild's hand and poured it on top of one of the wolfhounds.

'Who is going to look after the prisoners for the time it will take you to get to court, arrange for the guards and return?' Cynehild asked. 'Owain and the stable lads are liable to forget to do something vital and let the men escape.'

Unfortunately, what Cynehild said made a certain amount of sense. After earlier, she could not trust Owain or the swineherd to look after the prisoners properly for any long period. 'A tiny insignificant detail which can be solved later.'

'Not a tiny detail, Ansithe, but an insurmountable obstacle. If the prisoners escape before you return, I will never see my Leofwine again. And I do so want to see him.' Cynehild put her hand over her mouth to stifle a sob.

'You have the wolfhounds as a deterrent,' Ansithe offered.

Cynehild pointed to where they were examining the floor in search of more porridge. 'They'd sooner lick a Northman to death than bite him. It is why you put them in hiding with Ecgbert, Wulfgar and the maids, remember.'

The elder of the two wolfhounds sighed and covered her nose with her paw.

Ansithe made a face. 'The Northmen don't know that and I put the dogs away because they were my last line of defence.'

'You are needed here—not traipsing across the countryside, having an adventure.'

'One of us needs to go. It is the only way to be certain that the brooches are delivered to the right person and we don't get cheated,' Ansithe insisted.

'I refuse to be parted from Wulfgar. He's teething and he is always such a poor traveller.' Cynehild cuddled a squirming Wulfgar closer to her chest. 'You can have no comprehension of what a trial it was when we had to make our way here. This time I would not be able to lean on Leofwine.'

'Are you seriously suggesting that I go on bended knee to Cedric? He wants to cheat us, Cynehild.'

'I will go.' Elene's gentle voice resounded in the hall. 'I can do it. I can take the brooches and the weapons to court.'

'You are too young,' Cynehild snapped. 'I'd no sooner send you than send my baby boy on his own.'

'You need to stop thinking of me as the baby sister. I am older than you and Ansithe both were when you were married.' Elene's mouth became mutinous. 'I should have been married by now with a great estate of my own to manage if not for the war. One never knows whom I might meet if I go to court. Certainly someone far more eligible than the swineherd!'

'What do you want, Elene?'

Elene stuck out her substantial bosom. Surely it had only been a few months ago that Elene was chasing after butterflies in the meadow or making a muddle of her weaving. 'Treat me as though I am a grown woman, instead of a toddler.'

'Your marriage is something that our father

will decide,' Cynehild said, developing a sudden interest in the rushes.

'But I might be able to guide him.'

Ansithe exchanged glances with Cynehild. Elene would soon learn about their father and how he used marriage to further his own power, but she had also been their father's favourite and he might be more inclined to listen to her pleas. Ansithe had had no alternative to Eadweard's offer. She silently renewed her determination that her father would give way and concede her right to decide her own future after he returned. 'If Ecgbert accompanies Elene, I am sure all will be well. It is the perfect solution to our present dilemma.'

Elene's mouth dropped open. 'You agree with me?'

'It saves apologising to Cedric.' Ansithe wrinkled her nose. 'Besides, I can't think of anyone I'd trust more to do it properly. Don't you agree, Cynehild, the insurmountable obstacle has been breached?'

Cynehild shrugged. 'It seems as though you have a very good scheme.'

Elene took Wulfgar and danced about the room.

'I will obtain the brooches,' Ansithe said before Cynehild started issuing orders.

Elene did a twirl which made Wulfgar shout

with laughter. 'Ansithe has won over their leader. He admires her.'

Cynehild grunted.

'It's true—he thinks her beautiful.'

'He respects my archery skill which is different.' Ansithe concentrated on the rushes and hoped her sisters would miss her burning cheeks. However, Elene nudged Cynehild and they both burst out laughing. 'What is wrong with that?'

'Nothing, Ansithe. Your archery skill must indeed be what he admires about you,' Cynehild said drily.

'You two are impossible.' Ansithe retreated from the room with as much dignity as she could muster.

The opportunities to escape were slipping through his fingers as surely as the dirt slipped through the brooch Moir was using as a makeshift shovel. Neither Palni nor Bjartr would be fit enough to climb through the holes in the roof and it was only a matter of time before that Mercian lord returned with an improved offer or, far worse, the Valkyrie sent word to Guthmann. Remaining in this place was no longer an option.

'Can we do it? Release the stones, wriggle through the gap and steal some horses?' Palni went over the gist of the plan in a hoarse whisper. 'I don't know how far I can walk on this leg. It seems to be swelling even more.'

Moir knew the plan had far too many holes, but it was their best hope. 'We will obtain the horses. I heard them snuffling last night. Ideally, we'll find more than three, but if it has to be only one with both you and Bjartr riding while we walk, so be it.'

'How long do we have? It will take at least a day to dig our way out and that is assuming they fail to notice what we are doing.'

'I have to try. I refuse to give up. I refuse to accept any member of this *felag* giving up.'

'You mean like…' Palni jerked his thumb towards where Bjartr lay curled up in a small ball. Bjartr had consumed the lion's share of the gruel this morning and then collapsed down into apathy.

'He's been injured.'

'You are being too soft on him. He needs to grow up, if he wants to lead a *felag* properly.' Palni absently rubbed his bandage. 'Once we are free, how are we going to make our way back to camp? We remain guideless, thanks in no small measure to him.'

'Find Watling Street and follow it.' Moir pushed his brooch in. The pin buckled. He cursed under his breath. He'd been fond of that brooch. 'One step at a time. Freedom first.'

'Without weapons.'

The stone inched forward. Moir smiled. When his Valkyrie came to check on them tomorrow morning, they would be gone. He sympathised with her plight regarding her family, but his first duty was to his men and his *jaarl*.

'Someone comes,' Hafual, who kept watch through a crack in the door, warned.

Moir rapidly rose and refastened his cloak. He moved so that his bulk would block any casual glance into their prison.

The door swung open. The Valkyrie with her hair arranged in a crown of braids stood like an avenging fury. Behind her the sky blackened. He heard the faint rumble of Thor hitting the clouds with his hammer and tossing lightning bolts. He forced his breathing to be steady. She could not know about their scheme.

'Is this a good time for a social call? Thor appears to be losing his temper at Loki over something.'

Her brow knitted in confusion. 'Excuse me?'

'I refer to the thunderstorm—in my world thunder is Thor striking his hammer.'

'Are your men well?'

'They are recovering.' Moir kept his gaze studiously from the stone at the back of the byre. This storm was his best chance to get the escape preparations complete, ready for the time when they could go. And keeping his men together would ensure that, when the opportunity struck, he could take full advantage of it. Bjartr and Palni were recovering, he knew that in his heart. 'If I start fearing for them, I will let you know.'

The thunder rumbled again and still she stood there with a quizzical expression on her face. Moir frowned. 'Is there anything else we can help you with, my lady Valkyrie?'

She held out a slender hand, one which seemed far too fragile to have wielded that bow and arrow with such deadly efficiency. 'I require your brooches.'

'Our brooches?' Moir's mind raced. He had figured they would have more time before Guthmann arrived. Had he miscalculated? Had the Mercian lord returned?

'You stated that they would help prove your identity. You wanted to take them to your *jaarl*.'

He motioned to his men to remain where they were. There was no point in making a break for freedom unless all hope was lost and there was no other way to survive. 'Yes, I wanted to take them myself. My *jaarl* will know them.'

'But your *jaarl* will know them without you being there to tell him?'

Moir clenched his teeth. 'True, but—'

'Either a yes or no.'

'Has the Mercian lord returned, offering you more money for us?'

The Valkyrie blinked twice. 'Cedric? He seeks to exploit the situation to his advantage. He will return soon, but he hasn't so far.'

'Then why the sudden urgency? Has Guthmann sent another messenger?' Moir's brain raced. They could wait until the cover of darkness, then he could carry Palni on his back. The others could support Bjartr. He didn't want to, but it was better than being sheep led to the slaughter. The gods had truly abandoned them.

'I am sending my younger sister and steward to court.' She pressed her hands together, but not before Moir noticed a slight tremor. 'Your weapons and your brooches will prove your identity. Elene can hire guards from the new Mercian King who will then escort you back to court. A prisoner exchange, I believe it is called.'

Moir revised his opinion on their luck. The gods had smiled on them finally. Perhaps Thor with his thunder was signalling his approval. Perhaps his ordeal was about to end and he could finally regain his family's honour, the honour his father had thrown away when he'd abandoned his men all those years ago. He frowned and silenced the hope.

Right now, all he knew was that Lady Ansithe

was a woman who would listen and make up her own mind. 'What swayed you?'

'Guthmann cut off Leofwine's finger when he could have simply taken the ring off it and sent it. He is even likely to say that you are worthless just to be contrary.'

'He could do.'

'I had to consider it. And who my true opponent is.'

He gestured to the men. They unfastened their brooches and dropped them into a pile one by one.

He carefully undid Palni's, wiped the dirt from it and put on the top of the pile, alongside his. She stooped to pick them up.

'And your men? Are they truly improving? I could examine them again.'

'There is little need for you to do so, Lady Ansithe.'

'Suddenly I am a lady and treated with respect instead of being a Valkyrie.' Her hands trembled again as she turned to go. One of the brooches fell and Moir deftly caught it.

'You need to take all of them.' He placed it back in her warm palm. A pulse of recognition and heat raced up his arm, making his breath catch. Up close like this, he could see the light sprinkling of freckles across Lady Ansithe's nose and the way her mouth curved like a bow.

It took every ounce of self-control he possessed not to reach out and touch a freckle.

'That is all,' she said, breaking the spell. He relaxed his arm. 'I presume my sister should mention a specific *jaarl* when she speaks to the King. One other than Guthmann, I mean.'

'The *jaarl* Andvarr is Bjartr's father. Bjartr is his only child.'

Ansithe blinked twice. She had not fully realised how valuable her hostages were. She tightened her grip on the brooches. 'You weren't going to tell me that.'

'I told you when it became necessary.'

She peered around his bulk at the youth who lay curled up on the ground. His clothes were finer as she had noted when she'd attended to him. She wondered that she had not considered it before—the possibility that Moir was escorting someone of standing. His taking charge of the men so late in the day finally made sense. 'His parentage explains many things.'

'Have you heard of my *jaarl*? He is the man responsible for winning the Battle of Ashdown.'

'I thought it was won by a cousin of the Northman's King.'

'Just so. The cousin is my *jaarl*.' He shrugged. 'Guthmann and Andvarr are allies rather than friends. In my experience, Guthmann constantly seeks a way to gain the upper hand, but it will go worse for the Mercians if he is successful.'

Ansithe nodded, understanding what he was saying and why he'd sought until now to keep the boy's identity safe. 'How would he treat you?'

'Me?' The large Northman gave half a smile. 'Guthmann has sworn to kill me. However, if it is a fair fight, I believe I will emerge the victor.'

'Any particular reason why he has taken against you?'

'Moir Mimirson stopped Guthmann and his best warrior from raping a Mercian lady. He "interfered with their fun" as the *jaarl* Guthmann put it. He then refused to make an apology to Guthmann Bloodaxe, Lady Valkyrie,' the man with a mangled leg called out. 'Our *jaarl* considered it best if Moir made himself scarce for a little while.'

Moir glared at the warrior who shrugged. 'The Lady Ansithe did not require the precise detail of my quarrel with Guthmann.'

His friend laughed. 'You simply resent that Andvarr forbade you from formally challenging him as you had planned to do over such a trivial matter.'

'It may have been trivial to you, but not to the woman involved, I assure you.'

'What happened to the woman?' Ansithe asked.

Moir smiled. 'I sent her back to her husband. She went willingly enough.'

'The rumours said that she clung to you and implored you to kiss her,' his friend interjected slyly.

'Believing every rumour is not good for your health, Palni. But the fact remains, she returned to her husband.'

'Do you remember her name, Moir?' Palni teased.

'Her name has no meaning here.' A muscle in Moir's jaw jumped. 'The lady in question was simply in the wrong place at the wrong time. I did what I had to do, what I like to think any decent man would do. And in any fair fight, I stand a chance of winning.'

Ansithe tightened her grip on the brooches. One pricked her palm. A fair fight. Something which he would not have had if she'd sent him to Guthmann. And his words about the woman he'd rescued were a reminder that others found him attractive. 'And what did your wife think of that?'

The others laughed.

'Moir Mimirson is wedded to war, Lady Valkyrie. Always has been. Always will be,' Palni said in a carrying voice. 'It is the way of the world.'

Moir gave the man another stern glance before bowing to her. 'I'm not married, my lady, and have no plans to be.'

She took a step backwards and stumbled slightly. He leant forward, so their breath interlaced. Ansithe was suddenly aware of how long his legs were and the strength of his fingers. She had never seen such fine hands before. She wondered what they would feel like against her skin. She sucked her breath in at the brazenness of her thoughts. He had just confirmed that women panted after him, so much so that one had brazenly asked him to kiss her.

'Trust is the best thing which could happen between us.' The words were whispered with an intensity which made her breath catch.

Her mouth tingled as if he had touched it with his lips. His gaze caught and held hers. Everything went quiet and she seemed to be held in suspension.

She looked down at the flagstones on the floor, aware that her cheeks flamed. He had done it on purpose. He probably took pleasure in making her uncomfortable and off balance.

'Thank you for being cooperative.' Her voice was breathless and higher than normal. She cleared her throat. 'It makes my task easier.'

A dimple tugged at the corner of his mouth, making his countenance become impossibly handsome. 'My pleasure.'

She left with her feet tripping over each other in her haste. The brooches clanked dreadfully and she could feel all their eyes watching her like wolves eyed a deer. Or maybe just like men who'd thought they were doomed to die being offered a chance of life.

'Did you obtain the brooches without a struggle, my lady?' Ecgbert, her father's steward, asked from where he lounged just inside the hall. His weasel-like features were more contorted than ever as he attempted an ingratiating smile.

Ansithe pasted on a smile as fake as his own and shook the raindrops from her cloak. She had already guessed that she'd find him inside. He always seemed to find a reason why going out in a storm was the wrong thing to do, why any repairs to the estate should wait until it passed.

'They are all here. The leader of the Northmen was happy to give them to me.'

Ecgbert pressed both his hands together and made a calculatingly ostentatious bow. 'Perhaps it would be best if Lord Cedric examined them before taking them to court. I have been speaking of this to your sisters. I strongly advise caution in this matter, my lady. I am certain your father would approve.'

Ansithe scowled. There was little doubt in her

mind who had informed Cedric that they had prisoners in the first place. 'Remind me. Whom do you serve?'

The steward blinked several times. 'Your father, my lady.'

'Serving my father means accompanying my sister while she takes these brooches to the Mercian King for the attention of the *jaarl* Andvarr. You will remain with her while she arranges for the guards.'

'And you think this will give your family a better price than from Lord Cedric?'

'For the *jaarl* Andvarr's only child? I would trust and pray so.'

Ecgbert's eyes bulged. 'You captured someone of rank?'

'I hardly need tell a loyal member of this household what a relief it is to hold such an important prisoner and how imperative it is that we keep his identity a secret until the time is right to use it.'

Ecgbert stroked his chin. 'You bring up a point I had failed to consider before.'

'Shall I find someone else to accompany my sister?'

Ecgbert drew in his breath. 'I have always been your father's man, my lady. We will go as swiftly as possible—your sister and I.'

Ansithe heaved a sigh of relief. Ecgbert was

not going to cause any more trouble. And she would succeed in her mission to free her father and her sister's husband. 'Good.'

Chapter Five

Elene made her horse paw the ground, giving a whoop of excitement when she was ready to set out for court. Ecgbert's sour expression showed his views on the trip. He kept muttering dire predictions, including that the Northmen would try to escape while they were away. Instead of berating him about it, even Cynehild laughed, telling him that he was worse than an old woman and to enjoy the adventure.

Ansithe watched them until even the tiny sprays of dust their horses' hooves kicked up had long settled. Neither of them turned back to look at her.

She knew the reasons for her staying behind were solid ones, but it didn't make it any easier to see her younger sister depart on an adventure she would have liked to go on herself. She sighed. Standing there, she knew wishing solved little.

She had to keep busy and ensure the household ran smoothly until her father's inevitable return.

She wanted to see the pride in his face when he finally understood all that she had accomplished. She had to hope that Cynehild did not attempt any more of her so-called improvements during that time or otherwise her father would heap the praise completely on Cynehild and ignore her own contribution. He'd done that often enough after her mother died. She frowned, hating the slightly disloyal thought.

'It is fine, Owain,' she said, going back to the byre after she had gathered her bow and a quiver full of new arrows. 'I will take this watch. You have been here long enough. The cows need tending to.'

'But the Northmen might escape if I don't keep guard. I swear one of the stones at the back moved yesterday—just before the thunderstorm.' Owain tapped the side of his nose in a knowing manner. 'They are up to something, my lady. I can feel it in my water.'

'Owain, be about your business.'

Owain looked as though he wanted to object and say more, but appeared to think better of it and ran off.

She sat down outside the byre, placing her bow and quiver on her lap. The shadows were lengthening, but it would be a good while yet before the sun set. She started to mull over all the things she needed to have done before Elene returned with guards and, if God was kind, her father and brother-in-law.

'Can anyone help us?' Moir's voice resounded urgently through the byre's walls and interrupted her thoughts. 'We need help!'

Her nerves instantly became alert. An escape attempt? Moir knew they had fewer people now that Elene and Ecgbert had left. Her mouth tasted sour. If that were the case, he had another think coming. She placed her hand on her bow and drew an arrow. She nodded towards the other guards. They moved up behind her with their faces in a high state of excitement combined with abject terror at the thought of doing battle once again.

'Is there some trouble?' she called out when all was in readiness.

'Is that you, Lady Valkyrie?' Moir asked. 'Thank the gods. I have been calling for a long time now, but no one answered me.'

Ansithe glanced at the stable lads who looked away and shuffled their feet, muttering about Owain being in charge. Owain had to have heard Moir's pleas for help earlier, but Owain had suffered from selective deafness in the past. She would not put it past him to torment the captives as his brother had died fighting the Heathen Horde, knowing that she would check on the Northmen eventually. She firmed her mouth. Owain would learn a lesson about behaving better. 'No one came for me, but I am here now.'

'Good, then something can be done.'

She heard the relief in his voice.

'Lady Valkyrie…'

She cleared her throat. 'I prefer Lady Ansithe.'

'Not nearly as fitting as Lady Valkyrie. Shall we settle on Kyrie?'

'If you must.'

'But whatever you wish me to call you, I'm pleased you are here. You speak far more sense than most women.'

'Tell me what the problem is, instead of speaking nonsense,' she said forcing her voice to be hard. He thought of her as sensible. It was not a flirtation.

'I require your help. Immediately.'

'Require is a strong word.' She clapped her hands. The stable lads grabbed hoes and a pitchfork.

A great howl of anguish rang out from inside the byre.

Sweat ran down Ansithe's neck. Had she missed something yesterday? Moir had sworn his men were recovering, but she knew from her late husband how quickly infections could strike.

She should have insisted on checking the injured men more thoroughly and then this morning had been given over to getting Elene ready. 'What is your trouble? Who is shouting?'

'It is Palni, my friend whose leg is mangled. He is running a fever and has stopped making sense. Please, I beg you.' There was no mistaking the rising desperation in Moir's voice. 'Is there anything you can do? Or have the Norns truly decreed his thread of life is to be snipped?'

'You should have permitted me to examine him yesterday and all this could have been avoided.'

'I thought he was getting better, honestly I did.'

Ansithe swore under her breath. She put down her bow, undid the lock and opened the door. The men were huddled in the back of the byre while Moir stood over his friend. It was also clear that Owain had neglected to feed them or clean out the byre. He would be doing both very shortly. She knelt beside the warrior and rapidly undid the bandages. The wound was hot to the touch and appeared to be swelling up to the size of a small piglet.

'How long has he been like this?'

'Since before dawn.'

'If you had just let me examine him…'

'I am more concerned with the now than the

past. He mumbles about ships and the wind being far too fierce. He has started shouting and making wild accusations.' Moir's voice became bleak. 'He will die without help, Kyrie. I beg you—save my friend, even if you have to amputate his leg. I…we will be in your debt.'

Ansithe pressed her lips together. Her husband had been the same at the end—making little sense and threatening her with knives. Amputation was an option if everything else failed. Some day they might be able to control such things, but for now the best thing was to cut out the infection and hope it had not gone into the bone. For that she would need Father Oswald. 'Have you seen anyone die of infection?'

'Enough to know the signs. I've been a warrior most of my life. It is far from a pretty end and our seers often make matters worse unlike your priests who can sometimes save a life.'

'Our priest here has saved such lives in the past.' Ansithe nodded towards where another bundle of clothing lay. 'And the other one, your *jaarl*'s son. How does he fare?'

'Bjartr? He is asleep. At long last. His litany of complaints about the hardness of the straw and the stench made sleep a while coming.' The relief in Moir's voice was palpable. There was some mumbling from the others. 'It is Palni I'm worried about even if he would tell me that I am an old woman for doing so. That is if he could speak properly.'

The spoilt *jaarl*'s son was snoring on the ground, but she didn't like his shallow, interrupted breathing.

'Have you tried waking him?'

Moir shrugged. 'I thought it best to let him sleep.'

She shook Bjartr. He mumbled a few words, but refused to rouse.

Ansithe's heart sank. Her husband's final days came roaring back—always asleep and only half-waking to eat broth with great difficulty. This man could be suffering from a reaction to the bee stings as well.

These two men were the difference between getting her father and brother-in-law back alive or dead. Ansithe firmed her jaw. Father Oswald would have to give way. He had to understand how important it was for the entire estate that both these men survive. Refusal on the grounds of solidarity with his brother monks was no longer an option. He had a higher duty to fulfil.

'He needs to be in the infirmary as well.' She glanced again towards where Bjartr lay curled in a ball. 'They both need to be.'

'We can help carry them.' Moir stood up and nodded to his men. 'If you will permit us…

There are enough of us that we can do both at once.'

'That won't be necessary,' she said and dusted her hands against her apron. She called for the stable lad who ran off with her instructions. Within a few heartbeats, six of the farm labourers came in and bundled the men up and carried them out of the byre.

She nodded towards Moir, who watched the proceedings with an inscrutable expression.

'We could have helped,' he said. 'We would have taken more care. They nearly dropped Bjartr and Palni's leg banged against the doorframe...'

Ansithe crossed her arms. 'They will be in safe hands. Father Oswald is an excellent healer. I will send a message when I know more.'

He reached out and grabbed her arm. 'Why didn't he tend them before?'

'Because he refused to do so.' She drew a deep breath. 'He fears you and your kind. Several of his brother priests were brutally murdered when the Great Horde invaded. Now if you will let me go, I must inform Father Oswald why he must act.'

'He knows nothing of me or what I did in the invasion. I fight warriors, not unarmed men.'

'So you have said.' She waited for him to release her, but his grip tightened, firming around her upper arm. 'Moir!'

'Wait. I beg you to wait.'

He spoke in a soothing voice which she couldn't quite catch to his men. Several of the men grumbled and two expressed concern that they would never see their comrades again as everyone knew what Christian priests were like with their blood-drinking rituals.

Ansithe rolled her eyes. It was beyond her capabilities to explain the precise nature of Christianity to these heathens. That was a priest's job. And it was about time Father Oswald behaved more like a priest and less like a blindly prejudiced man. These men were frightened human beings, not feral beasts. But she could do something to ease that fear.

She gave his fingers a pointed look. Slowly he released them. She instinctively put her hand over where he'd held her.

'You may come with me if you like to see that your friends are settled, but your men must remain here under guard. I will see that they are fed.' She wrinkled her nose. 'And fresh bedding is supplied. I can't have anyone else getting sick.'

'That is beyond kind.'

'Not kind. I have seen what can happen when one man gets ill and how that sickness can rapidly spread.' She met his eyes with a refreshing directness. 'One other thing—you must have your hands bound.'

'Willingly.' He held out his scarred arms. 'It is a small price to pay to give my men peace of mind.'

She obtained a length of rope and tied his wrists securely.

He muttered again to his men which she had to strain to catch. The men appeared shocked that he was willingly going with her. Their smiles became genuine when he informed them of the promised food and clean bedding.

'My men listen to me,' he said when they had gone out of the byre and she had issued her orders to the remaining stable hands.

Her feet skittered into each other. 'Are you saying that I should as well?'

'Yes.' He leant towards her. 'I like to think I mean what I say. It saves me from having to remember which lie I have told.'

She ignored the sudden warmth which flooded through her and attempted to breathe normally. Moir must know how he looked with his long golden hair falling over his forehead and his eyes like summer sunshine on the mill pond. He was a man used to taking what he required from willing women, wasn't that what his friend had implied yesterday?

Men did not flirt with her except when they

wanted something from her. She'd learned that lesson a long time ago. And she was pretty sure despite his protestations to the contrary that Moir would lie to her if it meant it gained him an opportunity to escape. She was overtired and missed Elene with a deep ache in her soul as if she might never see her younger sister again. It had made her susceptible to his undeniable charm.

She forced her lips to turn up. 'You must forgive me my scepticism after you raided my home without as much as a preliminary enquiry about hospitality.'

'You are not ready to trust me. I can accept that.' He gave a half-smile. 'One day you will see that we men from the North make better friends than enemies.'

She wrinkled her nose. He seemed not the least put out by her response. He'd anticipated it. 'All of you? You told me not to trust Guthmann.'

'Guthmann is a Dane, not a man from the North country.'

His clear-eyed gaze met hers and seemed to bore down to that inner place in her soul which few ever saw, the one which knew she could try all she wanted with her father, but she could never repair the damage she'd inflicted on his life. She kept her back straight and did not flinch.

She had done nothing to be ashamed of since the day her mother had died.

'I want to earn your trust.' His voice flowed over her the way new honey flows out of crushed combs. 'I swear to you that I rarely break a freely given promise. I have every intention of keeping this one.'

'Why is it so important what I think of you?' she asked through aching lips.

He was silent for a long while. Ansithe was conscious of how her breath filled her lungs—in and out. And the way his blond hair fell to just below his chin. She knew she watched him for too long and far too intently.

'Because it matters to me a great deal,' he said finally breaking the spell. 'That is all the explanation you require.'

Ansithe's heart hammered. 'Is it?'

He gestured with his bound hands. 'Lead the way to the infirmary, I would see my friends. Keep pace with me as I wouldn't like to get lost.'

Getting lost. He meant vanishing before escaping. 'Worry not, there is little danger of you... *getting lost.*'

Father Oswald, the priest, was pacing up and down in front of the infirmary building when Ansithe arrived with Moir. The two ill men lay where the stable hands had abandoned them—

in the dirt. Moir made a disgruntled noise in the back of his throat.

'What is going on here?' Ansithe gestured towards where the men lay. 'I sent these men to be cared for by you, not tossed in the dirt like discarded rags.'

Father Oswald pointed a finger at Ansithe. His body quivered with barely suppressed rage. 'You, you have done this deliberately. You know I don't want these creatures here. They are barely human. I won't have it! I will speak to Lady Cynehild.'

'Shall I call her, or will you?' Ansithe pointed towards the hall. 'Cynehild wants her husband returned safely. The best way to ensure that happens is to keep these two men alive.'

'They are not men, but animals. It must be God's will that they die.' Father Oswald paused dramatically and raised his arms to the heavens. 'Would you fight God, Lady Ansithe?'

'To get my family returned alive, without hesitation.'

'That is blasphemy.'

'They are injured *men*. Use your eyes, man.' Ansithe bit out each word.

'I say they are not men, but beasts.'

'Keep calm, Kyrie.' Moir's breath brushed her ear. 'Losing your temper will simply give him another excuse to refuse. We will all lose. Me.

You. Your family, but most importantly Palni and Bjartr.'

She took a calming breath. Moir was right. There had to be a way of appealing to his vanity. 'I've failed, Father. Despite your teachings, I'm nothing but a miserable sinner.'

The priest shuffled from foot to foot. 'I didn't say that, Lady Ansithe. Your quick thinking saved us.'

'I considered my skill at healing would be enough to heal these men, but it isn't. I should have begged for your advice earlier.' She bowed her head. 'It was wrong of me and I most heartily repent.'

The priest coughed. 'You have a good heart, Lady Ansithe, but you've no real feel for healing.'

Moir went down on his knees and raised his hands in supplication. 'See to my friends even though they do not deserve it. Show that you and your God are merciful.'

The priest crossed himself and began to say the Lord's Prayer as he counted his rosary beads. Moir said it along with him. Father Oswald stopped midway through and stared openmouthed at him.

'How do you know these words?' Ansithe asked before Father Oswald exploded with rage at a pagan warrior saying the sacred prayer.

'I visited Constantinople when I was younger and had occasion to hear them in the great church there. They made an impression.' He smiled and a shaft of sunlight lit his hair. 'Do you think they will help in saving my friends?'

Ansithe turned firmly away from him. 'Help me keep them alive until the ransom is paid, Father.'

'I already have. I gave you the bandages and medicines.' He snapped his fingers. 'It is more than most would do.'

'I lack the skill to do more to help and Elene has gone to court.' Ansithe held out her hands. 'You alone possess the medical knowledge and skill to save these two men. I believe God gave you the skill so that you can heal people.'

'And that one? Why is he here, looking like the very devil himself? Reciting those words in such a voice?'

'He seeks to reassure his men. He will not harm you and he meant no offence. He thought to honour you, not mock you.'

'Honour me?' The priest frowned. 'Perhaps he did, but he makes me uncomfortable.'

'Will the priest do as you ask?' Moir asked, rising from where he'd knelt. 'He speaks too fast for me to understand.'

'Then let me speak.'

His eyes held hers for a long heartbeat. 'I will do as you request.'

'What is happening, Lady Ansithe?' Father Oswald asked.

'He wants to ensure his friends are cared for. He doesn't trust us.' She lowered her voice and spoke in Latin. 'His men are worried you might want to drink their blood. They were not entirely sure you'd try to save their friends, even though I told them again and again how skilled you are. He is their leader and he volunteered to come with me and check. I need them alive, Father. I need to get my father and Leofwine back—also alive.'

The colour drained from Father Oswald's face. 'The very idea! Drink their blood indeed!'

'It is amazing the sort of rumours that circulate.'

Father Oswald glanced once more towards Moir. 'They've never truly known the saving grace of our Lord.'

'They will see him working through you,' Ansithe answered skilfully.

The priest's face became lit with an inner fire. 'Maybe I can make them see the true path to the Light of the World. Maybe this is a test and trial for my personal faith. The heathen does appear to know something. Maybe I can try. The bishop did mention something about preaching to the heathen.'

Ansithe released her breath. The first hurdle was cleared. She'd worry about the consequences to her soul later. 'You're a good man, Father.'

Father Oswald examined both men where they lay and proclaimed that they should make it through if they received proper medical attention, instead of what they had been receiving. Ansithe started to call for the stable hands, but Moir indicated to Ansithe that she should untie his hands, then with Father Oswald's help he picked up his young charge and slung him over his shoulder, carrying him into the infirmary. He returned for his friend with the injured leg. Ansithe marvelled at his strength.

'I will use my skill as the Good Lord intended me to,' Father Oswald declared. 'I will demonstrate Our Lord is far mightier than any of the false gods the heathens worship.'

Moir glanced at him. 'Father, it seemed to me on the way over that the church roof needs to be rethatched. If Lady… Ansithe will permit, my men and I will assist in that task while you see to our companions.'

'Miracles can happen.' Father Oswald wiped his brow with the sleeve of his cassock, fell on his knees and offered up words to the Almighty in thanks that his prayers for a new church roof had been answered.

'Do you think you can save them, priest?' Moir demanded.

The priest stopped in his prayers and glanced up at him. 'I will do my best. They are in God's hands ultimately, but I dislike losing any patient, even heathen ones. Now leave and let me get about God's business while you set about fixing that roof!'

'How did you know about the roof?' she asked Moir quietly as they were leaving the room.

Lights sparkled again deep in his eyes and she wondered that she had ever considered them like ice. 'In my experience, churches always need new roofs.'

'Should anything change, you will be sent for, Northman.' The priest's voice floated after them.

Moir halted on his way towards the door. 'Will Lady Ansithe indulge me in this?'

Ansithe nodded, understanding what he was asking. 'You and your men will be given time to make your goodbyes to your friends should they be beyond saving, but my advice is to trust Father Oswald's judgement.'

Moir grabbed his pendant and felt the smooth amber against his fingers as he left the infirmary. *Duty before pleasure. A better man than his father.* The last words of his mother. They steadied him. He knew what he had to do.

Moir slowed his steps as they made their way back to his prison. He touched her arm, halting their progress.

'What is it now, Northman?' Her hand inched towards her eating knife.

'I owe you a great life debt for standing up to the priest and trying to save my friends. I know the power priests hold in Mercia,' he said quickly before she panicked.

Her hand stilled. 'Nothing special. I like to avoid unnecessary deaths.'

He breathed out. Crisis adverted. He tore his gaze from her.

'Palni and I go back a long way. He is one of my oldest friends. He is only on this expedition because I asked him to come. I have enough blood on my hands without adding his death to the tally.'

He choked back the words, acknowledging that she had taken a chance in examining the men in the byre. Someone else might have considered it an escape attempt and refused to help. He winced as he thought about the loose stone at the base of the back wall. If they had succeeded in escaping, given the state of Palni's leg, something he had not truly appreciated until he saw it in the sunlight, he would have been digging at least one grave before they returned to And-varr. Contrary to his expectation, Ansithe had helped them and had fought with the priest to get the treatment required. She had treated them far better than they deserved.

'We need to get you back to your men, so you can tell them that Father Oswald intends to save lives, rather than drink blood.' She gave a strangled laugh and started walking briskly towards the byre.

If they made it there before he could explain, Moir knew the chance would have slipped through his fingers. 'I promised to re-roof the church. I intend to keep that promise if you will grant me the freedom to do it.'

'It is a big task for one man.'

'Less for four. The men and I will work for our keep,' he said before she dismissed the offer. If they could do this, it solved many problems. 'We will work for our friends who are to be saved. Your buildings and lands cry out for attention. Let us help you get the manor ready for your family's return.'

Ansithe missed a step. Moir instinctively put out a hand to steady her. Her eyes betrayed myriad browns, greens and a few blues. A man could study them for a long while and never discern all the exact shades. After a long heartbeat, she pulled away. 'You will do what?'

'Keeping us locked away will do nothing for you or your lands except cause men to be idle guarding other men who do not need to be guarded. There are urgent things which need to be done on this estate in addition to mending the church roof. More than enough to occupy my men and me until the guards arrive from court.' He listed on his fingers ten items he had noticed during his walk there, starting with the sorry state of the byre's thatched roof and ending with the unsatisfactory condition of the threshing barn.

Her eyes narrowed. 'There are sound reasons why these things haven't been done yet.'

'Little reason for them to be delayed further. Your father will be impressed to see how well you have cared for the land while he was gone if they are done.'

She put a hand to her throat. Something flashed in her eyes, but was quickly masked. 'My father would be proud of me? He rarely is.'

Her voice trembled on the word *proud* as if she suspected that he wouldn't be. Moir frowned. After what she had done and the risks she had taken, her father should be. But it was not his place to become involved in her life. All his muscles tensed. Working was a way to keep his men fit and occupied for when the escape opportunity presented itself—after they had departed with the guards.

'A well-managed manor and lands is always an asset.'

Ansithe chewed her bottom lip, turning it the colour of a summer sunset before a thunderstorm.

He forced his eyes to focus on his prison rather than the curve of her mouth. She was not for him. Ever.

'And this will be how you repay your life debt? Fixing this estate?'

'Yes. You need these jobs completed before your father returns. And you have my pledge that my men and I will not try to escape while we complete the tasks.'

Ansithe made her gaze sweep the yard and see the estate with fresh eyes. Not the cosiness of the place or how well everything fitted together or how beloved it was, but the way there was a gaping hole in the byre's roof and the barn door hung by only one of its hinges and the walls about the sheep pens had fallen into disrepair. Shearing was coming up soon and the woods about the manor desperately needed coppicing or the trees would grow too big to be used.

Extra pairs of hands were needed. It would mean that these men were not just more mouths to feed, but contributing to the prosperity of the manor. It would also mean taking a risk and allowing them to move freely about the estate. Ecgbert would have argued against it and would have enlisted Cynehild's aid in refusing it. But he wasn't here. These prisoners were her responsibility so it was her decision to make.

Ansithe pressed a hand against her stomach and bade the sudden butterflies to be gone. Moir was right—if she could show her father that she was truly capable and the manor had prospered under her leadership, it would be one more reason why she should remain here as the trusted housekeeper, rather than being offered as part of an alliance to some lord her father wanted to cultivate.

'And you will give your pledge not to escape?' She paused and searched her mind for the correct phrase to make him agree to her scheme. 'As a life debt? Something which cannot be broken without dire consequences for your soul.'

He gave short laugh. 'You know more about my culture than you want to admit, Kyrie.'

The nickname and accompanying laugh warmed her down to her toes. She took a steadying breath, trying to ignore the fluttering which had started in the pit of her stomach. She was supposed to be immune from such things. She knew the limitations of her physical charms and rejoiced instead in her practical nature, the strength in her arms which enabled her to pull a bowstring and the way her brain worked. But his look had her wishing that she was somehow wrong and that he could see beyond the purely physical.

'I may not have travelled much, but I have listened.' She fixed him with her gaze. 'Will you swear your oath on penalty of death?'

'I want those men to live. I want all my remaining men to return to our *jaarl*. I want to be able to look him in the eye and say that I did what I vowed to do despite the odds being stacked against me.' He clasped one hand to his chest. 'You willingly have my pledge, Lady Ansithe. My men and I will not try to escape from you.'

Ansithe locked eyes with him. There was a warm spark in the ice blue she'd missed before. It would be so easy to tumble into his gaze. She put a hand to her temple. She had to think sensibly, rather than wishing for impossibilities. Robust common sense had saved her from falling into folly during her marriage and it would save her now. Men were not interested in her, not in that way. 'Why are you so willing to pledge that you won't try to escape?'

His eyes slid away from hers. 'I made a promise a long time ago and I intend to hold to that promise despite the daunting task in front of me.

I keep my men safe. I will do everything in my power to bring them back alive.'

She assessed him from under her lashes. There was more to this promise than he wanted to reveal.

'Do we have a bargain?' he pressed.

She tried to think of all the reasons why this was a bad idea, but right now they seemed trivial, particularly when she looked into his eyes. She held out her hand. 'We have a bargain.'

His fingers gripped hers with a firm but oddly gentle grasp. It was the sort of hand which offered safety, rather than harm. It was the sort of hand a woman could believe in. It bore no semblance to the flabby handshake of her late husband or to Cedric's damp one. He slowly raised her fingers to his mouth. His touch was butterfly light, but it caused a warm curl to develop in the pit of her stomach.

She hurriedly withdrew her fingers as if they were burnt. She had no business comparing him to her husband. At least her short-lived marriage had been advantageous to the family. Her desires were unimportant. Her duty was to her family, particularly after what she had done to them all as a young girl. She was the practical one. 'Do not give me cause to regret this.'

Her voice was far more breathless than she wished. And she knew her cheeks were far too hot. She simply had to hope that he assumed it was from the sun's final rays rather than any attraction to him.

'I am merely pleased you have seen sense, Kyrie.'

She opened her mouth to object to the name again, but burst out laughing instead. 'You are incorrigible.'

'I like it when your eyes sparkle.' A smile tugged at his mouth. 'You like being thought of as a woman to be respected, a warrior.'

Ansithe sobered. How many times had she longed to be the warrior which her father desired, to replace the one who had been so cruelly taken when her mother fell from her horse and lost what would have been her baby brother? 'That is something I can never be. I can never be the son my father desired. My sex precludes it.'

'I will never understand why you Mercians do not permit their women to fight.' The blue in his eyes deepened. 'There again, had the Mercians had archers like you at Ashdown, victory would have come at a far higher cost for us, if it had come at all.'

'Changing custom is beyond me,' she said firmly. She had tried hard to be worthy by helping to protect the estate with her skills, but got more criticism than thanks for it. 'Warrior women do not exist for Mercia. It has always been this way. My cross to bear.'

His slow gaze went from the crown of her head down past her meagre curves to her feet. 'It is not how it is in the North. It is not how it is the world over. There is nothing unnatural about you.'

'We are not friends, Moir,' she said with a crushing firmness that was directed towards him and her own heart. 'You belong to the North and I to Mercia. You are my captive. My only interest in you is the gold you and your men will bring when you are ransomed. My father's welfare must be paramount. And when he returns, I will go back to being what I try to be good at—running this house, rather than being any sort of warrior.'

'Are they worth freeing, your menfolk?'

She wrapped her arms about her middle. Her father—yes, without a question. Her duty demanded it. She could not be responsible for both her parents' deaths. Nor could she be the one to destroy Cynehild's happiness. She had heard Cynehild's whispered prayers and how she longed for her husband to return. Maybe if Leofwine did return, Cynehild would forgive her for her part in their mother's death. But Moir didn't deserve an explanation. He'd never expressed a desire to hear her life story. She was not going to be one of those women who filled the air with noise.

Liar, whispered a little voice, she simply didn't want him to see her as the mother-murdering monster that she was. After her mother died and before she'd married, her father had flung that accusation at her whenever he was in drink.

'My father is a good man. His tenants love him. He tries to do right by his daughters even when it is difficult for him,' she said instead.

There was a certain truth to her words. He had not abandoned her. He had permitted her to return after Eadweard's death when her stepson had demanded she leave because her presence was disruptive. And he had tried to care for her after his fashion, but he simply could not help shuddering every time he saw her.

The dimple again peeked out of the corner of Moir's mouth. 'You are the most intriguing person I've encountered in a long while. And I will fight anyone who says you are less than worthy for being a warrior.'

'We are at the byre.' Ansithe dismissed the fluttering warmth in her stomach. Men flirted with her for reasons which had nothing to do with desire. 'Tell your men about the oath you swore.'

'With pleasure, my lady Valkyrie.'

Chapter Six

'There are Northmen on the church's roof.'

Cynehild hurried into the apiary where Ansithe had retreated after giving more orders to Owain and the others regarding the Northmen.

She'd decided that once her heartbeat was steady, then she'd inform Cynehild about her decision. However, the honeycombs from the destroyed beehives had had to be crushed and left in buckets to drain. Ansithe squinted up at the sun. The entire process had taken longer than she'd considered.

'I know.' Ansithe transferred the last of the combs into the bucket. 'They are repairing it.'

Cynehild's mouth dropped open. 'You knew about this and didn't think to mention it?'

Ansithe set the skep down. 'I haven't seen you to inform you. I assumed you would be supervising the weaving and I'd see you in good time. I became distracted…with everything I had to do here.'

Cynehild's eyes narrowed. 'You set men who tried to kill us loose around the estate and didn't consider it important enough to let me know? Is it any wonder I despair of you and your ability to keep house?'

'I ran it perfectly properly before you returned.'

'People were far too scared of you. They thought you'd put an arrow through them if they dared disobey you.'

Ansithe slammed the skep down, absolutely furious. 'Truly? The first person I ever put an arrow through as you call it was the Northman who attacked you. Before that, I believe people laughed at me for daring to practise my archery or wasn't that what you told me on the morning of the attack?'

Cynehild put her hands over her mouth. 'I don't why I said that. I know you saved my life. You saved Wulfgar's, too. Everyone. Forgive me, Ansithe? My tongue runs away with itself sometimes. I really need your help and didn't know where you were.'

Ansithe concentrated on the skep. A lump formed in her throat. Cynehild hadn't said anything new, but somehow it hurt more. 'I need to get this skep fixed.'

'Ansithe, please. I want us to be friends. I just want to understand what is happening.'

'The only reason they are there is because Father Oswald desires the roof fixed before they make a start on the other jobs which need to be accomplished. We agreed that I was responsible for the prisoners and, in my judgement, this is the best use of them.'

'I never said you weren't responsible for them. It is why I came to find you—to make you take responsibility for what they are doing. They should not be there. They are disruptive and it is unseemly.'

'Out with it, what is wrong?'

'I wanted to pray to St Oswald and St Aidan for Leofwine's safe return.' Cynehild wiped her eyes with the corner of her apron. 'As I always do, every day since we had the news about his capture, but it was far too distracting.'

It was news to Ansithe that Cynehild prayed every day. 'Distracting?'

Cynehild frowned. 'Warn me next time, but first come and see what I mean.'

'I suppose I won't get any peace until I do.' Ansithe washed her hands in a bucket of water and followed her sister.

She stopped in the middle of the yard in front of the church.

Because of the heat of the day, Moir and his

men had stripped off their tunics and were fixing the roof half-naked. Moir's broad shoulders and well-defined chest muscles were particularly notable.

Ansithe's mouth went dry. Her hand tingled from the memory of his lips brushing her palm.

She became aware that Cynehild had continued speaking to her and had looked at her as if she required an answer.

'I see what you mean about the distraction,' she said, taking a deep breath and hoping her answer made sense.

'Yes, the noise. You can hear it from here. It makes my head spin.'

Ansithe tore her gaze from Moir's torso. 'The noise?'

'Yes, the noise. What did you think I meant? I can't hear myself pray.'

Ansithe licked her dry lips. 'The noise. Yes. I will see what I can do about it.'

'See that you do. I don't want anyone to say that I didn't do everything to get my Leofwine back.'

Ansithe covered Cynehild's hand with hers. She had not realised that Cynehild was that concerned about what people might think of her. 'No one who truly cares about you and whose opinion is worth caring about would say that.'

Cynehild smiled gratefully.

Ansithe went over to the church and called up to Moir. He immediately clambered down. Close up, the network of silver scarring which marred his gold-tinted chest was clearly visible, a reminder of what he was. And he wore an amber bead on a leather thong about his neck which moved with each breath he took.

'It is not nearly as bad as I first feared,' he said. 'It will take only a day or two at most, provided you have thatch and new poles for the roof.'

Ansithe fixed her gaze away from his chest. 'Father Oswald will be pleased. He complains of the rain dripping down his collar when he says the mass.'

'I hope he keeps his end of the bargain and does his best for my friends.'

'You are distracting my sister from her devotions. The noise.'

His dimple flashed. 'We will do the remainder tomorrow.'

He shouted up to his men who pulled on their tunics and clambered down.

'Would it be possible to bathe? I spied a lake from the roof.'

Her mind immediately conjured an image of him rising naked from the water of the fish pond and she swallowed hard. 'Bathe?'

'We've been working hard. Bathing revives

the spirit and the lake will do, rather than a sweating hut.'

'We don't possess a sweating hut as you call it and have no need of one either.'

He lifted a brow. 'Pity, but then maybe one day I can have the pleasure of showing you why these huts add so much to your life.'

'I will have the stable lads accompany you.'

His eyes danced as if he knew about her wild imaginings and fully approved. 'My men will appreciate it, this little bit of freedom you give us.'

She turned abruptly on her heel and marched away. If she had as little to do with him as possible, then this unsettled feeling would surely vanish like dew did before the summer sun.

Moir wiped the sweat from his brow, straddled the roof and considered his morning's handiwork. The church roof had been harder to repair than he'd predicted to Ansithe, but the final bit of thatch was now in place. Most of the others had worked hard as well but one, Hafual, a warrior who had encouraged Bjartr in his bad habits, kept finding reasons why they needed another pole or he had to go and find more thatch. Moir had the uneasy sense that Hafual failed to understand that they had to remain together as a *felag* rather than each man looking out for him-self. Moir pressed his lips together.

'Has anyone seen Haful? He is taking too long with the straw for the thatching.'

The remaining two did not meet his eyes and suddenly became busy with tying in the last few bundles of thatch.

'Tell me that he hasn't done something stupid.'

Again came the shrugs. The throbbing at Moir's temples increased. They knew what was going on. If Hafual went missing, they would be straight back in the byre again. His oath to Lady Ansithe would mean nothing. He clenched his fist. He wanted it to mean something to her.

'When did you last see him?'

'Right before we went up on the roof,' the other men chorused. 'He wanted to check on the poles as he thought we might need another few. He didn't like the look of the last two poles.'

The younger one shifted on his feet.

'Anything else?'

'He mentioned his woman, the one who is about to give birth again.' The older one punched the air. 'Good luck to him, I say, if he has gone.'

Moir ground his teeth. The answer as to why Hafual was not here was far too obvious—he'd succumbed to the same malady as Moir's father had all those years ago. He wondered what bribe Hafual had offered the others to turn a blind eye and why they had been fool enough to accept. 'I will search for him now and you'd better pray I find him before the Mercians do. Those stable lads are looking for a fight. You saw how they goaded us yesterday at the lake.'

'And us?' the younger one squeaked.

'Keep working. If anyone asks, you are doing what you are supposed to and I have gone to search for more materials.' He banged his fists together and willed them to understand. He'd give Hafual the benefit of the doubt for now, but if he had tried to escape, his actions had endangered every one of them. 'This is not about individuals, but us as a *felag*. We get out of this as a team, instead of one being free while the rest are delivered up for Guthmann's pleasure.'

The men nodded, suddenly realising the seriousness of the situation if Hafual was not found. Moir's mouth tasted bitter. He knew how his father's companions had suffered thanks to his father's actions. His mother had explained it to him as they'd watched his father's body being pecked by crows after his hanging.

He scouted about the yard, trying to think about what he would do if he were not very bright and trying to escape. Even he would not risk moving far in the open daylight. The yard seemed empty and desolate, but there was a muffled shouting coming from somewhere. His body tensed. He forced his arms to stay loose. He was becoming worse than Palni for jumping at shadows.

A queer shuffling and tapping sound made him pause as he was about to leave.

He went over to the pigsty and rapped his knuckles against the pen. 'Come out now, Hafual. It smells better out here.'

'Can't. The door is stuck. I've tried and tried. There weren't no poles in here, even though he said there would be.'

Moir noticed a stick propped up against the door. There was no way that it could have accidentally fallen there. He removed it and tried to ignore the prickle of unease. Someone knew one of the Northmen was in there. That person either wasn't certain or had gone to fetch Ansithe.

'Out now, be quick about it.'

The young warrior emerged covered in dung. 'How did you know I was in there?'

'You breathe too heavily and don't sound like a pig.' Moir replaced the stick. 'And poles are never stored in such places. Who told you they were in there?'

His lower lip stuck out. 'The fair-haired lad. He said I would find what I needed there. And then as I went in, the door swung closed. I thought I were finished for sure.'

Moir raised a brow. 'You weren't trying to escape, then?'

He puffed out his chest. 'My father's cousin was one of the men who died when your father escaped. I would not betray my *felag* in that manner.'

Moir flexed his fingers. 'I'm not my father.'

The other man hung his head, looking closer to Bjartr's age than to Moir's. 'I can see that.'

'If we stick together, we will all get back safely.' He spied a horse trough. He reached out and grabbed Hafual by the collar of his tunic. 'But first you need a bath. We are going to be locked up together tonight and I don't fancy sharing it with the scent of pigs.'

The man protested that he didn't smell that bad, but accepted his dunking.

'What is the problem, Moir? I thought you were fixing roofs, not playing among the pigs.' Ansithe's precise tones rang out over the yard as Hafual emerged, damp but no longer disgusting from the pigsty.

'Problem?' Moir glanced Hafual. 'My man ran into some difficulties when he went for some more poles to complete the roof. He made a mistake.'

'Indeed. I had heard there was trouble at the pigsty.' A light breeze moulded her gown to her body revealing her long, slender legs. She had slung her bow and a quiver full of arrows over her shoulder.

He enjoyed the view for a breath. Then he shook himself. He had no business admiring her figure. Acting on his growing desire towards Lady Ansithe would make matters extremely complicated, but she was someone he was starting to admire and, against his better judgement, like. 'Simply a misunderstanding.'

He willed her to believe it.

'A misunderstanding.' She pursed her lips and nodded. 'I will accept that. See that it doesn't happen again.'

Hafual gulped and agreed, then ran off to join the other men working on the thatching.

'The new thatch is nearly on.' Moir held a cupped hand up to the sky. 'All we need now is some rain to test my prowess.'

'You are hard workers—I'll give you that.' She put her hand on his arm. 'We need to speak. Alone.'

A knot of fear grew in his belly. Ansithe had not come out to admire his handiwork after all. She had another purpose. He motioned to his men to keep working. Hafual's remarks about his cousin dying because of his father's behaviour clawed at his insides. He renewed his vow—he would do better.

He went over to where Ansithe waited. Up

close he noticed the deepening furrow between Ansithe's brows and a slight pinching around her generous mouth.

'Who has died—Palni or Bjartr?' he asked before she had a chance to tell him the bad news. He steeled himself for the news that one or both had died. This trip had been cursed since they'd first stepped out of the camp.

'Father Oswald reports that Bjartr is conscious and eating porridge. His reaction to the bee stings was severe and he probably should never work in an apiary.' She bit her lip.

'And Palni?' His heart thudded. His friend deserved better than to die in a foreign land.

'Father Oswald fears the infection in his leg is spreading, possibly to the bone. One day, maybe we can fight such things, but for now it is in God's hands.'

Moir winced. Infections could take hold very quickly. If it had not progressed too far, the limb could be amputated and the life saved. 'Fears or knows?'

'It has gone beyond thinking,' Ansithe admitted. 'Father Oswald wanted me to find you before the operation to remove the infection, but you were looking for your missing man.'

'Has the operation started?'

'I gave the order, but...'

'May I see him?'

'Father requested peace to carry out the operation.' Her lips turned up. 'I am to keep you contained until it is over. He said to tell you that he has no intention of drinking Palni's or any other man's blood.'

Moir firmed his mouth. 'He judges me far too harshly.'

'He says to tell your men that provided he can cut all the infection out, Palni should survive but it will be Our Lord's will and not our own.'

'He is asking me to trust his God. I hope this God is more reliable than my father's.'

She stood there looking at him. 'And you will tell your men?'

'What is the problem? Are you seriously telling me that Father Oswald delays the operation because he fears my men and me?'

Her mouth turned down. 'Bjartr refuses to allow the operation. He insists we find you first.'

Moir took off at a run and threw open the door to the infirmary. There, Father Oswald cowered in a corner while Bjartr lay over Palni, who appeared pale as death. In his right hand, he had an eating knife.

'I see your health has improved immeasurably, Bjartr.' Moir fought to keep his voice even. 'Good, you can help with the repairs to the estate, instead of lazing in bed.'

'I am saving Palni's life,' Bjartr declared.

'This so-called priest wants to drink his blood for his filthy rite.'

'Nonsense.'

'What did you say?' Bjartr blinked twice.

Moir crossed the room and grabbed the knife from his hand. 'Nonsense, utter and complete nonsense. This priest wants to save Palni's life. If he says that he wants to demonstrate the power of his God, then I will accept it. I want Palni's life saved. Now get off him. That is an order.'

Bjartr scrambled off the bed. 'I am trying to save his life.'

Moir turned towards the priest. 'You and your God can save Palni's life?'

The priest sank down on a stool. 'I make no promises about his leg, but his life, yes, I believe so.'

'Do what you can.'

Moir tossed Bjartr over his shoulder as though he was a sack of grain. 'Let me know when the operation is over and I can see him.'

He carried the loudly squawking Bjartr to the byre and threw him in. At Bjartr's hammering and kicking of the door, Moir reached over and locked it.

The anger flowed out of him and he slumped down by the wall. A noise made him glance up.

'Father Oswald sent me to be with you,' Lady

Ansithe explained. 'He is grateful for what you did and doesn't want you to be alone.'

'Then the runes are cast.' He patted the ground beside him. 'I welcome the distraction.'

She sat down next to him, close enough that if he leant slightly towards her, their bodies would brush. 'Does your friend have a family?'

'A married daughter with a young son and another on the way. They have been estranged for years, but Palni recently mentioned that once things were settled in England, his family would come and join him on new and fertile land.' Moir concentrated on the newly thatched roof. An amputated limb. Palni would not be able to go warring again. And he couldn't tell how much his speaking about retiring to farm was the bravado of an ageing warrior and how much Palni just wanted his daughter there.

'And that won't happen now?'

'That will remain a dream for ever if he loses his leg. Why would a *jaarl* gift land to a man who can't hold it?' Moir banged his fists together. 'I told him a thousand times—don't dream. Actions speak louder than dreams. He will always have a place in my household if his daughter refuses him.'

'Why would she do that? Children have an obligation to honour their parents.'

'Their relationship is complicated.'

'Father Oswald believes he can save the bone. He is very experienced.' She put her hand on his arm. The light touch sent a pulse of warmth through him. A lump grew in his throat. He struggled to remember the last time anyone had touched him out of a need to comfort. His mother, just before she died, probably. 'Once he is healed, he may still have the future he desires.'

'Why did Father Oswald send you out?'

'I'm useless during any operation. I tend to faint. He will send word when it is done.' She gave a small shrug. 'Ironic, really, as my late husband thought I'd be an excellent nurse before we married.'

'Did he marry you so you could be his nurse?'

'One of my duties,' she admitted with a shrug. 'Unfortunately, he objected to my fussing as he called it, but at least I was able to run his household efficiently.'

'Your husband died in your care,' he said, suddenly understanding. 'And you were blamed for it.'

'It was an old wound he'd carried since that war fifteen years before with Wessex. Everyone agreed that except my stepson, but we never got on.' She looped her hands about her knees and stared straight ahead. 'I would not wish that sort of end on anyone.'

She lifted her chin, but her eyes held shadows. He hadn't realised that his Valkyrie was a widow. The thought shocked him. Never before had he thought of a woman as belonging to him or having a claim on him. His father had used the excuse of his duty towards Moir's mother as his reason for abandoning his men. 'Any children?'

Her mouth became pinched and the light fled from her eyes. 'Unfortunately, no. Mine was a marriage based on practicality rather than desire. I returned home as soon as possible. My father took me back because my stepmother had just died in childbirth along with her infant son and he needed me to run the household. He planned on marrying Elene off as soon as he returned from the war.'

'And your stepson?'

'In Wessex with his wife and young daughter.' Her hands pleated and re-pleated her apron. 'I say son, but he was five years older than me.'

'Your father married you to an old man?' Moir's fists curled. Her father had sacrificed his daughter on the marriage altar to achieve his own ends and had clearly been less than enthusiastic at her return. Despite all that, Ansithe endured terrible risks to get her father returned to her. He had to wonder what her father had done to inspire such devotion in her. It had to be more than a simple honouring of her parent.

She lifted her chin. 'Let's keep the boring tale in the past where it belongs.'

'I would like to see Palni as soon as he wakes,' he said, honouring her request to change the subject. What had happened to her was anything but boring. It would explain the paradox between her calm coolness in the face of danger and her evident fear about any attempt on his part at flirting with her.

She briskly dusted her hands on her gown. 'Shall we go now? These sorts of operations last only a short while.'

Moir shouted instructions to his men for the next tasks. They agreed to get them done before nightfall with Hafual shouting the loudest.

Men were better when they had something to do.

It was one of his mother's sayings. He could remember her sweet lavender scent washing over him as she handed him some rope to twist, a simple enough task for a young boy who had lost his father in terrible and shameful circumstances. And she had been right, it had given him some purpose.

'If your men accomplish all the tasks you have given them, this estate will be prospering by the time you leave,' she remarked.

'How long has your steward been with you?'

'Long enough.' She twisted the apron she

wore between her fingers. 'My father is fond of him and will not hear a word against him, particularly not from me.'

'There is much that has been neglected.' He gestured towards where the estate workers lounged, pretending to work but accomplishing little. 'It is not as if you lack the manpower, just the will to ensure everything is accomplished. I assume your steward countered your orders and encouraged the men to go slow.'

Ansithe nodded. 'I will discuss the situation with my father when he returns. Maybe this time he will listen, particularly as I can point to Ecgbert's collusion with Cedric. My father cannot abide disloyalty.'

'You have spoken to him about this before?'

'Several times since I returned to live here.' Her mouth curved into a sad smile.

Moir's brows drew together. 'You father put the steward above his own daughter?'

'Ecgbert can write. There are not many people who can who are not priests. My father requires his servants to act solely in his interests.'

'Once he returns, he will reward you for all you have done.'

'That is the plan. He will see I have value. All this will happen after you leave.'

Moir swallowed his anger. A reminder that the younger sister and the incompetent steward would reach the court in a day or two more at most. Then the King would send a party to take them to meet their destiny.

'Of course,' he murmured. 'It was merely a suggestion. It is hard when one can see ways to improve a farm and can do nothing. It helps to keep my mind from my friend's troubles.'

She put her finger to her mouth, silencing him. 'All seems quiet. Shall I see if Father Oswald is ready for you?'

Moir's feet became heavy. He stared at the closed door to the infirmary. 'It feels as though I have reached a dividing moment in my life,' he confessed. 'The bones have been rolled, but I am not sure I want to see the result.'

'Once you know what has happened, you can act.' She patted his sleeve.

Moir froze as the surge of desire at her touch nearly felled him. Lady Ansithe merely offered comfort, not an invitation to take her to bed. 'What was that for?'

'For luck.' Her cheeks flamed sunset rose. 'Don't worry. I won't do it again. I didn't mean anything by it.'

She turned to go, but her feet skidded into each other. Moir put his hand under her elbow to keep her from falling. She looked up at him with darkly fringed brown-green eyes. He reached out and touched her cheek, soft against the pads of his fingers.

'We can't have you in the infirmary as well. Who would keep order?'

'Nobody expects to fall.'

The words were little more than a whisper. And he knew he should step away from her, yet his feet refused to move.

'No, they don't,' he agreed, watching the way her mouth was shaped. Her tongue flashed out and wet her bottom lip, turning it to the colour of ripe berries, the sort he knew with a glance would be sweet to nibble. 'Most actively try to avoid it.'

Neither of them said anything. His fingers itched to draw her closer. He wanted to touch her lips with his and see if they tasted as good as they looked. She swayed towards him, her mouth softly parted. He groaned and gave in, brushing his lips against hers. His tongue met hers and the kiss deepened. He drank from her lips.

Somewhere a cockerel crowed, breaking the spell. She jumped and hurriedly stepped away from him. It took all his hard-won discipline— won through years of training—to release her and move back. There were so many reasons why it would be a mistake, starting with their exposed position and ending with the fact that he remained her captive. 'Lady Ansithe, I...'

'Go.' She pointed towards the infirmary. 'You were right. You are more than capable of behaving correctly in the infirmary. You don't need me there and, if I am not mistaken, I have a bee swarm to capture. One I spied earlier.'

Without waiting for an answer, she quickened her pace away from him. He watched her backside sway as her green gown rippled about her ankles, revealing their slenderness. He itched to discover the passionate woman who lurked behind her carefully constructed walls.

The apiary with its skeps and hum of busy bees was a place Ansithe always enjoyed being. She carefully tipped the swarm of bees she'd collected from the pigsty into one of the disused skeps.

Although she had lost a few colonies, the rest appeared to have settled back to their routine. She counted the functioning hives. Despite Cynehild's prediction, they would get some honey later in the year and still have five or six hives to overwinter.

'Concentrate,' she muttered. 'The bees know if your mind is elsewhere. It is when accidents happen. That unasked-for kiss should already be forgotten.'

But as she worked, she kept picturing Moir standing there with his body silhouetted against the sun before he went into the infirmary, alone but determined. He had needed comfort. Something had called her deep within, primitive and dark, and so she had touched him. Kissed him. Then realised her mistake.

She straightened the skep, trying to concentrate. She hadn't intended to stumble, but she had managed to keep from totally humiliating herself and demanding his mouth. Heat like a fire had spread through her veins. She'd never known a kiss could be like that—tempting and dangerous. Thrilling, making her long for more. And he'd walked away from her without a backwards glance.

'Nothing is going to happen,' she whispered to the hives. 'I haven't forgotten what I look like. Where my talents lie.'

The hum from the bees increased and it seemed as though they were disagreeing with her words and agreeing with her heart which kept whispering—what did she have to lose? He had wanted to kiss her as well. He might do so again.

Chapter Seven

'Is the operation finished? Does Palni live?'

The priest looked up from where he sat, scratching notes on a piece of vellum. 'You have returned quicker than I would like, but, yes, to both your questions.'

Moir put his head on his hands. Palni lived. 'Thank you and your God. And his leg?'

'Fortunately, the infection had failed to reach the bone. Flesh only, not bone. Understand? Good. But if we had delayed much longer...'

Moir's throat worked up and down. 'You saved his leg. Lady Ansithe said to trust you, but I didn't dare hope. I didn't even think it could be possible.'

Lady Ansithe. The woman he'd just shared a kiss with. He had not intended it to happen. He knew all too well what Palni and the priest would both say about it if they knew. She was the one woman he should not dishonour and he had.

'I am no butcher.' Father Oswald turned back to his writing. 'You may stay with your friend. All things are possible to my God.'

Moir crossed over to where Palni lay, white against the linen. Palni's eyes snapped open.

'How much of my leg have they cut off?' Palni whispered. His hand scrabbled at the bed-clothes. 'I swear by Thor's hammer that I can still feel it throbbing. And I can move my toes.'

'That's because it remains whole. The priest was able to cut out the infection from the flesh without touching the bone. He said it was to show you his God's power,' Moir said, crouching down. He touched his pendant and promised to anyone who might be listening that he'd be a better person now that Palni had been saved.

'His God's power?' Palni groaned. 'I should know not to argue with a priest.'

'Did you have words with him before this?'

'I may have done. Told him if his God saved my life, I'd give up my heathen gods.' Palni's eyes glistened with unshed tears and he raised his voice. 'It appears I was wrong, Father. I am as good as my word. Teach me about this here God of yours.'

'My God's mercy is great.' The priest put down his stylus and looked directly at Moir. Moir shifted uncomfortably. It was as if the priest knew all his faults, including his growing passion for Ansithe. 'He believes in forgiveness. Be better in the future. It is what I say to all who confess and truly wish to repent.'

The deepening colours of the sky never failed to fascinate Moir. The sunset this evening reminded him of the many shades of auburn in Ansithe's hair and how it felt against his fingertips. He knew he had no business thinking about such things or about their kiss. He should be thinking about how to apologise to her and ensure that it did not happen again.

The priest's words earlier clung to his mind. Forgiveness and mercy—two qualities his father's gods did not have. And he had much to do before he could demonstrate that he was worthy.

After leaving the infirmary, he had worked the remainder of the afternoon, hoping to encounter Ansithe and explain about his presumption in kissing her, but she had been conspicuous by her absence. Enemies, he reminded himself. She considered him her enemy. And all he could think about was the taste of her mouth.

'Shouldn't you be in the byre with the others?' Ansithe asked behind him, making him start.

'I like to watch the sunset. It reminds me that I've lived through another day.' He kept his gaze pointedly away from her mouth. Perhaps ignoring what had passed between them was best. He would ensure it did not happen again as it could put his men at risk. 'My man will recover, according to your priest. He thought my faith in him lacking.'

Her smile could have lit several halls. 'It can take some weeks to recover from such operations. If Elene returns before then I will keep him behind until Father Oswald deems him ready for travel.'

'You will do that?' Moir ran his hand through his hair. He understood her immediate unspoken words. Her sister should be at the court by now. Their time here was coming to an end. He doubted he had ever felt as at peace as he did here, watching the sun slowly sink and thinking about nothing more consequential than the precise colour of Ansithe's hair. He reminded himself yet again why touching her would be a bad idea.

'I made a promise and Palni will remain in my care. I've no wish to get on the wrong side of Father Oswald. He can be fierce when it comes to protecting his patients.'

'I will make my men understand that Palni is in safe hands if we must depart before he is ready. They understand I am not my father.'

Her entire body became alert. 'What does your father have to do with this?'

Moir silently cursed. 'A boring story about self-serving betrayal. I learnt from his mistakes.'

'Do you think your *jaarl*'s son will try to lead your men now that he has recovered instead of tolerating you to do it for him?' she asked instead of pressing further.

Moir's neck relaxed. He appreciated her understanding that there were certain areas in his life which he didn't want to talk about. It was possible she fully understood why the kiss they'd shared was best consigned to history. 'All Bjartr has done since I removed him from the infirmary is curl up in a ball and moan.'

'Maybe he is ashamed of how he acted. It can be hard to face people when you know you have let them down.'

'Do you know what it is like?'

Her eyes became haunted and he longed to remove the weary sorrow from them. 'Yes.'

'I believe your priest is right. There is power in forgiveness. I had not thought about it until today.'

'I like to think there is.' She put her hand on his sleeve and he covered it with his. They stood there for a few breaths watching the sun's final glow. The rays turned her skin a lovely rose peach. Then she withdrew her hand.

'Apparently Father Oswald and your friend share a love of King's Table. They have been playing it ever since he woke up. Father Oswald is pleased to discover someone with talent and a modicum of intelligence.' She gave a half-smile. 'Unlike me or my sisters. He says I deliberately lose when I get bored.'

'You don't enjoy playing it?'

'It reminds me far too much of when my late husband was ill. He forced me to play match after match. He took delight in lecturing me about what I was doing wrong.'

Moir nodded. 'I enjoy playing in the winter months. On days like today, it is far better to be outside…'

'A man after my own inclinations,' she said with a laugh. 'Cynehild gets annoyed that I spend so much time outdoors. She believes a lady's place is inside, attending to the weaving first. She told me that I'm becoming as brown as a berry.'

A small spray of freckles sprinkled across Ansithe's nose. He wanted to reach out and taste each one. He clenched his fists and concentrated. It was not going to happen.

'Your sister is too harsh. How else can you ensure the estate is well run?'

'My destiny is to disappoint my father.' She turned away from him.

'Is it important to have a future? To have your life mapped out in front of you as far as you can see?' His voice was as soft as the evening breeze which ruffled her hair.

'It is how my life has always been. I know what is happening when and what is expected of me. Where I have failed. How I will never measure up.'

'Sometimes I think it is more important to grab the present and be part of that instead. The future can take care of itself. It normally does.' He tried for a weak smile. 'Like earlier. With Palni.'

She turned towards him. Her enquiring brown-green eyes seemed far too large for her face. He doubted any woman had ever looked at him in quite that fashion. His easy words died on his tongue.

'Is that why you kissed me, because you were afraid for your friend and needed a distraction?' Ansithe asked, knowing it was now or never for the decision she'd made at the apiary. She needed to know why he'd kissed her earlier.

'Kyrie.' The word was a whispered groan. He held out his hand to her.

Her fingers curled about his. He tugged and she came within the circle of his arm. His mouth hovered a breath from hers.

'Kyrie,' he whispered again. She caught the whisper in her mouth and leant forward to meet him.

At his touch, Ansithe parted her lips eagerly. His arms came about her and pulled her tight against his hard body.

How long they stood there, tongues touching and tangling, she had no idea.

Someone coughed in the byre.

He stepped away. Her body shivered with a series of warm pulses.

'And that is your answer—another kiss?' Her voice sounded husky to her ears.

'Strictly speaking, you kissed me as well.' His eyes became blue flames in the lingering light. 'But as you require an explanation for my kisses—the first one was because you were there, looking like an angel.'

'And the second one?' She worried her bottom lip. 'You must require something else. I am not the sort of women men steal kisses from. Ever.'

'Because you were in the sunset's glow, standing close to me, asking me why I had kissed you. You seemed to doubt that I could desire you. I believe I have successfully demonstrated that to the contrary.' He put out a hand and touched her cheek. Rose-petal soft. 'How else could I convince you that you are a desirable woman?'

She removed her cheek from his warm palm. It was far harder to do than she had imagined. She wanted to turn back to him and touch her mouth to his again and see if his words of desire were the truth or designed to lull her into letting them escape.

'We have no future,' she said bluntly. 'I can't fail my family again.'

The words came out in a rush. She winced. It sounded as though she had expected a marriage proposal or declaration from him.

'I am not asking for for ever, Kyrie. I agree that it is impossible. Neither am I asking for more than you are prepared to give. I know your society views liaisons between men and women differently from mine. I know about the power your priests wield. I am asking only for the now. For whatever you are prepared to give.'

For the now. For whatever she was prepared to give. He did not know how tempting it was— to be held as if she might learn what it was to be cherished. To feel that she was wanted for more than being the person who ensured food was on the table and the bed linen was changed. Not to be the practical one. She sighed. She was the sensible one, the one who saw the problems and found the solutions.

She touched her mouth with her fingers. She felt far more alive from Moir's kisses than she ever had from any of her late husband's pawings. She had dreaded the marriage bed when she had been married. Now her insides felt as though they were made of liquid fire, all from this man, this Northman, a man who should be her enemy, but somehow wasn't.

'I should go.' Her feet stayed rooted to the ground and he was far too close. If she leant forward a little bit, her chest would brush his. Ansithe's mouth went dry at such a wayward thought.

'Then I will apologise. Profusely.' His eyes watched her intently in the owl-light. They were like beacons of pure blue heat. 'It won't happen again, but I need to know—did you like it? Tell the truth, Kyrie.'

'I did like it,' she admitted unable to lie as he started to turn away. 'It is just that…that it is complicated. You are supposed to be my enemy.'

'I don't consider you an enemy. Your actions saved my men's lives. You fed us. You have bound our wounds. You permitted us to retain our dignity by working for our keep.'

She bit her lip. 'My husband married because he needed practical support in running the household. He never desired me.'

'Your late husband was a blind fool if he didn't desire you.'

'Excuse me?' she gasped.

'Not all men's tastes run to curvy blondes with feathers for brains.' His knuckle brushed her cheek. 'I, for one, have become quite partial to flame-haired archers with well-trimmed ankles and eyes to drown in in recent days.'

'You are in the minority.'

'But my preference means something to me.'

She stared at the ground. Why couldn't she be one of those women who could easily share a kiss or flirt with any creature in trousers? Because this was surely what it was—a flirtation to pass the time.

'The sunset is over. Darkness falls. Cynehild will panic if I'm not there.'

Her voice faltered on the exaggeration. Cynehild enjoyed ordering Ansithe about during meal times while she kept Wulfgar on her knee.

A braying noise came from the byre. 'Is someone in distress?'

'Bjartr is probably objecting to something one of the others has said. We will continue *our* conversation another time, preferably when we won't be interrupted.' He leant towards her, but she moved so that his mouth brushed her ear. 'Thank you for the kiss.'

He strode into the byre, shouting for calm. The noise instantly ceased.

Ansithe put her hand to her ear. Kisses from Northmen could only lead to trouble. She had to forget them. And the best remedy for that was more work.

'What do you think you are playing at?' Moir asked Bjartr when he entered the byre. 'Screaming like a fury?'

'Nothing. Nothing at all that you need to be concerned about.' Bjartr gave a huge sigh. 'You were far too busy looking at the sunset to wonder about my health.'

Bjartr sat with his back towards everyone. The cheerfulness at the return of both Hafual and Bjartr had given way to tension crackling in the air as though a storm was about ready to burst. Hafual muttered a comment that Moir didn't quite catch. They were breaths from a serious quarrel, one which could irreparably damage the *felag*. He was going to have to work these men until they had no strength left to do anything except sleep.

'Nothing appears to be something to me.'

'I wanted more food and a soft place to sleep. You should never have taken me from the infirmary. Return me immediately.' Bjartr made an imperious gesture.

Moir scowled fiercely. 'Do you ever think beyond your own selfish desires?'

Bjartr's mouth flew open. 'You dare speak to me like that!'

The pendant swung against Moir's chest, reminding him of his duty to Andvarr. 'Do you understand what being a captive means?' he asked in a quieter voice.

'I want to find the blonde goddess of my dreams, the one who brought the ointment.'

Moir pressed his hands together. 'Elene is a daughter of this house and deserves your respect.'

Bjartr leant forward. 'Where is she, this goddess made flesh? Bring her to me.'

'She has gone to court with our brooches,' Moir replied truthfully. 'When she returns, we go, prisoners of whichever warlord paid the highest price for us. I only hope she took my advice and sought your father out, rather than seeking Guthmann.'

'The goddess is the woman who left. Oh.' Bjartr sat silently for a long time. 'I haven't been well, Moir. It's harder than you might think to be my father's son.'

Moir blinked in surprise to hear the faint note of humility in his voice. Ansithe spoke true. Maybe the lad could learn if he was given a chance.

'You need to remember that we are being treated far better than we could ever hope for. We've worked hard to earn our limited freedoms. I don't intend to jeopardise that now.' He glared at the other men who rapidly examined the straw which served as their bedding.

'My father will ransom me, won't he?'

Moir opted for a version of the truth. 'Most fathers would.'

Bjartr collapsed back on the straw. 'My father can never abide a failure and that is what I am.'

Moir regarded the lad. He was in truth little more than a boy, a boy with a powerful father who alternately praised him, berated him or ignored him in favour of his own ambition.

'I promised your father your safe return and I intend to do that. Trust my methods.'

'I see what you are on about with your little conversations with that fearsome woman.' Bjartr hoisted himself up on his elbow. 'Romance the Valkyrie and then betray her when we escape. That's what I'd do.'

Moir started towards Bjartr. 'Stop your mouth. You know nothing about it.'

'Don't like to hear the truth, do you? Funny that,' Bjartr said snidely. 'There again, your family excel at betraying their comrades. Maybe you intend to betray us as well.'

Moir flinched. Bjartr always seemed to know how to thrust the dagger into his soft underbelly. He thought he had kept his feelings for Ansithe well hidden. He needed to forget what her mouth had tasted like and to concentrate on important matters like keeping up his men's morale. He was not going to become his father and jeopardise the *felag* for a woman. He knew where his loyalty lay. 'I will keep my oath, Bjartr.'

* * *

After being released from the byre by the stable hand in the early dawn, Moir went to find more material for repairing the threshing barn's roof. The sound of the thump of straw hitting the ground surprised him.

In the nearly dark barn, Ansithe was moving great bundles of hay with a fork.

'It's a bit early for that,' he commented, trying to work out why she was out here, rather than tucked up safely in bed. He had thought to keep himself too busy to think, but now his mind teemed with images of Ansithe lying on a fur-covered bed with her auburn hair spilling out over the pillow, her eyes heavy-lidded with passion and wearing nothing but a smile.

'I need more straw for repairing the skeps. I must be prepared to collect more swarms.'

'Did you not want to be in the hall with your sister?'

She pitched another forkful of hay. 'What, doing things a lady should be doing? I prefer to do this. Since my father left with his warriors, it has become a necessity.'

'There are servants remaining to do it. My men and I are here.'

She paused. A wisp of straw was stuck in her hair. Moir itched to reach out and pluck it. He forced his hands to remain at his sides. 'I woke early, checked the animals and saw this needed to be done. I think better when my hands are moving. Owain and the stable lads have been busy guarding you. Between making sure you can bathe, and the byre is guarded at night, there has been little time.'

'I gave you my word we would not try to escape from you.'

'It pays to be cautious.'

'Are the animals sickening?' he asked, trying to discern her true reason for working that hard.

'The pigs remain in the forest and the cows are fattening on the grass. But the heat means it is ripening early.' She wiped a hand across her face. Her gown caught, revealing the contours of her breasts. Moir's mouth went dry. How could anyone think she was unattractive? 'We could do with some rain or otherwise they will eat all the winter feed before winter.'

'The atmosphere is rather heavy. Perhaps there will be another thunderstorm later.'

'Perhaps.' She turned back to her fork. 'If you don't mind, I have work to do and you have barns to repair.'

'One of my men could do this for you,' he pressed.

'It helps me to think,' she said again.

'Or keeps you from thinking? Did your dreams wake you?'

Her cheeks went rosy. 'You might say that. The heat makes sleeping difficult and Wulfgar is teething. Cynehild tries to keep him quiet, but his screams can be piercing. It is just as well that I will never be a mother.'

'It might happen one day.'

'It did not happen with my late husband and I am determined to avoid any future entanglements.'

Moir frowned and fought against the urge to draw her into his arms. She needed to come to him. He had offered her the choice in their physical relationship and he had to abide by her decision. It bothered him that he felt awkward and unsure. She looked at him as if she expected him to go.

'I wanted to speak to you about Bjartr,' he blurted out.

'Your *jaarl*'s son?'

'He fears returning to his father as a failure. I told him that it will make for a good story around the fire at Jul, in the winter. He pretended to listen.' He breathed again. A safe topic—winter.

'Will you winter on this island again or do you return North?'

'Nothing remains for me in the North. My *jaarl* negotiates for land.'

'And he is crucial to a successful outcome?'

'He is my *jaarl*. I trust his word.'

She rolled her eyes heavenwards. 'Will you take land or do you plan to be a warrior for the rest of your life?'

'Some day I want a family, children about my knee.' An unfamiliar ache developed in his chest. He had been alone since his parents died and had never thought it would change, except now the ache was there. This woman had put it there and it frightened him because there was no use longing for things which couldn't be. Ansithe had a life here. People who depended on her. He put his hand against his pendant and remembered his vow. 'But not yet.'

'I see,' Ansithe uttered before she remembered last night. Kneeling beside her bed, she had solemnly vowed to stop confiding in Moir. But before the sun had risen on a new day, she was practically inviting herself to be his wife. They had kissed, twice. No one had seen. She was safe, but she dreaded to think how Cynehild would use that knowledge.

She was supposed to be forgetting that she had enjoyed being in his arms. This was what doing the chores were about—keeping busy with her normal routines. In another breath, she would be throwing herself at his feet and begging him to kiss her again.

Now they were standing in a nearly deserted barn and she was intensely aware of the dream that had woken her, the one which had filled her with an intense longing to be cradled in his arms. Her entire being had thrummed and ached. She longed to feel his mouth against hers again. Hard, fast and engulfing. The work had been supposed to banish the dream.

Now he was here, standing far too close for comfort and looking better than any dream could. And her body ached anew.

'About yesterday,' he said and rubbed his hand against the back of his neck. 'I acted rashly. I don't want anything that happened between us to change things.'

'I, too, have reflected on it and it won't be repeated. We are best forgetting it ever happened.' The words sounded forced to her ears and she knew she said them partly to inform her own heart. Since they had kissed, she had been unable to think of little else. Surely forgetting would become easier as time went on?

'Can you forget?' he said, uncomfortably echoing her thoughts. 'It has preyed on my mind all night—I want to kiss you again, but I will abide by your decision. The last thing I want to do is to hurt you. You saved my friends' lives.'

'You didn't hurt me,' she said around the lump in her throat. 'Someone has to be sensible and I am always sensible. I look for the practicalities in every situation.'

He gave an uncertain nod. 'Then everything is fine.'

'Of course.' She turned back to the stacking of the hay. The rhythm of the task normally soothed her. 'I wonder that you even bring it up.'

He took the fork from her slack hands and placed it down. 'You appear upset. You shouldn't worry. I have never forced myself on a woman. I live for the present, remember. What may or may not happen is not worth worrying about. I value our friendship for as long as it lasts.'

Friends, not lovers. Friends. The word tasted bitter in her mouth. 'We can never be friends, Moir. I believe I made that clear earlier.'

'A pity as I was beginning to think of you as one.'

'Then have another think,' she said tartly.

'Lovers, then?'

She went completely still. She must have misheard. 'What did you say?'

'If you refuse to be my friend, will you consider being my lover?'

She remembered the young warriors her stepson had enticed into trying to steal kisses from her when she was a bride to show his father she was unworthy of him. Several had made improper suggestions like this one, while her stepson stood sniggering behind a post. The knowledge washed over her like a bucket of ice-cold water.

Her heart protested that she should stop because there was no comparison between them and Moir, but she refused to listen.

'This conversation ends now.'

'I beg your pardon. I was merely trying to discover what we were. I know what I'd like us to be.'

Rather than answering, Ansithe gave vent to her frustration by jerking the fork up from the ground, attempting to shovel more hay and having the fork fly out of her hands. It fell to the ground with a clang. She pressed her fingers to her temple and gained control of her temper. She was not sure who she was angrier with, him for attempting to use her or herself for wanting to believe him.

'You attacked my home,' she bit out, staring at the fork. 'There can never be anything between us except the life debt. My father's welfare must come before everything.'

'Why does your father come first?'

'Because I destroyed his life once and this is my opportunity to save it.'

He went over to the fork and held it out her. 'What did you do? I am trying to understand, Kyrie. Help me.'

She wrapped her arms about her waist. If she

touched him, she'd fall into his arms and demand his lips, demand to feel safe again. It was far better that he looked at her in disgust. 'I thought Danes were coming to attack us. We were escaping and my mother in her haste mounted a horse that was too strong for her. It reared up and she fell, heavily pregnant, and broke her neck. My father ordered the baby to be cut from her, but the little boy lived only for an hour. The worse thing was that it was only a group of monks from Wessex who approached, not Danes at all that I saw.'

He did not recoil, but looked at her with concern. 'How old were you?'

She tightened her grip on her waist and tried to banish the image of her mother's body with her baby brother beside it from her mind. 'Nine.'

'And your father blamed you for it?'

'I know what I did.'

'Did you make your mother get on that horse? Did you cut the baby from her? Your father must share some of the blame.'

'That is not the point.' She pressed her hands against her eyes before continuing. 'My father blames me. But this way he will have to be proud of me. He will have to listen before he tries to use me like a counter again to further his own standing.'

'It seems to me that he should already be proud of you.'

'Moir, you have never met my father.'

'But I know his daughters, particularly his middle one.' His lips parted, but he smoothed a lock of hair from her forehead before stepping away from her. Then he bowed. 'I will return to get the men ready. Today's task—rethatching the threshing barn. Be prepared for Bjartr's complaints to echo out over the yard.'

Ansithe exhaled. A hard knot within her eased slightly. He didn't consider her a monster after her confession. 'I will tell Cynehild to stop her ears.'

Ansithe sat down on the pile of hay. Forgetting that kiss and disliking Moir was proving far harder than she had considered. Telling him about her dark secret and hearing his reaction had made her wonder—was it truly all her fault? Or had it been easier for her father to blame someone else? She winced a little at the disloyal thought, but it remained.

Becoming lovers with Moir could not happen. It must not happen. She put her face in her hands and banished the traitorous thoughts about how his mouth had moved over hers and how he made her feel alive instead of a shrivelled-up barren woman like Eadweard had claimed she was when her womb had failed to quicken.

She dusted her hands on her gown and peered at her face in a bucket of water. The same awkward features she always saw peered back up at her. She knew what Moir was trying to do—he wanted to use her, to soften her up so she'd betray her family by looking the other way when he and his men escaped. He probably thought that a woman who looked like her would easily be swayed by a few kisses, just like picking a ripe plum.

She buried her face into her hands again. Just once, she wanted someone to like her for who she was, instead of what she could bring to the relationship.

Chapter Eight

'Baldwine has sent word. He requires advice and assistance. Urgently,' Cynehild said the next morning when Ansithe uncharacteristically had decided to stay indoors and concentrate on her long-neglected weaving rather than finding an excuse to see Moir. Cynehild sat next to her, spinning. 'He claims outlaws or Northmen broke in and stole his sheep during the night.'

'Baldwine actively dislikes me and thinks anything I say is suspect. Normally Ecgbert goes.' Ansithe put the shuttle down. Her heart sank when she thought about the *ceorl* who had once saved her father's life and had been rewarded with the tenancy of a farm nearby. And he would blame everyone but himself for the lost sheep.

'Ecgbert is busy doing your bidding.'

Ansithe ground her teeth. Cynehild had that superior older-sister expression on her face again, the one which she wore when she wanted to force Ansithe to do something against her will.

'You remember when I accidentally let the cows out of the top pasture and they trampled all over his vegetable garden. And he has never forgiven me for the incident. He was the one who proudly captured the monks that I had thought were Danes.'

'You were only nine.' Cynehild set her drop spindle whirling. 'That was over a decade ago, Ansithe. Few people recall your part in that now.'

Ansithe gaped in astonishment. That incident had defined her whole life and Cynehild was dismissing it as if it were nothing with a wave of her hand. 'Our mother died!'

'Our mother died because she fell off a horse that was too spirited for her to handle.' Cynehild's eyes softened. 'I know Father blamed everyone but himself, but our grandmother used to say that our mother should not have been on that uncontrollable horse in the first place. She used to advise us not to speak to you about it because you were apt to weep.'

Ansithe stared at her older sister in astonishment. They had never really spoken about that day. Elene was far too little to remember it, but Cynehild was right—their grandmother had always changed the subject.

'Cedric mentioned it when he called. His reason for why I could not be trusted to work out our prisoners were warriors from the North.'

Cynehild mistimed the spindle and broke the thread. She gave an annoyed grunt. 'Cedric should keep his opinions to himself and stop making mischief. And in any case, you shouting about the Danes was not why our mother mounted that horse.'

Ansithe stared open-mouthed at her sister. 'And you know this how?'

'Because I was there. I begged her not to get on that horse, but Father was screaming at her to do it, so she did as he instructed and then it reared up and threw her.'

'You've never said anything until now.'

Cynehild retrieved her spindle and reattached the thread. 'Our grandmother wanted it to be in the past. I thought you simply mourned our mother's death like I did and respected your right not to speak about it. Ask next time.'

She stared at her older sister. She was saying pretty much what Moir had said about people not blaming her. Other people might not, but she knew what her father still thought—that the ultimate responsibility for the accident was hers for sounding the false alarm. 'Our father married me off to an old man because he could not bear the sight of me.'

'He needed that alliance desperately with Eadweard. He thought it would protect him against Wessex. He never suspected the Heathen Horde would arrive.' Cynehild gave an exasperated sigh. 'It isn't always about you and your mistakes, Ansithe. Other people make them, too. You simply allow yourself to be defined by them.'

'You have never hesitated to mention them in the past.' Cynehild had to be wrong. She remembered her mistakes so she wouldn't repeat them.

'That was before you saved my life. You did more than that—you saved this estate and little Wulfgar, too.'

'I'd wait until Father and Leofwine return before praising me too much. Things I do have a habit of turning to mud in my hands.'

'They will return. And when they do I will ensure Father understands that you must be consulted before he tries to marry you off. Like he did with me about Leofwine.'

'My marriage was a disaster in many ways. We were ill-suited to each other,' Ansithe said.

Cynehild put her spinning down and gathered Wulfgar to her. 'Arranged marriages can work, Ansithe, if there is good will on both sides. Yours was simply unfortunate. Love didn't happen straight away for Leofwine and me, but after I gave birth, it blossomed.'

Ansithe concentrated on her tangled threads. Giving birth would not happen for her. 'I have never had a child.'

'That could have been your husband's fault.'

'He had several children already, remember?'

'You won't make me change my mind or make me feel guilty for having Wulfgar.' Cynehild put Wulfgar down. Wulfgar started to toddle away, talking about water. 'After what you told me about Cedric making mischief here, you need to go to Baldwine's and see for yourself.'

'Why? What does Cedric have to do with this?'

'Baldwine will have told Cedric about the missing sheep and you know what he is like. He will come here to check that all our prisoners are present in case they're responsible.'

Cedric was bound to come calling? Ansithe sighed. Cynehild simply did not fancy the journey to the farm. But she had a point—Baldwine was bound to send word to Cedric as well. 'Wouldn't that be avoiding my responsibilities?'

'You can't be in two places at once. Cedric only makes you lose your temper, so I will deal with him. I can be responsible as well, Ansithe. Will you let me help you without snapping my head off and barking orders?'

'I don't...' Ansithe paused. Maybe it seemed

that way to Cynehild. 'You are right—his lectures do bother me.'

Cynehild grabbed Ansithe's hand. 'Thank you.'

'You are also right in that we will have to do something about Baldwine's missing sheep. I will investigate. They could have strayed, but I will not put these lands in jeopardy just because my father is a captive. We will not become an easy target for all manner of outlaw.'

'Take that handsome Northman with you. He seems to have some good ideas about how this estate should be run. He might be able to tell what happened and where the sheep went.'

Ansithe narrowed her eyes. Cynehild could not have seen them kissing, could she? 'Why should I take the Northman?'

'Things have been unsettled hereabouts. You might need protection.'

'I have my bow and arrow.'

'He has a calming manner which is more than some.' Cynehild developed a sudden interest in the embroidered cuff of her gown. 'His men can finish the threshing barn. Trust me to look after them for the morning.'

The back of Ansithe's neck prickled. Cynehild was up to something. 'How do you know all of this?'

'Because you are not the only one who can

speak to him, sister dear. Now are you going to trust me or not?'

Ansithe's throat closed. She glanced up at the roof beams and blinked rapidly. She hadn't realised that Cynehild thought she didn't trust her. 'You are being impossible, but I do love you.'

After Cynehild's declaration about trust, Ansithe had been left with little option but to go the farm with Moir. The ease between them had vanished and the silence stretched out uncomfortably. Yet with every step she took, she was aware of the length of his legs and the way he moved with certain grace. Occasionally their hands brushed, causing her breath to catch, but she couldn't tell if it was deliberate or not. Every time she looked at him, he had a bland expression on his face.

She stopped in front of the farmhouse. 'Baldwine is like most of the farmers here. He despises all from the Horde. His eldest died in one of the battles.'

'I am not here to make friends. I am here to provide protection.'

'Protection? I can look after myself.'

Moir crossed his arms. 'Cynehild wanted to ensure you were protected. It is why she sent me.'

'Cynehild overreacts.'

He moved directly behind her. Her body instantly responded to the warmth radiating outwards. 'Sometimes it is good to have someone to watch your back. Your sister worries about you. I jumped at the chance to spend time alone with you.'

Ansithe pressed her lips together. He wanted to spend time alone with her. 'I will keep that under advisement.'

'It's the Heathen Horde, I'm telling you, Lady Ansithe,' Baldwine the farmer said, scratching his nose. 'Can't be anything else.'

'Why would they take seven sheep?' Ansithe asked. 'And leave the rest?'

Baldwine's ears went red. 'How should I know such a thing? I didn't get a chance to ask them… unlike you. You remember when—'

'Moir?' Ansithe said before Baldwine could finish. 'Is there something you wish to say?'

'Outlaws, not men from the North.' Moir crossed his arms over his chest. 'If it were men from the North, I could understand cattle or horses or even women, but not sheep or pigs. Those creatures are more trouble than they are worth to dispose of at market.'

Baldwine's face went a bright red. 'And your *friend* knows better than I about such things, does he?'

'He is the *jaarl* Andvarr's liegeman and my captive,' Ansithe said. 'I am sure you heard how I as a lone woman managed to defeat a band of Northern warriors.'

Baldwine whistled. 'I heard tell you'd done such a thing, but I didn't reckon it were actually true. I remember about the monks, my lady, and what happened then.'

'Damned with faint praise,' Moir murmured.

Baldwine bristled. 'Did you say something, Northman?'

'I did. Show your lady some proper respect. She has earned that right. The brilliance of her scheme and the way she deployed those bee skeps was something to behold.' Moir stepped forward with clenched fists.

Baldwine was the first to look away.

Ansithe stepped between them. 'I can fight my own battles.'

Moir gave a half-smile and briefly covered her hand with his before stepping away. 'Agreed, my lady, but you should not have to keep fighting the same one, particularly when you have already won. And you should always make use of the tools you have rather than letting them rust through lack of use.'

She stared at him. He spoke the truth. Baldwine and others were trying to use the past to make her cringe and cower. Practically, in the last year she had shown everyone, including her father, that she was more than capable of running the household efficiently. Moir was right. She did have the skills to handle the awkward Baldwine.

'Baldwine, I travelled here because of sheep, not to listen to you prattle on about what happened when I was only a young girl.'

The farmer stroked his chin. 'I reckon we will be happier when you are settled with your own man once again. It were a terrible shame when your husband died. Cedric, now he is a good lord. He promises—'

'What promises has Cedric made? I wasn't aware that he could make any promises to my family's tenants,' Ansithe said in a firm voice. Coming here was worthwhile for learning that nugget of information, if nothing else. 'Do not count on your future lord before he becomes your true lord.'

Baldwine did not meet her eye. 'Lord Cedric is concerned about you, my lady. He was going to see you today about this here stolen sheep. It were why I was surprised like to see you and your...captive. Perhaps we ought to wait for him. Get his thinking on this. A right sound fellow is Lord Cedric.'

Ansithe frowned. She could well imagine what Cedric would say and who he'd blame. She also knew if she opened her mouth before she counted to ten, she'd lose her temper with Baldwine.

'Perhaps we can discover another explanation through investigation, rather than waiting for someone who has nothing to do with this estate.' Moir's words cut through her descending red fog of anger.

Baldwine stared at him as if he'd sprouted an extra head. 'Is there another explanation?'

'I would like to see the pasture where the sheep vanished from,' Moir said. 'They can be the very devil for escaping. What with the recent troubles, I doubt anyone has had much time to mend walls. Your steward neglects his duties, my lady, but I know you have already discovered this.'

Baldwine looked about ready to bluster, but his wife shushed him.

Ansithe pressed her hands against her eyes and regained control of her temper. 'That is the best suggestion I've heard this morning—we will check the walls and the surrounding fields thoroughly.'

'I find it best to ascertain all the facts before casting blame,' Moir said, catching her elbow as she went out of the door. 'You did well, Kyrie.'

'With a little help from a friend,' Ansithe said. 'I thought I wouldn't need you today, but I did. I am glad you came with me.'

His eyes crinkled at the corners. 'All you needed was for someone to believe in you and I am happy to do that.'

If anything, the sun had grown hotter and huge thunder clouds formed in the sky, billowing overhead after they'd finished with Baldwine, having discovered the missing sheep had strayed to a top pasture through a hole in the wall.

As they walked back to the manor, the butterflies and damselflies played in the sunshine. By the time they reached the relative shade of a stand of oaks, Ansithe's gown was stuck to her back.

'Your prowess at finding sheep has been duly noted,' Ansithe said, skirting around a log. 'Expert thatcher and now sheep-finder. Are you sure your heart belongs to war? You would make a fine farmer.'

He stopped and looked at her quizzically. 'In order to farm, one must have land, something few have in the North with the new King.'

'Did your father lose your land, is that why you came on this expedition?'

'I don't usually speak about either of my parents, but my father did lose everything because he betrayed his men and his honour.'

'How did you know about the sheep?'

Moir gave a rueful smile. 'It is down to my

youth spent chasing goats over the hills, rather than any special power. I thought the pens looked a bit run down when we arrived. And since the new King took power it has become a common trick to hide livestock and make the tithe less in the North country.'

'You chased goats?'

'I had to eat. Both my parents had died.' He looked away from her. 'I was not supposed to become a warrior. Everyone had dire predictions about what I would become, but my *jaarl*'s lady, she had belief in me...despite everything. She vouched for me so I could join my first *felag*.'

'Bjartr's mother,' Ansithe said, wiping a hand across her face. She sat down in the shade of an oak on the cool moss. It explained much. There was far more to Moir looking after Bjartr than she'd thought.

'Ingunn was one of the greatest women I ever met. She was like a second mother to me. Unfortunately, she was taken far too soon.' Moir settled down next to her. 'I was never able to show her that her faith in me was justified. I wanted to. The summer she died was my first warring season. But I like to think my loyalty has been noted. It is why Andvarr entrusted his son to me.'

Ansithe nodded, beginning to understand why

he was so protective of Bjartr. 'But you did become a warrior. Her faith in you was justified.'

He looped his hands about his knee. 'It remains to be seen if I remain one once this journey ends. It has been a disaster from start to finish. I warned Andvarr of the danger of making Bjartr the *felag* leader on his first expedition, but he adores his son. Bjartr took liberties.'

'Adores or ignores?' Ansithe said shrewdly, crossing her arms. 'Bjartr reminds me a bit of my stepson. His father either lavished attention on him or ignored him. He fled when the fighting happened, rather than standing and fighting.'

'Andvarr wants him to become a great warrior, but sometimes Bjartr takes that too much for granted. He does not see how hard his father works. How many other people have calls on his attention.' Moir shrugged. 'It is a problem for another day. Soon I will have more than chasing reluctant sheep over the hills to worry about. Your sister will return and my time of grace as your priest calls it will end. I swear Palni will be ready to wear a monk's cowl if we don't leave soon.'

Ansithe stilled, waiting for the request for her to turn a blind eye to their escape. He looked at her, but she said nothing, holding her breath.

'You have kept Bjartr alive,' she finally said

into the silence. 'That has to count for something. Surely his father wants his son back alive.'

His lips turned up into a small smile. 'Hopefully Andvarr will consider that when we return rather than what happened before I left.'

'Who told me that I had earned the right to be considered more? Not to be defined by what happened when I was nine years old.'

'You sound far surer of that than I am.' He smiled one of his crooked smiles, the sort which made her feel as if she'd been surrounded by a thousand candles. It seemed strange that she looked for his smiles after such a short time together and that she already knew she'd miss them once he had gone.

She screwed up her eyes. He would be going. Soon. Her father and Leofwine would return and her scheme to win her father's respect and admiration would succeed. But her father had never truly appreciated what she had done before, so why would he start now? The thought made her unaccountably depressed. This time it had to be different.

'Let's not speak about what we are facing. What will you do if the war ends? They say your *jaarl* seeks peace.'

'War always happens. Men quarrel.'

'One day the fighting will end for you. It nearly did for Palni.'

'When that day happens, then I will decide.' He rubbed his hand along the back of his neck. 'If there is no land for me here, then perhaps I will travel to Iceland. A warrior I met told me that it was a good place with waterfalls and clear streams which suddenly turn boiling hot. Constantinople is also a possibility. The Emperor there told me that I could return.' He stopped. 'You are smiling at me.'

'I am thinking how different we are,' she said to cover her confusion at wishing she could travel to see the places he had named. 'You have travelled across the seas and I have barely left home. It seems strange that people think the men from the North are uncivilised.'

'Travel is uncomfortable and dangerous. Most of the time you are cold, wet and living in certain knowledge that each breath might be your last one.'

'But there are reasons why you still long to go.'

A faint breeze ruffled his hair. 'I never think beyond the sunset or the next sunrise. It makes travelling easier.'

'There always seems to be a reason why I can't go anywhere.' Ansithe stared at the leaves rustling on the branches. It was easy to make light of her disappointment at not being trusted to travel. Somehow with him sitting beside her, it no longer mattered as much as it had. 'I even contemplated becoming a nun until I learnt that my brother-in-law meant me living at one of the convents close at hand, rather than travelling to Rome.'

'When you married, didn't you have to leave the estate?'

'My late husband preferred his estate which was five miles away rather than the one in West Mercia. He was a friend of my father's. I doubt anyone else ever looked at me. I am not the beauty of the family. Cynehild had that honour first and then Elene. My husband wanted my dower portion and my abilities to manage a household, although my stepson claimed that ability was woefully exaggerated.' She forced a smile to show that it didn't hurt. And somehow sharing the story with him, it didn't. It was as if that humiliation had happened to someone else and it was now her stepson's problem.

'Who owns your dowry lands now?' he asked.

Ansithe frowned slightly. She had half-wished that he had told her that she was pretty, instead of asking about the lands that would form part of any future dowry of hers.

She gestured about her. 'They were returned to my father when my husband died. My stepson sold the other land to Cedric for a pittance.

Cedric only realised afterwards that these lands had some value as well.'

'I see. Your father sold you for his own purpose.' A muscle jumped in his jaw. 'And lied to you about your looks until you refused to believe even the evidence of your own eyes.'

She gave him a baffled look. 'Lied to me?'

He held her chin between his thumb and forefinger, turning her face this way and that. He let her go.

'To my mind,' he said slowly as if he wanted to make sure the words were right, 'you are beautiful, fearless and with a big heart, the sort of woman whom any man would long to have. Why your Mercian men are blind and why you persist in listening to them is a matter I do not care to explore.'

She closed her eyes. When he said it like that, he made her father sound selfish beyond all measure.

Perhaps Moir was right. Her father had uttered his ominous words about arranging a new betrothal for Ansithe on the morning of his departure. Getting the gold to pay his ransom would surely ensure such talk died? But it was beyond her to explain this to Moir.

'Are you going to answer me, Kyrie?' He caught a strand of her hair on the breeze and wrapped it between his fingers. 'Or are you going to call me a liar?'

'If I do, what will you do?'

His eyes crinkled. 'What do you want me to do? How can I make you believe something like that when you are clearly determined not to?'

His warm voice curled about her insides. He was going to kiss her. Her mouth ached as if it already felt his lips against hers. All she had to do was lean forward and he would make her feel beautiful.

'When I was younger, I liked watching the river and imagining all the places it must be going,' she said, jumping up in a rush to change the subject. 'I had a place up on the hill which made for a good lookout.'

He rose and put his hand on her back. The warmth that radiated outwards from his touch made the butterflies start in her stomach again. She longed to lean back and savour it. She remembered with a shiver exactly how skilfully his mouth had moved over hers in those kisses they'd shared.

He gestured with his other hand. 'Beyond the river, there is the ocean and foreign lands.'

'Have you seen many lands?'

'I have seen enough. There was little future for me in the North. When Andvarr recognised this, we began to travel first to Francia and then here. I want to become in control of my own destiny instead of just labouring for someone else.'

'I am sure you will get it. I just wish…'

'You wish what?' His breath caressed her ear. She watched his chest rise and fall. Propriety demanded she step away from him, but she was powerless to do so.

'That you acquiring the land you crave doesn't mean someone else has to lose it,' she said to his chest. Her voice was far too breathless for her liking.

His arms fell away from her. 'We won the war. Once there is peace, we will hold the land for ever. We can make it productive again.'

'Who started it?'

He gave a wry smile. 'That is a question which great lords can argue over.'

'Because you never look beyond the next sunset.'

'You know me so well.' He laughed. 'May I see your lookout spot? It intrigues me unless we don't have time.'

He was giving her an option. She felt as if she balanced on the edge of precipice. To keep on the narrow pathway of her life, all she had to do was to return to the relative safety of the hall and her family. It suddenly did not seem appealing in the slightest.

'There are sure to be a hundred chores which

need to be done when we return,' she warned. 'Cynehild has a genius for finding them.'

He laced his fingers with hers and raised them to his mouth. The gentle touch made her knees go weak.

'My men have their orders. They might even obey them, instead of listening to Bjartr's complaints.'

'Is he well liked?'

'I used to think so, but my men have little time for self-pity.'

A reminder if she needed it that he, too, had responsibilities.

Ansithe clenched her jaw. She might be brave when it came to defending her home, but when it came to being alone with this man, her stomach was a mass of nerves. She knew she wanted to be the fearless warrior, the Valkyrie he thought her instead of the dried-up shell of a woman she'd spent years thinking she was, but she was scared to take the chance.

He said nothing, but held out his hand. If they returned to the manor, she'd never know. She took a deep breath.

'My special place is this way.' Her stomach swooped as though she had taken a great leap from a cliff.

'I'm honoured.'

Chapter Nine

'This is my favourite place in the whole world,' Ansithe said and waited to see what he would say. If he could appreciate the beauty of it and understand what it meant to her, then maybe he'd understand why she wanted to save it for her family.

'Then I am honoured you have chosen to share it with me.'

The slight rise as they approached her lookout gave Ansithe and Moir a good view over the land around Baelle Heale. The river ran like a silver ribbon through the fields, woods and water meadows.

The sound of a cracking twig made them both freeze. Moir pulled her into the shadow of an ash. His hard body met hers. Ansithe struggled to take a calming breath. All about her she noticed his scent and the way his tunic gapped at his throat.

Her stomach knotted. For a few breaths she had forgotten the danger they were in. There were outlaws all around here. Then just when she was sure they were going to be attacked, his chest rumbled with barely suppressed laughter.

She flattened her palms against him, feeling his chest muscles ripple under her palms. 'Are you going to let me into the joke?'

He pointed with one hand, but kept the other about her waist. 'See.'

A mother boar with five striped piglets marched out into the clearing and looked at them quizzically. The nearest piglet had a very muddy backside as if he had been wallowing in a puddle.

The muscles in her neck eased. She breathed deeply. No outlaws or Danes to fight, but a boar snuffling about in the dirt.

'I thought it would be far worse. Would that life held nothing more than worrying about where to find the next mud bath?'

His hand cupped her face. Gentle fingers smoothed her cheek with light feathery touches which made her think again of butterfly wings. 'I would have protected you.'

'I can look after myself.' She barely recognised her voice. She wet her suddenly dry lips. Every particle of her was aware of him and how close they stood. How all she had to do was to lift her mouth…

'But you don't have to. You are far from being alone. I'm here.'

She raised her face, intending to say something, but the words died on her lips when she encountered the intense expression on his countenance. 'I know where you are.'

His mouth lowered and took hers. Unlike the hurried kisses from before, this kiss was deeper, slower and more questing. As if he knew he could take his time. She opened her mouth and accepted his tongue. Her heart wanted to stop beating and her bones melted into him.

Her back arched towards him, her breasts meeting his hardened planes. There was not an ounce of fat on him. This was the body of a man who worked hard, rather than that of an old and infirm man. She placed her hands on his chest as his hands roamed over her back. She was aware her couvre-chef had come off and he tangled his fingers in her hair, sending it cascading down about her neck.

A small cry escaped her throat.

He lifted his mouth from hers. His eyes were a stormy puddle of blue. 'We should go. Return to the hall before something happens that we might regret.'

Regret. She forced her fingers to release his

tunic. Her mouth tasted sour. He had done this for his men so that she would free them and now was regretting it.

'You regret this?' she asked with a wobble in her voice.

'Only if it makes you unhappy.' His voice held a husky rasp that sent a fire coursing through her.

Unhappy. Lying was futile. His kisses made her feel everything but unhappy. She had spent a lifetime thinking she was ugly, unworthy and incapable of ever being desired. His touch had shown her what a lie that had been. All these years she'd been wrong. Moir found her desirable.

'You were right about living in the moment.' She tried to ignore the way her mouth throbbed. 'My future might never happen the way I want it to. Everyone except me seems to anticipate it going in a certain way. I want to believe I can have a future which will make me happy.'

He covered her hand with his. 'Don't play cruel games with me. I've stayed away because I know how dangerous it might be for you should people discover that you and I were together. I refuse to risk your life.'

Her stomach tightened. He was talking about more than a faceless society disapproving of them. 'Because you have a feud with Guthmann?

Because you fear what he might do to me if he knew you and I had been together.'

'I won't always be here to protect you, but Guthmann is a powerful enemy. He swore a vow to kill me and harm those who were closest to me, particularly any woman I might care about.'

A frisson of cold ran down her spine. Guthmann had sent a severed finger to ensure his ransom demand was paid. He made promises, not threats.

'I doubt very much that I will ever meet Guthmann,' she said in a shaky voice. 'I want to be here with you right now, not thinking beyond the next sunset. I don't want to live my life in the shadows of fear. I want to live it in the light.'

He stilled. 'What are you saying, Ansithe?'

She sighed, wishing she'd kept quiet. Things were simpler before she'd realised his desire for her was as real as hers was for him. 'I like how my name sounds on your lips?'

'Answer the question,' he demanded, piercing her with his fierce gaze.

She kept her head high. She had already humiliated herself enough. She could not do worse. If he rejected her, then at least she'd know. 'I have found it impossible to forget about the kisses we have shared. They have occupied my thoughts and dreams. I find myself thinking about them at odd times. Like when I was trying to do embroidery or when we were chasing sheep.'

'Your dreams.' He gave a crooked smile. 'Do I behave properly in them? Do we indulge in kisses?'

Ansithe looked out at the silver river snaking below their feet, rather than tumbling into his gaze. Her arms tingled like they had before the Northman broke open their door. She was at a dividing place in her life. She could curl up small and have regrets for the rest of her life or she could be brave and bold. 'What I dream about is joining with you.'

The words hung in the air and suddenly she wished she could unsay them.

With careful hands, he turned her to face him. 'Why are you telling me this?'

'Because I want to do something just for me. I want to know what it is like to be desired when you are joining with a man.' He started to say something, but she put a finger to his lips. 'I know we have no future together. I'm not asking for one. I am telling you my dreams because you asked.'

Something flared in his eyes. 'Do you think that little of me?'

'Elene will return any day with the Mercian warriors and everything will change, but for once in my life I want to feel cherished. Your touch…makes me feel beautiful.'

She pressed her hands together. He made no move to take her into his arms or to kiss her.

She moved away from him and kept her gaze on the ground. A grasshopper hid under a clump of grass. A butterfly rose in the air, circled and flew away. 'I have made a mess of things again. Those kisses were given out of pity.'

'The last thing I feel for you is pity. Passion, desire and a longing to fully taste you, but not pity.' He raised her chin, so she was forced to meet his piercing gaze.

'Truly?'

He smiled wickedly. 'Your kisses kept me awake, too. All my dreams were of you and what I'd like to do with you. Your touch has nearly unmanned me and if you have any doubts, tell me now before we pass the point of no return.'

Her heart beat so hard that she felt it would jump out of her chest. 'That is a start.'

'I can't make any promises, but I vow—my desire for you has nothing to do with my duty towards my men. I will fight for them when the time comes, but I've no intention of manipulating you.' He caught her hand and held it against the front of his trousers. 'I get to be the judge of who excites my blood, not you.'

She withdrew her hand. Her palm tingled where it had touched his straining hardness.

'I'm not asking for promises and you needn't worry that there will be children. My late husband proclaimed me barren and unable to perform a wife's duty.'

He watched her with shadowed eyes. 'Your late husband was by all accounts a lying fool.'

'Perhaps we should go back. I may have had a touch of the sun.' She shaded her eyes. 'I would never have said such a thing out loud.'

He caught her wrist, holding her in place. 'I won't permit you to unsay it. I'm glad you said it, but why do you want this?'

'Because I don't want to lie to you. It was a simple enough dream.'

She tugged, but his hand slipped down and intertwined her fingers with his, keeping her at his side. Her fingers curled about his. They stood like that, watching the river, aware of each other's breathing, aware of each other's small movements.

'Then I agree.'

The words made her heart hammer. 'You do?'

His smile made her insides turn to liquid fire. 'Do you know how delectable you look when you ask this? How could a man like me refuse you anything?'

A thrill went through her. He desired her

body. He did not consider her shrivelled up. He wanted to join with her. She had to wonder if her husband had misled her about other things as well as her desirability as a woman.

'When it is over, we will part without regrets.' She gave a little laugh and knew she'd hug the memories close. She might never have a child to hold in her arms, but she could have the memory of being truly desired, whatever her future held.

He raised her fingers to his lips. His eyes peered into hers as if he could see deep into her soul and discern her growing feelings for him and that it would be something more than two bodies meeting for her.

She swayed towards him, licking her bottom lip. The fire in his eyes deepened to a brilliant blue.

'We will part when the time comes because that is what the fates decree. But this will be a private time for us and us alone.'

He took each finger into his mouth and suckled. Warmth shot through her, making her gasp and melting her bones. Her back arched. A great well of heat opened in her middle, searing her with its intensity.

'Do we wait for darkness?' he asked, pulling her to him so that her body had support from his. She clung to him like a drowning man clings to a spar. And the evidence of his arousal pushed into the apex of her thighs. Not soft or hesitant, but hard and firm. 'Or will you reveal your body to me in the sunshine? I have dreamt about how it must look—your long legs and firm breasts. The body of a Valkyrie, a goddess.'

'My late husband insisted on darkness. He doused the torches and threw himself on me,' she answered, straightening her spine. 'I want this to be different. I want there to be no secrets between us. If you don't like what you see, you must tell me.'

His husky laugh sent a warm pulse racing up and down her spine. 'Soon you will see what I see, what I can touch and then you will know that you could never disappoint me.'

His hand slipped down her back, cupping her buttocks and pulled her more firmly against his growing arousal.

His mouth tugged at her earlobe, making lazy circles on her neck before moving to her face. He rained small kisses on her temple before going back to administer to her ear. His hot breath teased her. The liquid fire built up within her. She had never expected such a simple touch would make a great well of longing open within her.

He fumbled at her cloak's fastening so he could lay it on the ground. She moved his hand and with a practised move undid the hidden clasp and shrugged it off. Then he eased her back against the sweet grasses. As she lay back, several small blue butterflies rose and circled up into the air. The air tasted of flowers and him.

He loosened her gown and pushed the material so that her neck and the gentle swell of her breasts were exposed. He pressed his lips against the hollow at the base of her throat, biting down gently.

Her body bucked upwards and her nipples hardened to points which rubbed against the fine linen of her under-gown. His fingers slipped down, capturing first one nipple and rolling it between his thumb and forefinger, then doing the same to its begging twin.

Her fingers pushed his tunic up and explored the contours of his bare torso. She felt the knots of old scarring and the hard sinew. Moir was a warrior who had fought in many battles, but he was also in the prime of life. She'd never touched a warrior this intimately before. Her hands revelled in how his muscles shifted and twisted as he moved.

He took off the tunic, naked except for the pendant about his neck. The summer sun blazed down on his golden-shot skin. He was all hard planes and delicious muscle. Her mouth went dry. This man, this beautiful shining male, desired her?

She reached out and touched the pendant. 'What is that for?'

'All I have left from my mother,' he said.

Before she could say anything more, he lowered his mouth and sucked her nipple in. Round and round went his tongue, wetting the cloth until all thoughts and doubts vanished from her mind.

He lifted her skirts so that they were gathered about her waist, revealing her long, slender legs.

'How could you think I would not like these perfect limbs? These round mounds? This inviting belly?'

He ran a clever hand along one leg, making the flames inside her lick higher until she knew they would consume her. Her body bucked and writhed against the cloak as his hand skimmed the apex of her thighs.

Her hands went to his trousers, worked on the tie, but managed to tangle it. He caught her wrists with one hand.

'You will knot the string. I am more adept at this,' his voice rumbled in her ear, sending fresh shivers down her spine.

He undid his trousers with the other hand and his erection sprang free. It was far larger than she had considered. She looked down at the grass instead of touching him.

'We go at your pace,' he said against her temple. 'It is far more pleasant. I want to erase all bad memories for you.'

'Please,' she whispered, hardly knowing what she was asking for, but for the first time in her existence her body was on fire and seeking relief. She knew now why women wanted this, instead of merely enduring it, why they might want to see the magnificence of their partner instead of hiding in a ball in the darkness.

His questing fingers went further up her thighs and found her nest of curls. She moved against his hand and his fingers went deeper, inside her.

Her body arched upwards.

'You're wet for me,' he rasped in her ear. 'See.'

He moved his damp fingers against her belly in a soft sensuous curve. The fire grew within her.

'May I?' he asked. 'Please?'

Incapable of speech, she nodded.

He opened her thighs and positioned his body carefully before entering her.

As he pushed, her body opened and invited him in. Instead of the intense pain she'd expected, a great warmth flooded through her. She tilted her hips upwards and he became fully sheathed. Giving into instinct, she began to rock back and forth. Faster and faster until the world swirled about her in total ecstasy.

A great cry rose up from Moir and then he collapsed back down on to her. She brought her arms around his back, welcoming the satisfied, boneless weight of him with a blissful smile on her face.

Moir smoothed the hair from Ansithe's temple. It had curled into small ringlets in the heat. He hadn't expected that intensity or the passion from her. He doubted he had ever seen anyone look as lovely as she did in that heartbeat—her dark auburn hair spread out on the cloak, her mouth slightly swollen from his kisses, her eyes heavy-lidded from the passion they had shared. For this one breath, she was his and only his. He drew a finger down her face and knew she'd ruined him for all other women. She was the one he'd always remember, always judge other women by, and he knew he'd never want anyone as much as he wanted her.

No thinking beyond the next sunset—wasn't that his proudly proclaimed motto? How silly it seemed now. He wanted to think beyond the sunset to many sunsets with her, but also not to think at all as he knew their sunsets would be limited. All he had was this moment.

He pressed a kiss against her cheekbone. 'Thank you.'

Her slow, knowing smile made his groin ache

again. 'I should be the one thanking you for making my dreams become a reality. You made me feel beautiful. As though I was worth something more than just being a nurse or a housekeeper.'

He'd made her dream a reality. Something tightened in his gut. He had never done that for anyone. A great surge of longing to protect her from harm washed through him.

'My pleasure,' he choked out, rattled by the feeling. He had never felt this possessive about anyone before.

'Now I understand what this is all about,' she continued, her lips curving up into a satisfied smile. 'Why minstrels sing of it. Why people do it so often. I never truly understood before.'

He rolled off her and stared up the darkening sky. Her husband had been an uncouth bastard and if he had been alive, Moir would have taken great pleasure in severing his head from his body for treating Ansithe in that fashion, for making her fear her femininity rather than embracing it.

He clenched his fist and wished he could take her with him. Slowly he forced his fingers to uncurl. Guthmann's last warning about what he would do to any of Moir's family, particularly his women, resounded in his ears. Until he ensured her safety, he would have to trust his instincts— she was safer at Baelle Heale than anywhere.

He wanted to see what she would be like if

she was brought to her full flowering of passion. And he knew he wanted to be the one to do it. He wanted to wake up every morning with her in his arms. He wanted to spin dreams and think about the future.

'Was your late husband blind?' He smoothed a tendril from her forehead. 'Don't answer that. He had to have been. Is that why you refuse to see what you look like?'

'He was older, older than my father if the truth be told, but his eyesight was still keen. I suspect my father thought he'd have an ally for rather longer than he did. In the event, the exertion of our wedding night made him take to his bed for weeks. He tried again with me, but I was inept.'

'Inept?'

'I never bore him a child. He said that it was all my fault, that my insides were shrivelled up. He ensured everyone in the household heard his accusation.'

His heart clenched at the matter-of-fact way she confessed that. The fault was more likely her husband's than hers. And he hated the man even more for humiliating her in that fashion. 'The last thing you are is shrivelled up. I know how wet you were for me. I know how alive your body is. Do I have to demonstrate it to you again?'

Her cheeks coloured delightfully. 'You are right. He lied.'

'I certainly have no complaints about your performance. How could I?' He ran his hand down her flank. 'It surpassed my wildest imaginings. The day remains young.'

She smiled and gathered her knees to her chest. Her curtain of hair fell over her face, hiding her glorious eyes. 'It is something I will remember for the rest of my life, but we need to return. Cynehild will worry.'

He reached and wound her silken hair about his hand. 'I would like to do it again if you are willing.'

She chewed her bottom lip. 'Is it possible?'

'Your sister hasn't returned from court yet.'

'She will be back soon.'

'Soon isn't today.' A few days more, a sunset or three, he silently pleaded. A few days with Ansithe and he would accept whatever destiny lay in store for him, even if that meant playing nursemaid to Bjartr until the end of his days or ending up as Guthmann's prisoner. None of it would matter—he would have held paradise in his arms.

She stood and smoothed her skirts down. He reached out and took some wisps of grass from her hair.

'I must seem as though I've been through a hedge backwards.'

He rubbed the back of his thumb across her well-kissed lips before he started to dress. 'You look like a goddess come to earth to torment the mortals.'

Her lips curved upwards. 'Thank you for that, but I'm not. I'm very ordinary. My late husband was frank about it—he'd purposely chosen the plain daughter. My grandmother's favourite saying was that I should be grateful that I was clever as I wasn't pretty.'

'My truth matters to me, not your late husband's or your grandmother's.'

She turned away from him. 'We had best return or otherwise people will be wondering what has happened to us.'

He caught her hand and raised it to his mouth. He made a vow—he would protect her and then he would return for her. But he would not tell her until that day happened. 'Some day, you will believe my truth. Some day I will show you what passion can be like in a bed piled high with furs rather than on the hard ground.'

'I am content with this ground.' She started to walk away with her backside gently swaying temptingly in front of him. 'What happened was for the moment, Moir. It doesn't change things. When the time comes, you will be ransomed. I have a duty to my family. I can't ruin their lives again.'

He wanted to throw her over his shoulder and carry her off somewhere where they could be alone without the entire world coming between them.

'But that time hasn't come yet. We still have this time,' he called. 'For as long as it lasts.'

She glanced back. Her eyes crinkled at the corners and nearly took his breath. 'For as long as it lasts.'

Chapter Ten

Ansithe stifled a gasp when they arrived back at the hall. In the lengthening shadows, she could make out a man, stripped to the waist and tied to a post. At her noise, he lifted his head and stared at them with a tear-streaked face. Bjartr.

Ansithe struggled to control her temper. She'd left Cynehild in charge and this had happened. She handed Moir her eating knife. 'You cut him down. I will see what is going on.'

'He stays.' Cedric's nasal whine rang out over the yard.

At Ansithe's gesture, Moir continued over to Bjartr, but two of Cedric's men stood in front of him, blocking him.

'I am warning, you, Northman, do not interfere with Mercian justice or you will suffer a similar fate.' Cedric said. 'This man tried to steal a child from this house and then denied it. I was about to take him away.'

Ansithe marched up to where Cedric stood and jabbed him in his chest. 'Under whose orders, Cedric? These are my prisoners, not yours. Cut him down, Moir.'

'Ansithe, Cedric is right. That Northman was caught leading Wulfgar to the lake. He was going to drown him. Then he struck one of Cedric's men.' Cynehild came out, wringing her hands and clutching a very damp Wulfgar who wriggled and squirmed.

'I saw it with my own eyes. And he attempted to hit me when I intervened.' Cedric gave an irritating laugh. 'He remains silent for now, but he will talk once I am finished with him. He is probably one of the ones who stole the sheep. He wanted to free his companions and crept in.'

'Impossible,' Moir roared. 'Now move out of my way.'

Cedric's men stood, hands on their swords, still blocking his way.

'You heard the man. What you are claiming is impossible,' Ansithe said.

'What do you mean impossible? The Northman made an unprovoked attack on one of my men. It is my right—'

'This man is my prisoner, one whom I captured as Cynehild knows full well. Now, move aside or I will consider it an act of war. We know who captured these prisoners.'

The men backed away, muttering.

'After you, my lady,' Moir said, giving her a significant look.

She took the knife from Moir, went up to Bjartr and cut him down. He fell to his knees and put his hand to his throat.

'What was he doing carrying Wulfgar?' Cynehild asked. 'Wulfgar was not supposed to be anywhere near the threshing barn.'

'Did you ask him? Or did you merely allow Cedric's so-called warriors to beat him until he was incapable of speech?'

'It was obvious what he was doing, my lady,' Cedric said. 'In any language. He was beaten for being insolent. You have no idea of how to look after prisoners properly.'

'Back. Bringing back,' Bjartr croaked. Now that he was down, the fresh bruising on his face was clearly visible. 'Danger. Lake.'

'Which way was Bjartr going, Cynehild, when you discovered him?' Ansithe asked.

'It happened so quickly. Wulfgar was missing, but only for a few heartbeats, I swear. We had started to search and then he appeared, carrying him.' Cynehild put a hand to her face. 'Oh, my goodness, do you think he was returning Wulfgar? Had he been gone longer than the nurse said?'

'He was insolent to me and my men whatever

he was doing,' Cedric said. 'Refused to hand the boy to my man. He raised his hand as if to strike him. My men had to subdue him.'

'Maybe he knew the man wasn't Wulfgar's mother or part of this family,' Ansithe retorted. 'Did your men strike first and ask questions later?'

'When you confront that sort of filth, you act and then ask questions. He didn't answer them.'

'What, so an unarmed man who saved a little boy from drowning in the lake was dangerous to your group of warriors? You had to beat him senseless because he did the decent thing?' Ansithe deliberately turned her back on Cedric before he made more than a spluttering noise. 'Honestly, Cynehild, what were you thinking?'

Cynehild appeared suitably shamefaced. 'It seemed so clear-cut when Cedric explained it. I waited until you returned home before letting him leave with that man. I owed you that much.'

'If he had left with Bjartr, you would never have had Leofwine returned to you,' Ansithe pointed out.

Cynehild made no answer.

'You choose to believe this piece of filth over me?' Cedric bellowed.

'Yes. If he was stealing a child, why would he be coming back to the hall with him? Your men are armed, he is not. Why would he attack them?'

'Since when do heathens need reasons?'

Ansithe pointed towards the gate. 'I would suggest you leave, Lord Cedric. Your services to justice are not required here.'

'What did he do?' Cedric sneered, looking Moir up and down. 'Kiss you? You have to know that he would only have one reason for doing that.'

'Excuse me?' Ansithe said, outraged.

'Well, you would not be the first to lose your head over a man, but it will end in tears, *my* lady,' Cedric continued.

Ansithe and Cynehild exchanged looks at his possessive tone.

'My sister asked you to leave, Lord Cedric,' Cynehild said coldly, moving to stand beside Ansithe. 'Earlier you and I agreed we should wait for Ansithe to decide her prisoner's fate. She has. You and your men may depart now.'

'When you lose everything after they escape, don't blame me. These Northmen only want to use you, my lady.' He touched his hand to his cap. 'Your servant, Lady Cynehild. I pray your husband arrives back quite soon. You are becoming positively ungovernable just like your sister.'

Cedric mounted his horse. He and his men rode away.

'Thank you, my lady,' Bjartr blurted out. 'For believing me. I saved that child.'

Ansithe glanced towards where Moir stood, still glowering. 'Where did you find my nephew?'

'By the lake. I saw him wandering around without a nurse. I knew it was wrong.'

Ansithe did not ask what he was doing by the lake. 'Cynehild is lucky you were there.'

'I will take you back to the threshing barn,' Moir said. 'The rest of my men will be wondering what has happened.'

Ansithe waited until he and Bjartr had gone. 'Explain, Cynehild. Explain how you nearly gifted our most valuable prisoner to Cedric.'

Cynehild gulped hard. 'It happened so quickly. Cedric was talking to me. Then Wulfgar was missing. We searched and I saw him in that man's arms. He refused to give him to Cedric's men. And…'

'And you did not stop to think. You panicked.'

'Wulfgar is my hope for the future. You wouldn't understand that, not being a mother.'

'Ask questions first. Do not jump to conclusions.'

'I was waiting for you to return,' Cynehild said. 'You were gone far longer than you should have been. Was everything well?'

'The sheep were eventually discovered. You can't put a time limit on these things.'

'I see.' Cynehild gave Ansithe a searching look which seemed to take in her mussed gown and creased couvre-chef. 'Will the sheep detain you again? You may not like what Cedric had to say, but you must be careful, Ansithe. People might gossip about you.'

Ansithe kept her gaze on the post where Bjartr had been tied. She suspected her mouth was redder than normal and that her clothes were badly rumpled. She stopped her hands from smoothing her gown and straightened her spine. Sometimes Cynehild saw too much. 'The problem with the sheep has been resolved. I know what is important and who is important.'

'I trust your word. Cedric...' Cynehild put Wulfgar down. Her cheeks flushed. 'You are right. Cedric is a fool. I just don't want my sister to get hurt.'

Ansithe kissed Cynehild on her cheek, making up her mind. She and Moir couldn't be together again. Some things needed to be remembered only in dreams, rather than being acted upon. 'You have little to fear on that score.'

'What do you think you were playing at?' Moir asked when he and Bjartr rounded the barn and were out of Ansithe's and her sister's sight.

Bjartr pulled away from him. 'I saved a child's

life and was beaten for it. Those men would not listen to me.'

'You were supposed to be working on the barn roof, not walking by the lake.'

'I didn't fancy it. Far too warm. And I have been injured.'

'And you think you can pick and choose what you do? You are fit enough to work.'

'My father—'

'Your father will hear of this. You were ordered to do a task by your leader, Bjartr Andvarrson. You failed. If Lady Ansithe and I had not returned when we did, I shudder to think what might have happened to you.'

Bjartr doubled over, suddenly appearing very young. 'I saved his life. I know I did. Do you want that little boy to be dead?'

'We are very grateful, I am sure. Now what exactly were you doing down by the lakeshore? Throwing stones into the water?'

'Nothing very much. I thought…'

'Let me do the thinking. It is why I have become your leader. You've already made too many mistakes.'

Bjartr hung his head and mumbled an apology.

Moir curtly accepted it. If he managed to get the boy back alive, it would be a miracle. And he had to do it, particularly if he wanted to have any hope of making a proper offer for Ansithe.

Ansithe twisted the hunk of straw and tried to concentrate on repairing the skep. She'd gone to the apiary after Cedric departed to recover her calm.

It angered her that he'd implied Moir was untrustworthy, but he was correct. People would gossip and she had no idea what her father would do when he learnt about their friendship.

'Once again, I discover you here,' Moir said. 'I've spoken to Bjartr—'

'I want to speak with you as well.' Ansithe put the straw down.

Moir stood near her. It took all her self-control not to lean against him and request that he cradle her even closer to him. She laced her fingers together.

He watched her intently, much as a cat might watch a mouse. 'Is there a problem? Bjartr has faithfully promised not to leave the others again. However, he did save your nephew and that needs to be taken into consideration.'

'About what happened earlier. Out in the woods.' A lump formed in her throat, forcing her to stop, but she had to explain. He deserved an explanation of why it could not be repeated. 'It feels wrong somehow.'

'Is this because of what that Mercian lord said? What we shared together had nothing to do with how my men are treated and everything to do with my desire for you.'

Ansithe tucked a strand of hair behind her ear and focused on a spot beyond his head. His desire for her. No mention of his feelings. Desire faded. She had seen that happen many times before. Her stepson and his mistresses. Her father and her stepmother. She was right to end it now before her heart got hurt.

'What I am trying to say is—that thing which was between us? It must be in the past. A beautiful dream, but it must not happen again.'

He pinned her with shrewd eyes. 'And if I don't want it to be in the past?'

'It doesn't matter what you or I want.'

'It only matters what people are saying,' he said in a flat voice and she knew she had put it badly. 'I thought you didn't care about what other people thought. It is one of the things I liked most about you.'

Her throat became thick with unshed tears. She waited two heartbeats and regained control. 'I must be able to think about what is best for this estate, instead of…well…other things.'

She hated that her voice caught on the last word and rose sharply. Her entire traitorous body wanted him to take her in his arms and hold her tight, but that would cause far too many complications and he'd rapidly realise that her words were all lies.

His eyes became wary. 'Other things?'

'I'm not asking you to make any promises,' she whispered, backing up so her thighs hit the stand where she had balanced the skeps. 'I'm asking you to understand. We both have duties that go beyond our desires. You said that I could end it if it was what I wanted, and I must. I can't betray my family. Not again. Not ever.'

His hand dropped to his side. 'I keep my promises as best I can.'

A shout prevented Ansithe from answering. 'Someone needs me. My duty—'

'Duty or fear?'

She wondered if he could see right down to that deep part of her and knew exactly how much her growing feelings for him scared her. 'My duty to my family has to come first.'

He put his hand on her arm. His breath fanned her cheek, making her body tremble. 'We will continue this conversation later, Kyrie. You and I…do not have to end because someone has tried to make you feel small.'

Following the sound of her name being screamed, Ansithe went rapidly into the main hall. Cynehild was seated in front of the banked fire, tears streaming down her face.

All the workers and servants had assembled, crowding the hall, and their facial expressions ranged from stunned to out-and-out grief. Ansithe's insides twisted.

Cynehild held Wulfgar so close the boy was squirming and pushing her away. Her maid looked on with an anxious expression, but Cynehild appeared determined to hang on to the boy. Ansithe's heart clenched. It was too late. They must have had word from Guthmann who had grown tired of waiting. Her father and Leofwine were never going to return.

She gave a low moan.

'Breathe,' Moir said in an undertone, his fingers supporting her back. 'You will help no one if you panic.'

Ansithe looked up at the soot-blackened rafters and attempted to regain control of her emotions. He was right—she was panicking before she knew the true facts. 'What is wrong? You all appear to have seen a ghost.'

'You are finally here, Ansithe,' Cynehild gasped, gulping back her tears.

'What is wrong?' she asked. 'Cedric hasn't returned, has he?'

'Elene has been kidnapped. That is what is wrong,' Cynehild screamed and Wulfgar began to cry in loud shuddering sobs. 'I need you and your bow, Ansithe. You must get Elene back immediately!'

The words hung in the air and Ansithe wanted the floor to open and swallow her. She'd inadvertently let her sister down. 'I was in the apiary,' she whispered.

'Why can't it be like it was in the days before the Heathen Horde arrived?' Cynehild wailed.

'I will find Elene, Cynehild.'

'We both will,' Moir said, stepping forward. He made a salute to Cynehild. 'My men and I volunteer to help rescue the Lady Elene from her plight. I owe her a life debt for helping with my men that first night.'

Ansithe pressed a fist into her forehead. Elene was in danger, danger which Ansithe alone could not rescue her from. 'Show me the ransom demand. How do we know it is Elene?'

Cynehild pointed to the fire where Ecgbert, the steward, lurked, warming his hands with a peevish expression on his face. 'He was there and he told us.'

'Where did the attack happen? What went on? Why was she unprotected? Why did she send you back alone rather than returning with you? Why did you allow your lady to stay behind alone?'

Ecgbert wrung his hands. 'Where to start, my lady, that is the problem.'

'Start from when you arrived at court. Leave nothing out.'

'We made it to the Mercian court all right,' Ecgbert said in a nasal whine. His face showed signs of light bruising, but nothing too serious. 'We had started out back here again when we were attacked. The Horde. I am certain of it. A good three days' march from here.'

'And the guards?' Moir asked. 'Did they fight or run off? Where did it happen? Did you notice what they wore?'

Ecgbert flushed a deeper red. 'What gives you the right to question my story, heathen?'

'This man has given his oath to me,' Ansithe said between clenched teeth. 'Be civil.'

Ecgbert looked her up and down. 'Then the stories are true, my lady—you are in the thrall of a Northman. It can only end badly.'

'If you took the time to visit Lord Cedric instead of venturing straight here with your news, it *will* end badly—for *you*,' Ansithe retorted.

'I agree with my sister,' Cynehild said, rising to link arms with her. 'Tell the tale and then we will see what is to be done with you.'

The steward spread his hands upwards as if imploring the heavens to give him strength. 'Most of the guards ran once we encountered trouble. They were from Wessex, you see. Those who remained fought, but without much vigour, if you get my meaning. The Danes retreated thanks to my brilliant tactic of screaming like a banshee. Elene sent me to get help while she stayed with the wounded. She was in an extremely bossy mood when I left—ordering the warriors about as though she was the lady of a great warrior. Lady Elene considered it would be quicker for me to come here than to return to court and the summer gathering. She has become a force of nature, just as you are, Lady Ansithe,' he concluded with a sigh as if it were something to be ashamed of.

Ansithe whispered a silent prayer of thanksgiving. Despite Cynehild's fears, Elene had not been kidnapped, but had remained to help the wounded. It was an important distinction. Elene had done the right thing in sending Ecgbert here rather than having him return to court.

'Why did you come here rather than returning to court?' Moir asked, lifting a brow. 'Surely it was quicker to go back there.'

Ecgbert raised his fists. 'Because if anyone can rescue Lady Elene, it is her sister, Northman. Them at court, they wouldn't believe me, see. I'm not one of them. I'm not a Mercian warrior. I'm just a steward whose father was a blacksmith. They'd say there was no hope for Lady

Elene, but Lady Ansithe wouldn't say that—she'd say *I have a plan. Let's get Lady Elene home*. That's why!'

A loud cheer went up. Ansithe examined the rushes. She had been ready to be extremely angry with Ecgbert because he had gone to Cedric first, but he had returned here with good reason. It was wonderful that Ecgbert had such faith in her. She'd never guessed.

She went over to the iron-bound chest and withdrew her grandfather's precious parchment map of the area. She unrolled it on the table. 'Where exactly did it happen? Where is Elene now?'

The steward pointed with his finger. 'In these woods, just after that bend in the river, I reckon. They were going to make for a disused charcoal burner's hut that we'd passed.'

Ansithe nodded. The point was indeed about three days' walk from where the manor stood. Elene was sensible and she did have a few warriors with her, even if they were injured. She'd know how to survive until Ansithe could reach her. She wished she knew why they had been attacked. The group should have been large enough not to be bothered.

'Do you know who they were? The ones who attacked?'

'They spoke like the Northmen. Maybe.' He

scratched his ear. 'But different somehow. They weren't from Mercia, that's all I know.'

'The Northmen rather than the Danes?' Moir asked.

'They all sound the same to me.' The steward's mouth became a tight white line. 'You all want to murder me in my bed that's all I know.'

'Were they well provisioned?' Moir asked, leaning forward, his eyes suddenly alert. 'How many of them were there?'

'How am I supposed to know?' the steward asked with a peevish note returning to his voice. 'It is probably some of your comrades come to murder peaceful folk going about their business. We should ask Cedric for help. He will welcome the chance to help. He told me...'

'So you did go to him first,' Ansithe said, struggling to contain her sudden rage. Even after her capture of the Northmen, and despite his words just now, the steward refused to see her as capable. 'You did not come straight here, to me.'

The steward thrust out his chest. 'I encountered him on the road. I tried not to say too much to him, but he asked about the Lady Elene. And there never has been any reason to hide things from him.'

'Interesting that your precious Cedric did not ride back with you to see you home safely,' Ansithe said, crossing her arms.

Ecgbert's gaze flickered everywhere but on her face. 'He told me about your pet Northman and that was why his help was now unwelcome here. He expects you to come and ask for his aid on bended knee, my lady.'

'It will be a cold day in hell before I ever ask him for anything,' Ansithe muttered and tried to focus on the parchment. She could not go alone—that would be suicide.

'My men and I will go and fetch the survivors,' Moir said into the silence. 'They are hardened warriors, the sort who will not be fazed by outlaws. We will find your sister and bring her back safely. You have no need to rely on your neighbour.'

The breath went out of her lungs in a great whoosh. Despite everything, Moir had volunteered. 'Thank you.'

His fierce gaze caught and held hers. It felt as though he had wrapped his strong arms about her and held her tight.

'Ansithe,' Cynehild said in a quiet voice, 'you are in charge here. It is your decision, but I believe you should go as well. After what happened with Wulfgar earlier, I am not minded to trust Cedric either. And I would hope, Ecgbert, that you will not say I am in the thrall to any Northman as my love for Leofwine is beyond question.'

The steward stood, open-mouthed. 'You are seriously entertaining what he says? That is a Northman. He is your hostage. You shouldn't listen to him. He will use this as a chance to escape and then where will we be? You would be much better to go to Cedric. You just need to say that you made a mistake. It is by far the best option, my ladies. You see if...'

Ansithe firmed her jaw. 'While you have been gone, that Northman has repaired the farm buildings,' she said, listing off the various jobs that the steward had sworn he had no time to complete. The steward began spluttering. 'He has done more in a few days than you managed in the whole of last year. Why shouldn't I trust him?'

The steward flushed and tugged at the neck of his tunic. 'There are reasons why I did that. Your father—'

Ansithe held up her hand, stopping his words. 'Once my father returns, you may deal with him and explain how this estate has fallen into such disrepair. Why you refused to listen to me.'

'Unless you get the Northmen to the court in time, your father will not be freed and they will escape without guards,' Ecgbert predicted. 'The gold Lady Elene received for selling the weapons was enough for the guards and not much else.'

'First let us get Elene back and then we will

worry about claiming a ransom for our hostages.' Ansithe fixed Ecgbert with her gaze. 'You returned because you trusted my judgement. I have to believe we will get them there.'

'Did the outlaws see you escape? Where did you hide?' Moir asked the steward. 'Were you allowed to go free as bait? Will they be lying in wait for us?'

The steward rolled his eyes. 'I know how to travel with caution, Northman. My loyalty to this family is beyond question.'

'We will have to trust that Elene is somewhere safe,' Ansithe said, making sure her voice carried to all parts of the hall. 'If she has been kidnapped in the time it took for Ecgbert to make his way here, there may well be a ransom demand. Cynehild can deal with that and stall until we return. But right now, I must believe we will find her and the men she is trying to protect safe and well. Elene is intelligent. She won't take any chances.'

Her words sounded like the pleading of a child. The desire to lay her head against Moir's chest and feel his arms about her shot through her. She ignored it and instead she concentrated on keeping her shoulders straight. Cynehild was the clinging vine, not her. She was the sensible one whom people relied on. She had spent the time since her mother had died learning how to be that person.

'We will leave as soon as is practicable,' she said to Moir. 'You, your men, Ecgbert and me.'

'Will you send us out to face your enemy without protection?' Moir asked.

Ansithe glanced towards her sister, who nodded. 'You shall have what weapons we have, but Palni must stay here. He is not fit to travel. He will remain safe, regardless of what happens to you.'

His eyes hardened to ice. And she knew she had just irrevocably killed the tender shoots of friendship between them. 'I thank you for the consideration, my lady,' he said drily.

Chapter Eleven

Moir struggled to act normally when he went into the infirmary to let Palni know what was happening, but he felt as though a great big hole had developed inside his chest where his heart had been. Ansithe wanted to end things between them. Or rather she thought she did. It was up to him to try to persuade her otherwise. They could be together for the time they had left.

It might be easier if he let her go, but he knew he couldn't and that frightened him. What if he made an offer for her and she refused him?

Palni glanced up when Moir cleared his throat. The priest seemed greatly embarrassed that he'd been caught fraternising with the enemy, but Palni showed little remorse.

'Am I interrupting something?' Moir asked, pushing the hurt from Ansithe's cold words away from him. 'It appears as if Palni is losing as usual.'

Father Oswald stood up. 'We were having a friendly conversation. It helps to pass the time. Boredom is the great enemy.'

'We speak about religion,' Palni said. 'That priest makes some interesting observations, things I'd never thought of before. He makes me see the world in a whole new fashion. It is as if I have been reborn into the light.'

'Does he?' Moir pressed his lips together. If the situation wasn't so serious, the fact that Palni, the die-hard follower of Thor, was interested in Christianity would amuse him no end. 'We must speak. There have been developments.'

'Something is up or otherwise you'd be busy romancing the Valkyrie,' Palni said, struggling but failing to rise.

'Our paths collide every now and then. I'm not romancing her.' He pinned his friend with his gaze. 'Remember that. I will fight any man who speaks ill of Lady Ansithe.'

'It is the first time I have heard you defend a woman to a friend. Intriguing.'

'I have no time for this.' Moir rapidly explained what was going on with the ambush and Elene's presumed kidnap. The priest threw his hands up in the air and started muttering about the saints preserving them. Moir gave him a hard glance and he quietened.

'You are going after her and you want me to

come too,' Palni said, trying but failing to rise. 'The Valkyrie has given her permission.'

'I have to, but not you.' Moir looked at his friend. 'You would only slow us down, my friend.'

'If you needed me, I would go. I always will.'

'I know what can happen to women who get taken. Lady Elene helped to save our lives in the aftermath of the raid. The fool of a steward thinks there will be a ransom demand, but I think we have a chance of finding her alive and well. Lady Ansithe believes me. She will be travelling with me.'

A smile tugged at Palni's mouth. 'She intends to hold you to your oath. Lady Ansithe is a good woman. Keep her safe. Things like this take time.'

'I intend to.' Something punched Moir in the gut. He could have used Palni on this venture. The warrior was good at tracking. He seemed to have a second sense about danger. But there was no way he could travel yet, even on a horse. He would be more of a hindrance than a help. 'But I'm going to have to leave you here.'

'There will be opportunities for *friendship* between you two.'

'This is hardly going to be a picnic for two. We are going to find her sister and the missing guards.' Moir was aware that his cheeks were flaming as the priest, Ansithe's priest, gave him a hard stare.

Palni adopted a falsely innocent face. 'If you make her unhappy, you will have to answer to me.'

'I have no intention of making her unhappy. There isn't a…' He paused. He was not in the habit of speaking about his intimate relations with women and did not intend to start with Ansithe. What they had shared was far too precious to be bantered about. 'Friends means friends. I want to speak about other things. More important than any fancy you might have about me and Ansithe.'

'It is you who keeps bringing it up.' Palni gave a delighted laugh before he sobered. 'I have a great deal of respect for Lady Ansithe. I don't want her to be hurt, whatever there is between you. It is going to be dangerous if these outlaws were confident enough to attack an armed group of travellers.'

'She wants to go. She wants to protect her sister.'

'These things have a way of happening.' Palni waved an airy hand. 'She has the soul of a Valkyrie, but she also is flesh and blood, not a creature from a *skald*'s tale. Remember that before you put her in harm's way.'

The priest made a few protesting noises

about Ansithe having the soul of a Valkyrie and crossed himself.

Palni smiled. 'Some people just do, Father. And you should be glad, or otherwise we would not be playing King's Tafl here.'

The priest stopped mid-complaint. 'In that case, I am very glad for Lady Ansithe's prowess with her bow.'

Palni grabbed Moir's tunic and pulled him closer. 'She is a good woman and good for you from what I can see, but think about what sort of future you can offer her before you go any further.'

Moir's guts twisted. He wished he could punch something hard. He jerked away from Palni. 'Tell me something new.'

'If you harm one hair on Lady Ansithe's head, I will have your guts for bowstrings.' Palni gave a nod. 'I bet you wouldn't think that I'd do it, but I will. She and the good Father here saved my life.'

'She is a grown woman, a widow, able to make her own choices. We both know what we are about.' Moir shifted uncomfortably. His joining with Ansithe was far too new to think about without wanting her immediately. He had hoped for more time with her, but now there was this obstacle in his way. Palni seemed to have read him with a single glance. He had to hope that no one else had noticed.

'What does that have to do with anything? I know what you are like with women—too dedicated to Andvarr's *felag* ever to settle down.'

'You don't need to worry about me. Everything will be well. I have no intention of hurting her.'

'No, you never do, but you refuse to suffer people, particularly women, interfering in what you see as your duty. If protecting her means you not fulfilling your vow of loyalty to Andvarr, which one will you choose? Are you in truth his hound or your own man?'

His insides ached at Palni's question. It had been the same one which had circled his brain ever since he'd watched Ansithe sleep in his arms and knew he had deep feelings for her which would never vanish.

And he was still no closer to the answer, not one which made any sense. He wanted an honourable future with Ansithe. A longer future than the one which was currently on offer. One which would last many sunsets. He wanted to hope and plan. She made him want to live, instead of just existing, waiting for the next battle, the next order from Andvarr. Moir clenched his fists. He had to be better than his father who had betrayed his commander's trust. He wanted both—his position in Andvarr's *felag* and Ansithe.

'I devotedly hope I never have to make that choice.'

Ansithe stood outside in the yard, rather than remain in the hall where Cynehild kept bursting into tears and declaring that this family must be cursed to suffer more than its fair share of bad luck. She had listened until the prophecies of doubt and doom became too much, made her excuses and had left the maids to try to console Cynehild.

The air was far cooler than earlier and the sky had darkened to a jet black. A crash of thunder reverberated two heartbeats before the rain started to pelt down in great silver sheets.

Ansithe sighed. Setting out in this was a recipe for getting lost, Cynehild was right about that if nothing else. Ecgbert would not be able to see his hand in front of his face, let alone be able to guide them to where Elene was sheltering, even if they used smouldering torches. They would have to wait until morning.

The storm matched her mood and her sense that everything was ending, before it had properly begun. She and Moir were a fleeting dream, with no more substance than a wispy summer breeze.

Having a relationship with Moir was simply not going to work, particularly not now that Elene had been kidnapped. It changed everything. It reminded her that Moir was one of them, the Great Heathen Horde who raided and took women for slaves. Had she been in his thrall like Cedric claimed?

Her heart protested that there had been another reason for his travelling deep into Mercian territory. She simply did not know what it was and she wanted to know. Desperately. And did she trust him enough that he would not escape once they were clear of the manor house?

'You wanted to see me,' Moir said. He stood very tall and correct. His voice held more than a hint of steel.

'I wanted to go over what supplies we will need and if you think taking horses would be a good idea or not.'

He came over to her, put his arm about her shoulder, but she stepped away from him. He peered at her with a quizzical expression.

'I meant what I said earlier about ending it. I wasn't waiting out here hoping you'd take me in your arms,' she said, hating the great leaden lump which now occupied her stomach. His holding her was precisely what she wanted. If he did that, then the choice would be taken from her and she could draw comfort from him.

He watched her with wary eyes. 'We will get soaked if we stay out here, discussing supplies.'

'It won't take long but I wanted to get the benefit of your experience.'

'The stables?' Without waiting for an answer, he started towards them. 'We should be able to speak without interruption there and can keep dry.'

Her stomach went into tighter knots. She knew she should find an excuse and go. Being alone with him in a private place where she was aware of every movement he made was a poor idea except she needed to speak to him about the plans for the expedition and the rain was getting heavier. 'The stables make sense.'

The scent of dried meadow grass and the sound of the soft snuffles of the horses filled the deserted stables. Moir put his hand out as if to draw her into his arms. But Ansithe backed away and wrapped her arms about her waist. If he touched her, she'd break all the promises she'd made to herself about how, if she behaved with propriety, Elene would be rescued unharmed.

'I understand you spoke with Palni,' she said, drawing her brows together and putting on her serious face as Cynehild often called it. 'Cynehild has promised to look after him until we return.'

She didn't add *if* they returned. It was possible that the outlaws could strike again, but she doubted they would be that bold. She and Moir would find Elene and the injured men quickly. It was when they did that her time would be nearly at an end with Moir. She'd have to send him back to court with the guards for the ransom. And goodness knew what would happen to him then.

'I've spoken to him.' Moir watched her with hooded eyes. 'Father Oswald believes it is good you are going to find your sister. He has gone to the church to offer prayers for her safe return.'

'Father Oswald thinks I am beyond redemption.' She gave a little hiccuping laugh and inwardly squirmed. So much for being nonchalant or stand-offish. She sounded pathetic and needy. She pressed her lips together and became more determined than ever to sound in control. 'I rarely pay any attention to what he says.'

'You do. You worry too much about what other people think, even though you pretend you don't. And you remember the criticism, rather than the praise. It is why you ended things between us. It was easier for you to believe what an arrogant coward said than trusting your gut instinct about what is good and true in your life.'

'I have no idea what you are talking about,' she protested, hating the truth in his words. Her own feelings about him terrified her. They went against everything she'd ever been taught, yet being in his arms had taken her beyond her wildest imaginings.

The silence grew. Ansithe could hear the steady drop of rain on the roof. 'I must make sure everything is in order. We need to make an early start.'

His eyes flashed blue fire at her change of subject. 'You wanted to speak to me about supplies rather than the composition of the party.'

'I know what is required.' Ansithe ticked the various items off on her fingers.

He coughed. 'My men and I will be ready to go but…can you trust Ecgbert?'

'We need him. He is the only one who knows where the attack happened and is our one link to Elene.'

'A man like him managed to escape with barely a scratch but a host of warriors was injured? That doesn't strike you as peculiar?' When she looked unsure, he added, 'He has not proven himself loyal to you. For a start, he is too friendly with your neighbour, the one who wanted to take us off your hands and who had Bjartr beaten.'

She pursed her lips together. Moir had made valid points. 'So you are saying that the attack was by design rather than chance? I am not certain. Ecgbert may shrink from violence, but he is no traitor. He is very loyal to my father and tells him everything.'

'He is either a coward who refused to risk himself to save your sister, or he is in collusion with whoever attacked them.' Moir crossed his arms. 'He could be leading us into a trap. You could authorise us to go on our own. Keep yourself safe here. You have Palni as my guarantee to ransom for your father and brother-in-law should the worst happen.'

'Elene is my sister. I go.' Ansithe flattened her hands against her gown. 'Your promise not to escape specifically stated as long as you and your men were under my control.'

His face fell slightly. 'After what we have shared, you still don't trust me to keep my word to you.'

'My archery skill matches any,' she said and willed him to understand that this wasn't a question of trust. 'I can be of use, rather than sitting back at the manor, tending my bees and waiting for news.'

'Promise me if the fighting starts, you will go somewhere safe to shoot those arrows, rather than being in the heat of battle.'

She watched him under her lashes. 'Would you?'

'I'm a battle-hardened warrior. There is a difference.' He reached out and entangled her fingers with his. The touch made her forget everything about propriety and what she should or shouldn't be doing and remember how safe she'd felt in his arms. She knew she should step away, but all she could do was to gaze up at his piercing blue eyes and cling to his hand. 'I want to protect you. I want to make sure you are safe.'

'I am safe. I will be safe. I can look after myself,' she whispered, but her fingers remained curled about his.

He tugged her hands. Her body collided with his. He swore softly and put his mouth against hers, nuzzling her. She instantly looped her arms about his neck, pressing her lips to his. He brought his arms about her, holding their bodies close. And she gave herself up to the kiss.

'What do you truly need?' he growled in her ear. 'Tell me the truth rather than giving me some lie.'

'Your arms about me,' she confessed, laying her head on his chest and listening to the comforting thump of his heart. Tomorrow, she silently promised, tomorrow she'd be strong, but for tonight she needed him. 'I was wrong earlier to think this thing between us was finished.'

'Are you using me to stop thinking?' he said against her ear. His tongue tantalised while his teeth nibbled, sending sparks shooting through her.

'Is that wrong of me?' she murmured.

He nipped her chin. 'I'm not proud. I will have you any way I can get you.'

His fingers went to where she had carefully braided her hair. With a few tugs, he had the arrangement down and her hair floating about her face. He buried his in the silken curtain.

'Can I stay here with you?' she whispered. 'Being alone right now frightens me more than I can say. I don't want to think. I keep remembering about when my mother died. You make it easy to keep the demons at bay.' She placed her hands against his chest and felt his hard muscles move under her palms. 'Is that possible?'

He pressed a kiss to her cheek and gave a deep laugh which reverberated through her body, making a curl of liquid fire flicker and dance about her insides. 'I believe that can be arranged. The physical exists between us, denying it would be wrong.'

'I won't deny it again.' She pulled his face down to her mouth.

Their mouths met again. Lips on lips. Tongue twining with tongue as the fire deep within her belly grew and raged.

He nibbled along her neck until he reached her gown.

He cupped her breasts over the material, drew small circles with his fingertips, teasing and tormenting them until her nipples became hardened points.

'We are rather overdressed,' he breathed in her ear.

She tugged at his tunic and lifted it over his head. His skin shimmered silver in the faint light. She ran her hands over the indents from his many scars. His skin was warm silk under the pads of her fingers. She brushed his nipples and they became tiny nubs. She bent her mouth and suckled.

He groaned in the back of his throat.

His hands captured hers and eased her gently down among the clean hay. The lingering scent of summer flowers and new grass filled her nostrils.

He rapidly undid her gown and pushed it up, revealing her body to his avid gaze.

Then his lips feasted on her breasts, teasing the nipples while he kept one hand lightly holding her wrists. Her back arched to meet his mouth and she knew she needed this. She wanted this. Her head thrashed about as wave after wave of heat coursed through her body. Then gently, like a feather, she settled back down to earth.

He was watching her with an intent expression.

'Thank you,' she whispered, reaching up and touching his cheek.

She'd been wrong earlier to push him away when all she had wanted was his touch to drive away all her fears and anxieties.

'We are not done yet.'

His mouth went lower, stopping at her belly button where his tongue played, lapping round and round until she was convinced the liquid fire would consume her once again. Her body writhed against his and she pulled at his shoulders.

'A little longer,' he murmured, releasing her hands and going lower still to the nest of curls at the apex of her thighs.

He slipped a finger between her folds, caressing her.

'I need… I need…you,' she cried as her body writhed against the sheer seductive movement of his fingers. He made her feel beautiful and desirable, as if she could accomplish anything.

He put her hand against his trousers. The hard length of him strained to get free. With fumbling fingers, she undid them and pushed them down. He pulled them off.

She held him and marvelled at his silky strength.

'Put me where you want me,' he growled in her ear.

She nodded and placed him between her thighs. He surged forward, sheathing his length completely in her. Her body opened to welcome him.

He collapsed down on her and then began to thrust. She joined him joyfully and together, the world exploded around them as the thunder reverberated in the sky.

Gradually, Moir became aware of his surroundings—the pebble pushing into the small of his back, the faint starlight infusing the stable now that the thunderstorm had passed.

He gave her neck a nuzzle before rolling off her and staring up at the roof. He'd lied to her—their joining was not just about physical desire. He desired her mind. He desired the way she cared deeply about her family. She awoke protective urges in him that he didn't know he'd possessed and for the very first time he could begin to understand why his father had been so determined to reach his mother that he'd betrayed his fellow prisoners.

With great difficulty he kept his mind away from making halls in the sky and spinning dreams about how he wanted to spend the rest of his life with this woman by his side. How could he ask her to share anything when his future was so uncertain?

She had come to mean so much to him in such a short span of time. She had made him want to dream of the gentler things in life. She made him want to consider a life beyond war and his oath to Andvarr. He wanted to keep her in his arms for ever.

He knew what she had done earlier—used his body so she could forget her fear, so she could have a few moments of peace. He'd done it often enough himself—finding an accommodating pair of thighs to keep the bad dreams at bay. He'd been happy to oblige.

His heart clenched. This time, he wanted it to mean something more than just two bodies seeking solace in the night. He wanted it to mean something to her, just as it had meant something to him.

He froze. He wanted to ask her if she'd wait for him until he could return to her, until he could make his world safe for her. Until he could ensure Guthmann would not carry out his threat and harm any woman he cared about. With her father and brother-in-law in Guthmann's custody, he could not take the risk.

Pushing the thoughts away and forcing himself to concentrate on the present, he kissed the tip of her nose. Her eyes instantly flew open.

'Was I asleep?'

'Adorably so.' He cupped her face between his hands. 'If I can, I will find her.'

'We both will.'

He gave her a significant look. 'I intend on keeping you safe.'

'I know it is dangerous, Moir, but I have to go.'

'Don't you trust me to return to you?'

She gathered her knees to her chest. 'I trust you to return if that is what you are asking. You are an honourable man. I'm willing to say my beliefs about Northmen were wrong where you are concerned. You keep your promises.'

'Did I ask you to remain behind?' Her trust in this matter meant more to him than he could say. 'I want you there. Your skill with the bow surpasses anything I've seen a Northman do.'

He kept quiet about wanting to spend more time with her.

She started to re-braid her hair, making her become the ever-efficient Lady Ansithe again, instead of his Kyrie. 'It isn't your choice. Elene is my sister. What she did was a brave thing. I have to wonder—if I'd gone, would the outcome have been different?'

'Second-guessing your past is as profitless as dreaming about your future. Live in the present.'

'Easy words to say, Moir, but hard to do in practice.'

'I know,' he admitted, wondering if she knew the words had been for his own benefit more than hers. He'd spent nearly a lifetime trying to live by them. 'My father was a dreamer who never accomplished anything except being drunk and my mother always kept trying to work out where things had gone wrong. I discovered that living in the present works best.'

'Your father was a dreamer?'

'He is not important. He belongs to the unlamented past. In the end he lost all honour. His word was not even worth the spit it took to give it. I vowed on his grave to be different—I would keep my promises or die in the attempt. I need to show Andvarr that he was right to put his faith in me.'

'Families are always important. They define who we are.'

'You are wrong. We define how we behave. No one else.' Moir ran a hand through his hair. Andvarr's last words before he left—*do not become weak like your father*—resounded in his brain. She didn't make him weak; she made him stronger. He put his hand against her cheek. She leant into it. 'What we experienced today wasn't a goodbye or an end, but a beginning. The present, Ansithe, and we don't know how long it will last.'

After returning Moir to the byre and tiptoeing past the slumbering Owain, Ansithe opened the door to the hall with a steady hand. The slight creak resounded in the stillness. The fire had burnt down to embers.

'Ansithe.'

Ansithe froze. Her mouth still throbbed from Moir's fervent kisses. Cynehild was bound to notice. She steeled herself, ready for the recriminations. She refused to lie to her sister, but neither could she make promises that she refused to keep. 'I didn't see you there, Cynehild. I… I was making sure everything was ready for the morning. It took longer than I expected.'

Cynehild gestured to the bench with a weary smile. 'Come sit with me. Who knows when I will get a chance to sit with one of my sisters again? I don't bite. Before you say differently, may I remind you that was a long time ago when we were children. I was five and you were three and had just thrown my favourite doll on the fire.'

Ansithe went over and sat beside her. 'I always have time to talk with my older sister.'

She was surprised that she meant it.

Cynehild gathered Ansithe's hands in hers. 'Do you think you can find Elene? Ecgbert has little sense of direction on a good day.'

'I have every hope, particularly with Moir's assistance.'

'But from what Ecgbert said—those outlaws could have returned. The guards are injured. Elene is unprotected. I've been barely able to sleep. I could have gone to court in her place, you know. Maybe I should have.'

Ansithe firmed her jaw. 'Elene is our sister. I will not abandon her. I will find her. Moir and I will deal with any outlaws. Together.'

'You really believe that Northman will help us, not just escape as soon as you are in the forest?'

'He is an honourable man, Cynehild, despite what Cedric implied.'

'And if this is all a trap?'

'What sort of trap?' Ansithe willed Cynehild to think logically. 'How could Moir do anything to plan ahead? Who could he contact? He would not abandon his best friend either. He cares about his men, even Bjartr.'

Cynehild covered Ansithe's hand. 'I don't want you to get hurt. I have no wish to lose either sister.'

'What are you saying?'

'I have eyes, Ansithe. I see the heated looks you and that Northman exchange when you think no one else is watching. How you look at him when he is directing his men. It reminds me of how I used to watch Leofwine before I knew how he felt about me. Out there, alone.' Cynehild grabbed Ansithe's hands. 'Come back to me, Ansithe, whatever happens. Don't run away with your Northman.'

Ansithe attempted to fill her lungs with life-giving air. 'Are you accusing me of something?

Do you think I am in thrall to him like Cedric claimed? I promised you would get Leofwine back. You will have him.'

Cynehild gripped Ansithe's hands tight. 'Accusing you? No. You may be reckless, but you know there are certain bridges not to be crossed. I trust you to do the right thing when the time comes. But keep your heart safe, Sister.'

'I know the future and have no wish for it to change. Getting my family—our father and your Leofwine—back means everything to me. It is why we took the Northmen prisoner,' Ansithe said around the lump in her throat. She knew she spoke at best a half-truth. Moir had already claimed her heart and he would take it with him when they parted.

Chapter Twelve

Ansithe looked back at the manor where Cyne-hild stood with Wulfgar, waving madly with a bright smile on her face. Her throat tightened. This might the last time she saw her sister or her home.

'We will find Elene,' she called back to Cyne-hild and Wulfgar. No answer. She took one final glance back, but they had gone back into the hall.

'We will do our best. It is not an easy task, Ansithe,' Moir said, keeping step beside her. 'And it is better that Bjartr stays to look after Palni. Another hostage, in case the worst should happen.'

'The worst isn't going to happen,' Ansithe said around a lump in her throat. 'I refuse to believe that.'

'The lad will be a hindrance. He sows discord,' Moir said in an undertone. 'Trust my judgement on this.'

Ansithe closed her eyes, suddenly under-standing the unspoken message. Leaving Bjartr behind was Moir's pledge that they would not escape no matter the circumstances. She appreci-ated it, but she knew deep down it was unneces-sary—Moir was a man of his word. 'I trust you.'

He gave a smile which lit her world. 'Prog-ress.'

Ansithe felt jumpy as if unseen eyes were watching her as they went deeper into the for-est, following the track Ecgbert claimed was the correct one.

She matched her steps with Moir's.

He paused and then nodded. 'Then let us hope your steward is a better navigator than he was at keeping your lands well tended. These woods have not been worked for many years and appear easy to get lost in.'

'I have my grandfather's map, but this wood is not as he knew it.'

'Who did the recent civil war benefit? The one between the Mercians? The *ceorl* or the *eal-dorman*? Look around you, you can see how this forest has been abandoned. Where are the char-coal burners? The swineherds? The woodcut-ters? Trees this big take years to grow and they are hard to fell with simply a swing of an axe to be of much use. And it is not just this forest, but the woods all over Mercia which have become like this.'

Her heart thumped. She knew the importance of the underwood in providing the poles that they needed for building and how the forest had changed since she was a girl. And some of that change had happened because of disputes with the kingdoms closest to them—Hwicce and Wessex—not just because of the Heathen Horde or the civil war which preceded their arrival. They had simply accelerated the decline. 'Everyone is sick of war except for a few.'

'Good borders will make for good neighbours, yes?'

'All I want is my family safe.'

She wanted much more than that, but confessing that to him was impossible.

'Let's not count on the future until it happens.'

'All I should worry about is the present.'

'Something like that.' He put his hand on her shoulder. Warmth radiated out, comforting her. 'First let's find your sister and then the rest will follow.'

'If your ransom is paid, what will you do?' she asked, watching the path in front of them, rather than his face.

'My ransom will be paid. I have left enough with my *jaarl* for that to happen. Provided whoever buys me thinks to ask.'

'What will you do next?'

'I never think beyond the next sunset, but maybe I've seen enough war. Maybe I will find some land to build on.'

Ansithe's heart skipped a beat. With great difficulty she held back the words asking if he would need a companion and if he'd consider returning for her. They had different pathways and destinies to follow which had only crossed for a little while, she reminded her heart. 'I can see you as a farmer. Maybe in that Iceland place you spoke about.'

His eyes crinkled at the corners. 'Thank you.'

In that heartbeat, she could also see him with a pretty wife and a gaggle of children crowding about his legs, listening to his stories. She had no doubt they'd ask about the time when he was captured by bees. She wondered if he'd ever tell them about her or even think of her—the woman he'd once considered had the soul of a Valkyrie.

'Your eyes seem sad.' His voice invited her to confide her thoughts. Confessing that one would lead to more complications. It would be easy to wish that she'd never kissed him, but that would imply regretting his touch, the way his hands felt as they roamed over her body or the taste of his mouth. She could never regret being with him in that way, but she could not hold back time either. With each step they took, she knew she was coming closer to their parting.

'I miss my sister.' She half-stumbled over a tree root. His fingers were there immediately, preventing her from falling. She gave a swift intake of breath as warm pulses of heat jolted up her arm. She jerked away. 'I should have been the one to go. Elene isn't like me.'

'Changing the past is impossible and the future belongs to the gods. The present holds the possibilities.'

'But you still dream of being a farmer? How is that living in the present?'

His barking laugh rang out, warming her down to her toes. Despite her resolutions, she liked him. Being around him made her day better. 'I have only started to think about it since being with you.'

And when it came time for them to part? Would it make it any easier that it wasn't her decision?

Ecgbert raised his hand. 'We need to turn slightly here. I remember crashing through the brambles here.'

'You said nothing about brambles earlier,' Moir said.

The steward's cheek flushed crimson. 'I tried to forget them, but my arms are scratched, my lady.'

He held out his hands. His wrists bore several long angry gashes.

'Before you went through the brambles, how did you find your way back?'

'I followed the river. I planned to jump in if they appeared again.'

'Then we shall do the same. There is a crossing a little way from here,' Ansithe said. 'No point in everyone getting scratches to match yours.'

Ecgbert's mouth turned down. 'I'd forgotten.'

'But I hadn't. I've spent years studying my grandfather's map, Ecgbert. I know where the old roads go.' She firmed her mouth. 'I want to make good time. We have wasted enough as it is.'

'Wait! Wait!' Bjartr raced after them. He carried a stick and was waving wildly. His face was covered in sweat.

Moir swore loudly. Ansithe motioned for everyone to stop.

When he reached them, his chest heaved, as he put his hands on his knees.

'What are you doing here?' Moir asked, lowering his brows before the lad had a chance to say anything more. 'I gave you orders to stay and look after Palni.'

'I am coming with you.' His bottom lip stuck out. 'It is the goddess of my dream who has been kidnapped and you are going to fetch her back or die in the attempt. She saved my life and I've never thanked her. Not properly. I owe that woman a life debt. The Valkyrie's sister agreed. She gave me a token to show Lady Ansithe that I come with her blessing. She'd rather have me out here looking than back there making a nuisance of myself at the manor. And I did save her son's life.'

He held out the small wooden cross.

'It is the cross Cynehild normally wears,' Ansithe said. 'It belonged to my grandmother. Cynehild did indeed send him.'

'You can stay at the manor and keep it safe.' Moir pointed back towards where they had come from. 'Go. Lady Ansithe does not need you on this quest. She has plenty of other men who will be of far more use.'

Bjartr remained where he was standing. 'No. I stay. I will be useful.'

'What can you contribute? You have caused enough difficulties already.'

'All my life everyone has been telling me— don't do that, Bjartr, it is risky. Let someone else do it. My father does it and now you are starting to do it, too. That stops now. I don't need anyone making excuses for me.' He drew himself upright. 'I start pulling my weight and take my place, not as the leader, but as the least important. You need warriors if you are going to rescue Lady Elene and I know how to fight. You saw to that, Moir, even if you only wanted me to use wooden swords. I am no longer a toddler following in your footsteps. I am nearly a man grown. You were fighting when you were my age. I should be as well.'

Moir stared at the boy, torn between annoyance and pride. 'Your mother—'

'My mother would want me to become a man. My father wants this as well,' Bjartr said in a loud voice. 'I lied yesterday—I went to the lake with the intention of drowning myself because I had disgraced everyone, but then I saw that little boy in trouble and knew I could do something to save him, but no one recognised it. Instead I was beaten for my trouble, but Lady Ansithe saw me for what I was and saved me. She treated me with dignity when no one else would. I want to help her and pledge my oath to her for saving my life. I explained this to Lady Cynehild and she listened. Why can't you? Why can't you see I can change? I want to be better because of Lady Ansithe.'

He stood tall, facing Moir. A faint breeze ruffled his hair, but there was a determination to his jaw Moir had not seen before. Moir touched his pendant—wasn't that all he'd wanted to do once?

'Not my decision,' Moir said at last. 'It's Lady

Ansithe who will make this choice. She leads this *felag*. I obey her orders.'

Ansithe looked at the youth. He had a pleading expression on his face. He had come on this journey of his own free will, wanting to help. She, too, knew what it felt like to be the one who had disgraced everyone. He deserved another chance.

If she sent him back, she'd also have to send someone to accompany him and they'd lose even more precious time. And he'd lose whatever courage he'd gained in the night.

'Will you obey me? Will you pledge on your sacred honour that you will not try to escape? That you will obey my orders to the best of your ability?'

'Give me the opportunity to make amends, Lady Ansithe,' he said, holding out his hands. There was a dignity in his face she hadn't seen before. 'Please. You have taught me about the power of forgiveness when you and your sister saved my life. You showed it to me when you argued with the priest so that you could save Palni. And when you cut me down and defied the Mercian lord. I will do all you ask and more.'

When faced with such pleading, how could she refuse? He did appear to want to help. Cynehild had given her endorsement. Sometimes, all it took was someone taking a chance for forgiveness to happen.

Ansithe held out her hand. 'I welcome all who wish to help free my sister.'

His hand curled about hers. 'You won't regret it.'

'She had better not,' Moir growled. Ansithe gave him a quelling look.

Moir was pleased to see they made good progress on their journey after Bjartr joined them. He'd half-expected Ansithe or Bjartr to complain at the pace the way her steward kept doing, but Ansithe made no mention and whenever they stopped, she wanted to get going again before anyone else. Bjartr kept quiet.

The weasel-faced steward kept bleating on about how he wasn't sure that he was up to the task if he couldn't rest one more time. Moir's feelings of distrust and unease grew.

'How much further?' Moir growled on the third day, fixing the steward with a dark gaze.

'It is here. I told you I'd find it. It is what your countrymen did, not mine,' the steward said, pointing to a glade where the grass was trampled down. Sweat poured down his face.

A sweet sickly stench hung in the air, the sort which hangs over battlefields. It was clear in a glance that something had indeed happened here. Moir's stomach clenched.

'Ansithe?'

'Where did you hide?' Ansithe asked, putting her hand over her mouth. The smell was awful, but she was not going to disgrace herself. She was battle-hardened. The thought made her straighten her spine and stare straight ahead when all she longed to do was walk into Moir's arms and draw comfort from him. His eyes turned tender.

The steward pointed to a hollow in the tree. He had gone a funny shade of green. 'I was too scared to even breathe. After they went, Lady Elene said they would make for the charcoal burner's hut we had passed.'

'Where is that hut? Precisely?'

'I can't remember. I thought I knew the one Lady Elene mentioned, but I've racked my brains on the way here and it is a blank. I should have gone with them to see precisely where it was and then left.' Ecgbert collapsed in a snivelling heap. 'I'm a miserable coward, my lady.'

'If you hadn't returned, we would never have known this happened,' Ansithe said. 'We have a slim chance of finding her, but it is a chance. The hut should be close by.'

Moir bent down and started to examine the grass. 'The outlaws did not cover their tracks.'

'There was definitely a battle here. I have found some of the missing Wessex warriors,' Bjartr called out. 'It is not a pretty sight. And I think there is a Dane as well.'

Moir cursed loudly.

'How can you tell the Danes were involved?' Ansithe asked, wrapping her arms about her waist.

Moir held out a broken axe he'd found. 'It is Danish. It is unlikely an outlaw would have it.'

'But we don't know that for certain.'

'How many dead?'

'Two Wessex and three Danes. There is also the body of a woman. Not the Lady Elene, my goddess, but a woman with a large mole on her upper lip and grey hair.'

Ansithe recognised the description and closed her eyes in grief. Gode had been their mother's servant before she was theirs and she had volunteered to go with Elene. She silently said a prayer for her.

'How many guards were sent with you?' Moir asked.

The steward pursed his lips, 'Eleven, I think. I kept telling them they needed more to look after fierce warriors like you, but they said that was all our gold was worth. They couldn't even fight off those outlaws.'

'They fought off the attackers or you wouldn't be here,' Moir pointed out.

'Elene didn't waste time burying the bodies,' Ansithe said. 'She wanted to get away. She showed sense.'

'Let's find this hut.'

When the shout came, Ansithe raced towards it, but Bjartr was standing by the hut, shaking his head. 'There is no one here. They have already left. I can tell by looking.'

Ansithe's knees threatened to give way, but Moir instantly put an arm about her waist, supporting her.

'No one there,' she whispered. 'How could it be? Ecgbert swore she was going to make for safety.'

'Do we know they were here?' Moir went in and emerged with a dark green cloak.

Ansithe gasped. 'It belongs to Elene.'

She looked up at the clear blue sky and blinked rapidly. Her sister wasn't dead. She was sure she'd know deep down within her soul if that had happened. 'Do you think they were followed and attacked?'

'Do we have to know how they were taken?' Bjartr asked. 'Isn't it enough to know they left?'

Moir glanced at Ansithe. 'The lad is on to something.'

'These men are prepared to stop at nothing,' Bjartr said. 'It takes guts to attack a force that large.'

'They were not prepared. We are,' Ansithe said, her hand going to her bow. 'We can hunt them. They can't be that far ahead of us.'

'This is a great huge forest,' Ecgbert bleated. 'They could be anywhere within it.'

Moir leant over to her ear. 'It does not look good for your sister.'

'I know, but I'd sense inside me if something had happened to her. She is somewhere out there and still alive.' She lifted her chin up. 'As long as she is alive and we can free her, I will be content. I do know what happens to women who are captured. You don't need to coat the truth with honey for me.'

'We will find her,' Bjartr declared.

'I agree.' Ansithe started to search the ground. 'We had worked out a scheme about what to do if one of us was taken and I am sure Elene will have implemented it if she could.'

'Was that down to you?'

'It seemed sensible.' Ansithe's eyes glittered with unshed tears. 'I just hope she was able to leave a trail.'

'I wish I could return to Baelle Heale.' Ecgbert wiped his face with his sleeve. 'I'm no warrior. I'm no good at this. I prefer ledgers and books.'

'Absolutely not,' Ansithe answered before Moir had a chance to voice his concerns. 'We can't spare anyone to take you back. And you never know when you might prove useful.'

'I was worried about that, Lady Ansithe. Your father…'

'My father would be furious if I didn't try to rescue my sister.'

Ecgbert crumpled under her gaze. 'If you say so, my lady. I had always considered he valued his own life more than his children's. He'd want to be ransomed first and then take charge of any investigation. But I may be mistaken.'

His words held a certain amount of truth. But it didn't change things. 'I need time to think. What did my sister do when she had to leave? She would have known that Ecgbert would try to lead us here, but might get in a muddle afterwards. She may have left the cloak on purpose.'

Moir rapidly detailed men to bury the bodies while he left Ansithe to ponder. He had a quiet word with Bjartr and explained that the steward needed to be closely watched. Bjartr seemed to grow two inches when Moir told him that he was the only person who could possibly undertake such a task.

'You care about her.' Bjartr's eyes widened.

'Palni said to remind you of Guthmann's threat to any woman you might care about.'

Moir rolled his eyes. 'Palni becomes like an old woman. I can handle Guthmann in a fair fight.'

'Is that what you want? A fight with Guthmann? My father wants to prevent that from ever happening.'

'I want to make sure her sister is safe. If we free her and somehow find Lady Ansithe's father in the bargain, we will be free and can go back to your father in triumph.'

Bjartr made a noise as though he wanted to say more, but Moir gave him a hard look.

'We need to be searching, not speculating, Bjartr, about what your father intends.' Moir turned to examine the ground. A small bit of metal winked out at him a short way from the hut. He rapidly crossed to it and picked it up. 'Ansithe.'

Ansithe hurried over and took it from his outstretched palm. Her cheeks were wet with tears. 'It is one of my sister's earrings. The bracken seems to be more trampled down beyond and I think I can see a bit of thread hanging off a fern.'

'Then I suspect she was able to escape.'

When the mist came down and it became too dark and dangerous to travel, Ansithe reluctantly decided they had to halt for the night. Progress had been slow going, particularly as Bjartr had the habit of declaring that he had seen something and running towards it, only for it to be nothing. As a result, they had lost the trail several times. Before the mist came down, Ansithe was convinced they had merely gone in several overlapping circles. At her orders, they had pitched the tents and bedded down for the night.

After a simple fish supper, most had retired to the various tents. Bjartr had been no trouble, not even baulking at having to help catch the fish or cook it. It was as if, in being given the slightest of chances, he had decided to change.

However, Ansithe found it difficult to sleep alone in her tent. The hoots of a tawny owl taunted her.

Every time she closed her eyes, she saw Elene's features. Elene would never have been in this position if Ansithe had not insisted that the brooches be taken to court.

'Can't sleep?' Moir's soft voice came through the velvet darkness. It amazed her how attuned he was to her. It was as though they were two halves of the same whole.

Ansithe gathered her knees to her chest. 'I wish I could. Even Ecgbert is sleeping. I am certain I can hear his snores. The ground is hard, but no one else seems to mind. I wish the mist hadn't come down and we could have gone further.'

'You get used to sleeping on hard ground. Even Bjartr has become accustomed. His snores have joined those of your steward's. It is a luxury to have a tent.'

'But you don't sleep.'

'Sleep evades me.'

She rose and peered out of the tent. Moir sat on his own beside the embers of the campfire. Other than them, the entire camp appeared to be shrouded in sleep. Somewhere far away a tawny owl hooted.

He patted the bare rock beside him. 'Come sit. I can use the company. My watch lasts a while longer yet.'

She pushed her feet into her boots and wrapped a fur about her shoulders before going out into the misty night air. 'Do you think anything will happen tonight?'

He shrugged. 'Nothing moves in this mist. Our quarry will be sheltering, waiting for it to clear. I've been keeping watch for years. You learn to read the weather.'

'You wanted Bjartr to stay at Baelle Heale,' she said. 'You were annoyed with my decision for him to join us. Cynehild would never have given him that cross if she doubted his sincerity.'

'He would have been safer there.' Moir ran his

hand through his hair. 'But maybe he is right. Maybe we have all treated him like a child. It is why he tried to prove himself.'

'Why did Andvarr entrust him to you?'

He turned towards her. 'He did it because Bjartr has acquired the habit of annoying people and I had had a fight with Guthmann. Andvarr killed two birds with one stone.'

'And he felt that your quarrel with Guthmann would have blown over by the time you returned?'

'Andvarr felt it would. I assumed there would be no need for Guthmann and I to encounter each other again this summer.'

She drew her upper lip over her teeth. Two very different views. 'But you expect to fight him.'

'I never look to the future. I live in the present, remember?'

'Even warriors have to plan ahead when they go into battle.' She leant forward. 'You think about the future even when you proclaim you do not. You would not have stayed alive as a warrior or been made a warlord if men did not believe in you.'

She did not mention that she believed in him as well. It would be revealing far too much.

He sat for a long time. The tawny owl began its hooting again.

'I had never considered it in that respect,' he said, breaking his silence. 'You are right—I do think about war and strategy. I just don't think about my own future. There is a difference between planning and dreams.'

Ansithe's heart knocked. She wanted to ask him why he was like that, but the last time he had refused to speak much about his past.

'I saw the look the others gave you when you discovered the Danish axe. Could Guthmann have attacked my sister?'

He stilled. 'To what purpose?'

She noticed that he didn't deny the possibility. 'You had a fight with him. He swore vengeance. It is possible that he learnt who my captives were when Elene handed the badges over to your *jaarl*?'

'Why attack your sister going back to the manor? Guthmann or one of his minions would know that I was not in the group. I could have understood waiting until my men and I departed Baelle Heale to attack us then, but attacking before that makes little sense.'

Her stomach tightened. He was definitely keeping secrets from her. 'But it is why you are sitting up, puzzling over it, is it not?'

'We were lost in this forest, starving for over a week when we stumbled upon your manor. It is possible that there are other groups of North-

men or Danes in a similar position. They saw
the convoy and attacked.'

'That is one explanation, certainly.'

'Whatever happens I am determined to keep
you safe.'

His words had a fierce ring to them.

She gave an uneasy laugh. 'I am in no danger
from Guthmann. I doubt he even knows I exist.'

Moir sat silently for a long time. 'We have no
idea what he knows or doesn't know. He would
probably thank you for capturing me.'

'What did you do to make him hate you that
much? It can't just be that you stopped him from
taking that woman.'

'Guthmann is a predator and I deprived him
of his prey. He felt I was arrogant and should
show more circumspection given my heritage.'

'Your heritage?'

'Unlike Bjartr or Guthmann, I did not have a
jaarl for a father. Nor did my family have lands.
My father betrayed his comrades and left them
to rot. At first when he returned, he was lauded
as a hero and made the *jaarl*'s hand. A year later
two of his fellow prisoners made their way back
and the truth came out—how he had given up
their leader in order to walk to freedom. He tried
to claim that he had intended to return and free
them, but his new responsibilities had prevented

him. There was a trial and he was found guilty, stripped of everything and executed.'

'How old were you when this happened?'

'Eight. My mother died the following spring and her last act was to give me the amber pendant that I wear so that I would remember to be a better man than my father. I swore on her grave that I would always be loyal to my *jaarl*.'

'Did your father ever give you an explanation?' she asked in a whisper, trying to understand what it must have been like for Moir as a child.

'He told me he wanted to be there for my name day, but I discovered when I was older that he'd told others he'd returned for my mother, so I don't really know what to believe. In the end, it doesn't really matter why he did it, only that he did.'

Ansithe pressed her hands against her eyes. That was a terrible burden to lay on a young child. Much as her father had made her feel responsible for her mother's death, a little voice inside her said.

'And then what happened? You are clearly a warrior now.'

'I held true to my mother's wish and made my name by my sword. The way to rise in the North used to be based on one's prowess in war.' Moir shrugged. 'I have been Andvarr's man and shown my loyalty many times. I hope in time he will see I am not my father.'

'Bjartr's father entrusted his son to your care.'

'And see how I have repaid that trust? Bjartr is a captive and has been shown to be a coward, rather than the future leader his father required.' He made a disgusted noise. 'And it is my fault.'

Ansithe put her hand over his. 'He is old enough to make his own mistakes and to learn from them. It was never your choice, Moir, but mine to bring him on this rescue attempt. He will be helpful. He already has been on this journey.'

'What, making us go around in circles?' Moir laughed. 'I swear he is worse than Ecgbert with his seeing of new trails in the bracken.'

'He is young and he does look up to you even if you refuse to see it.'

Moir laced her hand through his and brought it to his lips. 'You are good for him, but I am not sure you are for me.'

Her heart pounded. 'Me?'

'Yes, you. You make me want to dream and plan about my future, not just what will happen in the next battle. You make me think of what could be, instead of what is. That can be fatal when you are a warrior. My mother used to tell me not to have my head in the clouds. Weaving cloth out of air, she called it. She told me that it would get me killed. I had to be better than my father. I had to know what my duty was.'

Her mind began to build halls in the clouds. She could see them with children and a farm, somewhere where it didn't matter that he was a Northman and she a Mercian.

'Is dreaming and planning for your future such a bad thing?' she whispered when the silence grew too much for her.

He picked up a stick and stirred the fire. Tiny sparks flew up into the sky, flaring for a brief time and then fading to nothingness. 'Possibly.'

'What are you going to do after this…after you are ransomed?' she asked in a small voice.

'That's too far away to start planning for.' He let out a large breath of air. 'Let us find your sister first.'

Ansithe hated to think of the unknown woman from the North who shared his heritage who he'd eventually marry and with whom he'd settle down on the lands he'd won. 'I agree. My sister must come first.'

They sat in silence for a while. Ansithe didn't want to consider that her long-term future would have no Moir in it. Against all expectation she liked the large Northman. More than liked him, she knew she cared very much about what might happen to him. And she most definitely did not want him to become a captive of Guthmann and face his wrath, but she also had a duty to her family. She couldn't live with herself if she failed them again.

Moir turned her face to look at him. His eyes were intent in the darkness of the night. 'We will find her, Ansithe. I won't stop looking until we do. No matter what anyone says.'

'Thank you.'

She leant forward and his mouth lowered to hers. Her lips instantly parted and their tongues met. His touch was instantly soothing. She moaned in the back of her throat.

'You are bad for me,' he rasped against her earlobe. 'I am supposed to be keeping watch rather than being entangled.'

'I should say sorry, but I'm not.' She moved a little way away from him. 'I will be good now.'

He tangled his fingers with hers. 'Stay with me. It will make the time go quicker.'

A lump formed in her throat. She didn't want to confess that while she wanted to find her sister, she also wanted to stay with him. Once they discovered her sister, then her time with Moir would end and she didn't want it to. She wasn't sure she wanted to go back to the life where everything revolved around duty and trying to make her father like her. She doubted if he ever could and that wasn't her fault, that was his. Moir had made her see that she was worthy of respect if nothing else. But she also knew she would not be happy until her family was safe.

Chapter Thirteen

They followed the trampled-down bracken for what felt like hours the next morning, leading the horses through narrow passages. Occasionally someone spotted something else glinting in the dirt which gave everyone hope, but then the trail appeared to peter out in a glade.

'I think they may have camped here,' Moir said. 'There are the remains of a fire.'

'Warm or cold?'

'A faint bit of warmth. It is possible the rain or the mist held them up or they were waiting for someone.'

'We have no real idea if Elene has been captured, just that they are no longer at the hut.' Ansithe pressed her lips together. She had almost given up hope of seeing Elene alive again. She had to have been captured by the Danes like her father and Leofwine had been. It must have been around here where her father met his misfortune.

Ecgbert sat down on the ground, groaning. He loudly proclaimed that going further was impossible, that they needed to get back to court with the Northmen for the summer gathering or her father would die.

Ansithe shook her fist under his nose. 'Is there a problem? Paying Guthmann's ransom demand will have to wait until my sister is found.'

'You are prepared to betray your father?' Ecgbert countered, shocked.

'We have time.' She glanced towards Moir. 'We must have time!'

'Hush, everyone,' Bjartr said, holding up his hand. 'I hear something.'

A brief clanking noise like metal striking metal sounded.

'It has stopped now,' Ecgbert said with a frown. 'It will be nothing. I wish they'd stayed where they said they'd be. I repeat, my lady, we don't have time to waste, particularly on this young man's fantasies.'

Ansithe held her tongue with an effort. Shouting at the steward was not going to solve any of her problems.

'It didn't sound like nothing to me,' Ansithe said. 'It sounds human rather than an animal.'

'I believe it came from over this way,' Bjartr said. He rushed off before anyone could stop him.

'He will be wrong and we will waste more

time searching for him. Again,' Ecgbert remarked with a sigh, sitting down on a fallen log.

Moir gave him a sharp look. 'At least the lad
appears to be thinking about others rather than
just himself. He will be back.'

'We should stay together,' Ansithe said.
'Sound can travel oddly in the woods, particularly in the early morning, but I could have
sworn I heard my sister's voice.'

'Careful.' Moir put a hand under her elbow.
'Don't get your hopes up.'

She leant into him and he instantly put his
arm about her waist. She listened to his steady
heartbeat while Ecgbert glowered at her. Her
own heart was beating so fast that she considered
it must surely jump out of her chest. She kept
thinking that her sister must be hurt or worse.
But with Moir's arm about her she felt she could
withstand anything.

Bjartr returned, panting hard, to say that he'd
found them about a quarter of a mile away.

Ansithe breathed again when they reached
the small cave. Elene was there and seemingly
unhurt. She was seated outside the cave, comb-
ing her hair and singing very off-key in a low
voice while two warriors practised with swords.

'We have been looking everywhere for you,'
Ansithe said. Relief combined with annoyance.

She'd been all set to rescue Elene but her sister was alive and unhurt. Making loud noises when she should have been silent. 'It is well that it was us and not someone else who discovered you with all the noise you are making.'

Elene jumped up and rushed to her, throwing her arms about Ansithe's waist. At her touch, all of her annoyance faded to nothing and Ansithe folded her little sister into her arms.

'You came! I knew you would! My sister never gives up. After we left the hut, we were trying to get back to court, but got into a hopeless muddle. Round and round until each tree appeared the same. Eventually we discovered these caves.'

'We followed the trail you left until we reached the glade,' Ansithe said. 'Then Bjartr followed the sound of the sword practice.'

Elene rapidly explained everything that had happened since Ansithe had last seen her. It sounded as though the journey had started uneventfully, but had become an adventure. 'The outlaws came again. They burnt the hut. We just got out in time. I knew if we ran, we would be followed, but I had no choice. We stumbled across this cave two days ago and thus far they have not attacked. I'm not sure why.'

'Are you sure they are outlaws?' Moir asked. 'We found a Danish-made axe.'

'I thought they were Danes from the way they spoke,' one of the Wessex guards came forward. 'But I couldn't be certain. Lady Elene kept saying her sister would arrive, more than likely in the company of Northmen. I bow to her expertise.'

Elene rapidly made the introductions. Of the eleven guards who had started, seven remained. Three of those had suffered terrible injuries. The man who spoke was the acting captain of the guard, Nerian.

'We are grateful to your sister, my lady. Her quick thinking allowed us to escape or otherwise we would now be prisoners,' Nerian said after Elene finished. 'We understand we are to escort the Northmen back to the Mercian court.'

'All that can wait,' Ansithe said. 'The important thing is to get you to a place of safety where your men can recover. That means getting you back to the manor at Baelle Heale.'

'And the outlaws who attacked us? They are still out there, my lady.'

She glanced at Moir. 'They will be dealt with. I have a strong hunch about who they might be.'

'We were certain you were them,' Elene said. 'We are fairly sure they know we are here.'

Moir and Ansithe exchanged glances. 'You think they are from around here.'

'I think they are waiting for us to come out.'

Elene worried her bottom lip. 'Ansithe, there was another thing. I thought I heard one of them mention Baelle Heale, but I could be mistaken. Why would anyone be interested in Baelle Heale?'

'I have no idea. Maybe you misheard.'

'At least one of them was Mercian, my lady,' Nerian interjected. 'I'd recognise that peculiar nasal twang anywhere. It is how you lot say certain words.'

Mercian. The air went from Ansithe's lungs in a great whoosh. She'd half-hoped they were part of Guthmann's *felag*. They could have used them for ransom rather than the Northmen if they'd defeated and captured them. 'Cynehild is well protected. She knows how to defend the manor. But I would feel better if we end this threat once and for all.

'Their hideout will be close to here,' Moir proclaimed. 'Can I see your map again?'

Ansithe produced the vellum she'd secreted away. 'I am not sure it will help. I marked with a bit of charcoal where we were and how far we have gone until yesterday. I wanted to be able to find my way out, but...'

Moir's smile made her toes go warm. 'The practicalities of my Valkyrie never cease to amaze me. And we can use this map. See, the caves are marked. We are far closer to Watling Street than I had thought.'

Ansithe knew she should rebuke him for calling her his, but she couldn't. She pointedly ignored Elene's questioning look.

Moir regarded her charcoal scratchings. 'Some day, there will be proper maps, but this will do for now.'

'They first attacked back at the clearing and then rapidly found the hut,' Ansithe said in a rush. 'But they didn't follow Ecgbert when he made his way back to the manor. And no one has tried to attack us on our way here.'

'I say that they will be operating there. It is near enough to the river and the road.' Moir looked again at the map, seemingly oblivious to the interplay between Bjartr, Nerian and Elene. 'I suspect they will be there.' He pointed to a spot near the river. 'Waiting for any traveller who happens to pass by.'

'Can we go around them to get back to Baelle Heale? To warn Cynehild?' Elene asked.

Moir's mouth became a tight white line. 'I've no idea, but we will be vulnerable to any passing war band. We will have to move slowly because of the wounded. We have no idea what they intend to do or who they are.'

Ansithe remembered his earlier disquiet about Guthmann, but it made no sense for him to attack Elene. Neither did it make any sense that they would be particularly interested in the manor when they must know the Northmen were going to the summer gathering to be ransomed. There had to be a solution to the problem. She studied the map carefully.

'We have to do something. Remaining here for any length of time is asking to get attacked,' she said.

'You have a suggestion?' Moir asked. 'Lady Ansithe does have a brain for strategy un-equalled by most men,' he added to Nerian.

Ansithe glowed under his praise.

'Ecgbert was correct earlier,' she said.

The steward's eyes bulged. 'I was? I mean, of course I was, if you say so, Lady Ansithe.'

'If you look at the map, it will be quicker to go to court than to return to Baelle Heale. We can cut down here and encounter the road.' Ansithe pointed to where Watling Street was drawn on the map. Her heart constricted. Going to court meant saying goodbye to Moir even sooner.

Moir frowned. 'You are supposing the map is correct.'

'My grandfather was meticulous. He wanted to know precisely where his outlying farms and fields were. He had lands near here.' She pointed to several smaller portions of woods. 'It could be they are known locally as Baelle Heale lands still. It would explain why the outlaws spoke of the manor.'

'Those farms were sold back when I first became your father's steward,' Ecgbert remarked. 'Your father liked to have his farms closer in.'

Ansithe's neck eased slightly. Ecgbert was proving useful after all. There was a logical reason why those outlaws would mention Baelle Heale. And there would be a logical reason why they had had a Danish axe, something which did not have anything to do with Guthmann and his feud with Moir.

'It appears continuing on to the court will be easier than returning.'

'Going to court is the best suggestion I've heard,' Nerian said. 'It solves a number of problems. I agree with Lady Ansithe and her steward.'

'Before we do that, we need to destroy this nest of outlaws whoever they are.' Moir stepped forward. 'They will only grow and prey on the innocent if they're not dealt with. Ensuring the Lady Ansithe and the Lady Elene's home remains safe can only happen when the outlaws are captured or killed. We are only supposing that they might have been talking about fields which were sold years ago. We can't know for certain.'

Nerian put his hand in Moir's. 'Agreed. I want to have another go at them, make sure they understand that Wessex is far from a weak country.'

'With my men as well, I believe we can do that.'

Nerian nodded his agreement.

'I have a plan about how we might entice these outlaws to appear. We need someone to be the bait,' Moir said.

Ansithe bade the butterflies in her stomach to be gone. Moir had faced battle many times before and survived. After they parted, he would face danger again and she would not know about it. And she knew deep in her heart that it was the knowing about it and that he had decided to risk his life for her family which made it so hard to bear. She knew she had to be a part of it and not simply stay with the injured as she should.

'I think I should be the bait, the enticement to get them to attack,' she said. 'Ecgbert and I together, if you think they might not attack a lone woman, but I can do it.'

Moir's face became like thunder. 'That is not happening.'

'It would be better, my lady, if you and your steward stayed with the more severely injured men,' Nerian suggested.

'No.' Her quiet word silenced everyone. 'Ultimately I have earned the right to help. It is my *felag* unless you wish to fight me for it, Moir.'

She stood there in the tremendous silence, waiting.

Moir's fingers closed around her upper arms. He leant so close their noses almost touched. 'I want to protect you. If I'm thinking about your safety while I'm trying to fight, I don't know what will happen.'

'I go with you, Moir, or this does not happen at all.'

After a tense pause, he bowed his head. 'I yield to you, Ansithe, but if nothing happens, you will go to the summer gathering unarmed.'

Moir watched Ansithe as she climbed a bluff after they had finally come to an agreement on the plan to trap the outlaws. Lady Elene along with Ecgbert had shown sense and stayed, tending the most severely wounded of the Wessex warriors.

Instead Ansithe had climbed to the top of the bluff to get a better view, along with him and the rest of the warriors, ready to sweep down if the attack happened on the men who she'd agreed would be the bait for the trap instead of her.

Moir fervently prayed his instincts were wrong and the outlaws would not appear.

The more he thought about it, the more sense it made for them all to go to court. Palni could travel there when he was well and Bjartr would be back under his father's care. Although under

Ansithe's guidance on this trip, he already seemed to have become far more mature.

But having Ansithe at court with him meant it might be easier to arrange their future. He could speak to her father…

The cracking of a twig echoed over the small wooded valley and Ansithe froze.

'Did you hear that?' she whispered, her hand going for her bow.

'It will probably be a boar,' Nerian the Wessex captain grumbled. 'Women always jump at the slightest sound. You should have stayed with Lady Elene, my lady.'

'Lady Ansithe has a cool head and good aim,' Bjartr said from where he brought up the rear. 'I'd trust her instinct over yours any day.'

'Just so, Bjartr,' Moir said. Ansithe gave Moir and Bjartr a grateful look. 'Our lady is a better warrior than most other warriors I've encountered. She has earned her place on this expedition.'

The Wessex captain's mouth turned down in disapproval.

'Far too steady for a boar.' When the second and third twigs cracked, with a practised hand she reached for an arrow and notched it to the bowstring.

Moir peered into the deepening shadows. He

thought he could see the shape of a man. He blinked and the shape had gone.

The birds ceased their twittering and the breeze died.

Moir waited another heartbeat. The shadows shifted again. Shapes of men moved. He hoped they hadn't noticed the group on the bluff. They headed straight for where the men who formed the bait rested.

Ansithe's brows drew together and her jaw jutted forward in concentration. His Valkyrie. His heart lurched. Some time in the last few days, he'd gone from thinking of Ansithe as being separate from him and instead considering her as belonging to him. 'Remain here.'

'I will be of more use to you nearer the action.'

'You will have a better view from up here. That's an order. If the tide turns against us, you are to immediately return to your sister and make your way back to Baelle Heale to warn your family. You must do that for me.'

She nodded as if she understood.

Nerian gave the pre-agreed signal to show his men were in place, preventing Moir from extracting a verbal promise from her. Within the matter of a few breaths, his men had assembled. Moir noted with pride that Bjartr was there straight away. They moved swiftly down the slope, leaving Ansithe behind. As they reached the clearing, Moir jerked his head. The men whistled under their breath. The outlaws had been unable to resist and were about to start looting the injured men.

When the attackers reached the bait, Moir sprang the trap, racing down the few remaining yards so that he was the first one to reach the attackers. He shouted his war cry.

At the sound of Moir's voice, the men from Wessex who had been lying on the ground, pretending to be injured, rose in attack formation.

The outlaws halted, confused. One met Moir's focused gaze. A hard knot of fear settled in Moir's stomach. He had to get to them before Ansithe felt a need to take part in this. He wanted to keep her safe and out of harm's way. He wished he'd argued harder for her to stay with her sister, but she was determined to play her part—as a watcher.

Nerian shouted. One of the outlaws had driven him to his knees and his helm had come flying off. Moir reached him in two strides.

His battleaxe hit the outlaw's sword before it could reach the Wessex captain's throat. He knew the force should have sent the sword spinning from the man's hand, but he blocked it.

Moir frowned and redoubled his efforts.

This time the sword spun from the man's hand. Moir dealt with him.

A sudden shout made him turn his head. Bjartr. Moir prepared to run. But his erstwhile charge was in the thick of it, swinging his sword left and right. The lad appeared to have found his courage.

Moir smiled, losing concentration for a heartbeat.

A blade cut into his shield arm. He turned and saw the leader of the outlaws standing in front of him. A Dane if ever Moir had seen one. The blade dangled over him. Time slowed to a crawl. He knew the next thrust would be to his heart. His arms ached. Raising his shield any higher was beyond him.

He'd always known a time like this would come. He'd expected it more than two dozen times before. Always he had welcomed it, but this time, he hated it. He wanted to live, not die. There were things he wanted to tell Ansithe, things she should know.

A roaring sounded in his ears. He tried to shout, but no words came out. The blade drew closer.

But just when he thought it must reach him, using the last ounce of strength he had, he pivoted. The blade sliced through air instead of flesh.

'Ha. Missed.'

He turned to meet his assailant and felt his ankle buckle, sending him to the ground.

Ansithe watched the unfolding battle with her heart firmly in her mouth. It was far harder than she had realised to remain above the action and just watch people she cared about fight, get hurt and possibly die. She had thought the battle for Baelle Heale was hard, but this watching was far worse.

Moir was in the middle of the melee, fighting as if he had a death wish. Nerian, the Wessex captain, fought alongside him, but Ansithe's unease grew.

These attackers were better prepared than anyone had considered. Moir and his team were outnumbered. It was almost as if the outlaws had expected this trap and welcomed it.

She pressed her lips together and sent an arrow flying towards the melee, towards the outlaws' position. It fell well short of her intended target, the tall warrior who appeared to be bearing down on Moir. But it did make him glance up and pause. That hesitation gave Moir the opportunity to spin around.

Ansithe ran forward, notching her arrow in the bow as she did so.

When she reached a better position, she allowed another arrow to fly. This one landed closer, but again missed as her target moved at the last possible breath. Ansithe cursed, loudly.

Moir fell to the ground, stumbling.

The next blow from the man would mean his certain death.

She fitted her next arrow to her bowstring and whispered a prayer.

Moir knew he had not rolled far enough and prepared himself for the next and final blow, but heard a strange gurgle instead.

His opponent fell forward with an arrow neatly through his throat.

Ansithe had struck true.

'Watch what you are doing, Moir.' Bjartr held out his hand and pulled Moir to standing. 'You were nearly killed. And we can't have that.'

Moir ignored the searing pain in his arm. 'Let's finish the job.'

Bjartr's eyes bulged. 'Together?'

'Yes, together.'

When the fighting finally stopped, Ansithe ventured on to the battlefield on shaking limbs. She counted several bodies, but none which appeared to be her Northmen or any of the Wessex warriors.

She heaved a sigh of relief.

'Has anyone seen Moir?' she asked.

'He's been hurt, but is making light of it,' Bjartr called out from the other side of the glade.

Ansithe ran to his side. Moir was cradling his arm. His face was smeared with dirt and blood, but Ansithe had never seen anything more handsome or welcome. She ran to him and threw her arms about him. He gathered her in and held her close.

Ansithe put her hands against his chest. 'You're hurt.'

'You should see the other man,' Moir dismissed her concern with a laugh, but his face was grey from the pain. 'Bjartr exaggerates as usual. It is but a scratch. I owe you a life debt once again. Your arrow killed the outlaws' leader right before he could finish me off. You are, in truth, a Valkyrie, Ansithe, but one who is determined to keep me from feasting at Odin's table.'

A sudden lump formed in Ansithe's throat. 'I wasn't sure if any of them hit their intended target. I... I had to move closer to get a better shot even though I know what I promised.'

'More than hit. You felled him. You saved my life.' His hand gripped hers. 'I thank you for it.'

'Who were they? They fought better than we expected.'

'Those who are alive are refusing to speak either in the North language or Mercian. They wear no identifying brooches either. No identification of any sort.'

Ansithe slung her bow over her shoulder. An air of desperation hung over the men. They were a motley bunch wearing patched cloaks and boots which had seen better days. Looking at them, it was hard to figure out who they were working for. A frisson of fear went down her spine. She could not rule out the possibility that they were working for Guthmann. 'We need to take them to the summer gathering and see if anyone will exchange them. They will have a reason for keeping silent.'

'The Northman did not lie, my lady. You have the intellect and cunning of a man,' Nerian said, coming up to them. He looked her up and down. 'Combined with the elegance of the finest lady. A formidable combination indeed.

'I will take that as a compliment rather than an insult.'

'It was meant as one.'

Chapter Fourteen

The remaining outlaws stood with their hands behind their backs. They appeared to have lost their appetite for fighting, but also continued to appear very reluctant to speak beyond grunting a few words denying that they were working for or were aligned with anyone.

'Do we know anything more?' she asked Moir.

'We don't know for sure,' Moir said in an undertone. Despite his protestations, Ansithe had insisted he wear a sling to support his injured arm. 'Their leader is dead. It could be that your neighbour Cedric hired them to cause problems for you while your father was away, to encourage you to rely on him for help.'

'It is worrying.' Ansithe concentrated on the ground. She could see Cedric doing that. He had mentioned the possibility of outlaws attacking them, almost from the first time she'd seen him after her father and Leofwine had departed. And they should have been safe when they'd travelled back from the fighting, but they had been captured instead. Could Guthmann have been working with Cedric? She banished the thought as pure speculation. 'I thought once they realised their leader was gone, they would be eager to tell us everything they know.'

'We will learn soon enough who they are. They cannot harm you or your family now,' Moir said.

She frowned. 'It is more important than ever that we get these men to the summer gathering as soon as possible and discover precisely who they are. Because even if they talk, they might not tell the full truth.'

'My thoughts precisely.'

'We have more hostages, Ansithe, isn't that wonderful?' Elene said, clapping her hands together and interrupting the conversation.

Ansithe hurriedly stepped away from Moir and investigated the folds of her gown. 'Yes, I know, Elene. I was there, remember?'

Elene grabbed Ansithe's hand, her face shining with excitement. 'Don't you see, Ansithe? We can send these in place of Moir and his men. They deserve to be free after what they have done to protect us. Capturing these men means we can return to court with our heads held high, but with different captives.'

Ansithe took a deep breath. Elene had given voice to her burgeoning hope. There was a solution and maybe a future for them after all.

'Impossible,' Moir said flatly before she could agree with Elene.

'Why?' Elene asked.

'The court officials have our brooches,' Moir explained in an overly reasonable tone. 'They are expecting us. My *jaarl* will have paid good money for me and the others. And we have no idea if these men are valuable warriors or worthless *ceorls*. Your father and brother-in-law still need to be ransomed, Lady Elene. And Palni remains in your care.'

'We could say the brooches were stolen,' Elene suggested. 'That we had no idea who you were.'

Moir bowed. 'I know the anger which would ensue when people discover they were tricked and the revenge they'd take. You want your father back and your lands safe. I have no wish to spend the rest of my life as a wolf's head or being accused of cowardice. You and your sister must trust me on this.'

A hard pit settled at the base of Ansithe's stomach as she remembered what he had told her about his father's betrayal. He wanted to be a better man. 'But you can be taken straight to your *jaarl*, rather than to the court?'

'There is no need for you ladies to worry about the exchange. I will ensure it happens,' Nerian said, bowing low. 'I will do my best to see these men safe. I owe them a life debt for saving me and my comrades.'

'We are still going to the summer gathering,' Ansithe said, crossing her arms. 'We will see the exchange.'

Nerian frowned. 'There are many features about this incident which bother me. When I mentioned Baelle Heale to the captives, several exchanged glances. They definitely know the name.'

'It could be because of my grandfather...' Ansithe's voice trailed away to nothing. She paused, trying to think. 'But that would mean local knowledge and these men are not locals.' Her stomach knotted. What if they had not dealt with the entire nest of outlaws and more attacks were planned? Cynehild could not defend the manor on her own. 'Oh, no.'

A loud shout resounded from the caves.

'Lady Elene,' Nerian said. 'One of your patients is calling for you. I said that I would get you for him and I became distracted. We can continue this discussion later.'

Elene pressed Ansithe's hand. 'We do whatever you think best, sister, but I need to see to my patients.'

'He is right,' Moir said after they had gone. 'There is no need for you to go to court. Return to Baelle Heale. Ensure Lady Cynehild and the others remain safe from any possible attack. Your father will join you in due course.'

'You truly think that it will happen?' Her voice wobbled. He had made no mention of his future intentions towards her. He wouldn't. He was the man who lived in the present, after all. He'd made no secret of that.

'I don't pretend to know the future,' Moir said, lifting her chin. 'But my instinct tells me that it is no longer as simple as capturing these outlaws to keep your manor safe. Baelle Heale is in danger. You would never forgive yourself if you didn't return, if you weren't there to protect it.'

'But—' There was more to his request. She could hear it in his voice.

'We don't have the time to spare. Your father needs to be freed. You heard Ecgbert and occasionally he does speak sense.'

A great black hole opened in her chest. Her vague hope that Moir would demand her hand once her father was released vanished. Earlier, waiting for the attack to begin, she had even halfway wondered if she'd ever return to Baelle

Heale. Moir had been right—dreaming was pointless. He had been honest about how long things were going to last between them. She'd accepted it, never really thinking about the consequences, never thinking she'd give him her heart.

'Cynehild will be going mad with worry. And we don't know if the outlaws will attack Baelle Heale.' She firmed her jaw and wrapped the tattered shreds of her dignity about her. She refused to beg. She'd never forgive herself if something happened to Cynehild and Wulfgar before Leofwine could return. Her sister's happiness mattered to her. 'I'd thought to go to the summer gathering first, but I trust your instinct—someone needs to inform Cynehild about what's happened here. Someone who is better at navigating than Ecgbert. If Elene and I go back with Ecgbert, it means there are more men to guard our recently acquired captives. We can ride the horses which will greatly speed our journey.'

His fingers squeezed hers before letting go. His eyes were inscrutable. 'It must be your choice, Ansithe.'

She wrapped her arms about her middle. She wanted to scream that she wasn't sure about anything any more, that her entire world was shifting and she wanted to return to her safe world, only she feared it didn't exist any more. Moir had made her see that she should want more than she'd settled for. 'We need to tell everyone my decision.'

'We will leave in the morning for the court,' Nerian said, giving Ansithe and Moir a significant look. 'My men could use an extra night of rest and we will cover more ground that way. If that is all right with you, Moir?'

'Shall we share a tent, Elene?' Ansithe asked before she was tempted to find a way to take more time alone with Moir. *As long as it lasts and no regrets when it ends,* she repeated silently over and over.

Her sister regarded her hands. The colour in her cheeks flamed. 'I'd rather stay and look after the injured men. I would hate to think I might lose one after all this effort. You are not very useful when it comes to nursing, Ansithe. Admit it. Your stomach churns too much at the sight of blood.'

'I see,' Ansithe said. Her heart thudded in her ears.

Elene put a hand on her arm and gave a conspiratorial smile. 'There might be a handsome warrior who wants to share it, if you are frightened of being on your own.'

Ansithe looked at her sister in shock. 'Elene!'

'Just saying. There is no harm in asking and

his eyes have been eating you right up ever since you arrived.' Elene gave a quick smile. She gestured about her at the makeshift camp. 'Out here, everything is different. Normal rules don't apply. Once we return home, then we can go back to being how we were, but for now, I have a duty towards those men and leaving them tonight would be wrong.'

Ansithe pinched the bridge of her nose. Her heart called Elene's advice sound. Her head whispered to consider the consequences. 'The rules always apply.'

'Then break a few.' Elene leant over and whispered in her ear, 'It is clear there is something between you and the Northman. I saw how you looked at each other. Everyone says you saved his life which meant he could save everyone else's. How attuned you are to each other. Why should you always wonder what if?' Elene put her hand on Ansithe's sleeve.

'I never wonder.'

'When my maid died in that attack, I didn't know what to do. I thought a woman on her own? How would I manage? But it has worked out. I enjoy looking after those men. They are alive because of me. I have proved my worth.'

Ansithe hugged her sister tight. She had never realised that Elene suffered similar sorts of feelings to hers. 'You didn't need to. You have always been precious to me.'

'Yes, I did need to. For me.' Elene seized Ansithe's hands. 'Sometimes, you must seize your destiny, Ansithe. And don't preach to me about obeying rules which you know in your heart are wrong. We both have that enough from Cynehild.'

'And you and this warrior? This Wessex captain, Nerian?'

Elene blushed and plucked at her gown. 'I do not wish to discuss it, except to say that nothing untoward has happened. He is a very honourable man, but his prospects are not what Father would wish. We should leave it at that.'

'Moir is Mercia's enemy,' Ansithe said.

'But he isn't yours. How could he be considered your enemy when he risked his life for everyone?' Elene kissed Ansithe's cheek. 'Put yourself first tonight. For once in your life.'

Ansithe's mouth went dry. She'd been extra-careful since they had found Elene. 'Elene, are you making an improper suggestion?'

'Someone has to.' Elene gave a resigned sigh. 'I swear, Ansithe, sometimes you overthink things far too much. Right now, I suggest we use that stream for a wash. I want to make you beautiful, Ansithe. You look as if you have gone through a hedge backwards.'

* * *

Ansithe lay down on the furs which made up her bed. Elene had brushed her hair until it shone like burnished copper. She had even insisted Ansithe put on a clean under-gown before leaving her with a smile.

Despite Elene's prediction, she doubted Moir would come to her. He had barely looked at her throughout supper.

Then he had disappeared off somewhere with the Wessex captain before she had the chance to speak to him. Some good Elene's attempt at beautifying her had done.

The niggling thought curled about her brain— had she done something wrong again? She had used her judgement in moving down the slope. She had saved his life, but maybe he had intended on using the confusion of battle as a chance to escape.

The flap moved and Moir entered. In the dim light she could see the tiny droplets of water clinging to his hair like diamonds or stars. Her mouth went dry.

'You retired unexpectedly early,' he said. 'I didn't get a chance to say goodnight.'

'You were elsewhere.' Her throat tightened. 'You and the Wessex captain were engrossed in conversation. No doubt you had to see to the new prisoners.'

'Nerian is a good man and a fair one. He has posted guards about the prisoners.' He held out his hand. 'He said I was to have the night off. I'd already saved his life enough for one day.'

'Indeed.'

He came over and lifted her up so that she was standing. Her breasts brushed his chest.

'Are you angry with me?' she whispered. 'For not staying where I was supposed to during the battle?'

He smiled. 'How could I be angry when you saved my life? A good leader allows his people room to make their own decisions. But you take far too many chances, Ansithe. Don't do it again. Your life is too precious. People depend on you.'

His mouth loomed over hers. 'I knew the risks.'

'As do I. I want you alive, Ansithe, because I want to do this to you. I have wanted to do this all day.'

His lips came down and captured hers. It was a fierce kiss, but one which also explored and roamed, intoxicating her with its intenseness.

She moaned in the back of her throat and looped her hands about his neck and the passion of the kiss increased.

He loosened her hands and stepped back. 'Your sister? When will she return?'

'Elene has other plans tonight,' she whispered

against his mouth. 'She is deliberately staying away, claiming that she needs to look after the injured men. A lie, of course. She is giving me an opportunity.'

He stared into her eyes. 'Does it bother you that she has guessed about us?'

'I wasn't sure whether she had or not,' Ansithe admitted. 'She insisted I make an effort and gave me a lecture about men and their ways. I think she is secretly hoping that you will come here. She has a romantic soul.'

He loosened his hold and leant away from her. 'And you? Is that what you want?'

A lump formed in her throat. She knew that she loved him, but he had never made any pretence that their relationship was to last. It had been a summer's romance for him and, for her, it was something she'd remember for the rest of her life. She knew heartache was coming, but she wanted one last night with him.

'We are living in the present and it is a while yet until the next sunrise,' she said and hoped he wouldn't hear the lie. 'I am not going to think about tomorrow until it arrives.'

He rubbed her cheek with his knuckle, sending little shivers through her. 'No tears when it does.'

'I will treasure our time together in my memory.' Ansithe choked back the words that would

confess her love for him. It was far too dangerous a feeling. She had nearly lost him today and
she was losing him tomorrow, but that would be
a different type of loss—she'd know at least that
he would be alive and one day might even think
of her with a smile.

'You are wearing your serious face.'

She ran her hands down his arms and tangled
his fingers with hers. She leant towards him and
brushed her lips against his. 'Am I? It is only because I am trying to decide what to do with you.
One last night to enjoy.'

His fingers tightened and pulled her towards
him. 'What to do with me?'

'I don't always want to take. I want to give
as well.'

He nuzzled her earlobe. 'I would like that very
much.'

Her fingers quickly undid his tunic. He pulled
off his trousers, so he was standing there naked
in front of her.

She drew in her breath, reached out her hand
and encountered the warm muscle of his chest.

'You are so beautiful.'

He captured her hand and raised it to his lips.
'You are a flatterer. I bear many scars and im-
perfections.'

In response she trailed her mouth down his
chest, exploring, tracing the outline of his nip-

ples with her tongue. They tightened to hardened points under her ministrations. His swift intake of breath and the rapid hardening of his member against her thigh showed her his rampant arousal.

Trailing her tongue down his stomach, she rejoiced in her power. She was doing this to him. Any remaining doubts about her lack of feminine charms vanished. For him, she was woman enough.

She moved her mouth lower still, licking and stroking him, cupping him until he groaned and tugged at her shoulders.

His face had a fiery intensity to it. 'If you keep this up, I can't make any guarantees about how long I'll last and I want it to be good for you.'

'With you, it is always good.'

'You make it so easy.'

She pushed his chest with her hand and he tumbled backwards on to the furs, taking her with him. They lay there, her body on top of his, his fingers cupping her buttocks.

Then she straddled him, teasing him with her nest of curls, making little circles about his erection as the primitive fire deep within her flamed higher.

His hands gripped her on either side of her hips, held her there, helping her call the rhythm.

Faster and faster. Circles and figures of eight. His groan echoed through the tent and his groin arched upwards.

When she could stand it no longer, she opened the apex of her thighs wider and sheathed him. He went deep and then even deeper until she felt he must have touched her inner core.

She began to ride him. Slowly at first, but gaining momentum until the world became nothing but him.

She poured everything into that moment, letting her body tell him secrets that she had only half-understood herself and was too frightened even to whisper.

His body instantly responded. She teetered on the edge of the abyss, knowing what was coming and thought she must have been born for this.

His mouth caught her cries of completion.

Moir floated gently back down to earth. He remained buried deep within her and she was collapsed on top of him, barely breathing.

He put his arms about her and knew that he would never again be as happy as he was in that moment.

From a brief heartbeat, he allowed himself to dream about what life would be like with her always at his side and how their children would be. A girl with flaming red hair who could shoot straight like her mother and a boy with her eyes and maybe his hair. They would grow strong and free without the dark shadows he'd experienced as a child.

He could almost reach out, touch them and gather them into his arms. He ached to hold them, the children that he hadn't realised he desperately wanted until he'd met this woman.

He blinked and the vison vanished as if it had never been. Wisps of dreams.

He opened his mouth to say something about looking after any child of his that she bore, but at her half-awake, half-asleep expression he closed it again. She had claimed to be barren, but he wondered again if it had been her late husband's age and infirmity that had been the problem. The last thing he wanted was to cause a quarrel. They would know soon enough if there were consequences to their passion. He allowed the words to be unsaid rather than disturb her.

She murmured something indistinct. He chose to believe it was his name.

He knew he had lied earlier. He didn't want her for the moment or the next day. He wanted her for ever, but it had to be done honourably. He had to make an offer to her father, before he asked her to abandon her life for the uncertainty of his.

'I love you,' he whispered against her hair.

'You have given my life meaning. I will not fail you. I want to return to you. Wait for me.'

She muttered gently in her sleep and he tightened his arms about her.

The light shone a dull grey when Ansithe woke suddenly. The place next to her was vacant, but still just warm. She glanced up and saw Moir, fully dressed, watching her.

'It is far too early.'

'It is owl-light. Dawn will be coming soon. We should speak properly, while we are alone. There are things which need to be said. Things we didn't say to one another last night.'

She stood up and went over to him. Her entire being ached. Her throat was thick with unshed tears. Whatever happened she refused to disgrace herself. Weeping was for later when no one could see.

'You are going to do it just like Elene suggested. You are going to save yourself and leave in the dead of night. You are going to escape. The outlaws will provide enough gold. They will believe the brooch story as it was me who captured you.'

'No. I know what I need to do. I gave my word to you I wouldn't try to escape.'

Ansithe cupped both hands about his face, forcing him to look at her. 'Run. I thought about it most of the night. The guards will not stop you or your men.'

'Running away was my father's trick. Not mine. I'd lose the little honour I have left.' His mouth became a thin white line. 'I'll not deny that I didn't think about escaping at the beginning, but I could not do it now. I would not endanger your family. I'm determined to protect you.'

Ansithe's breath caught. He was right. She could not ask him to betray his code. 'To protect me? From the outlaws? You think they will attack my family?'

His mouth turned down. 'I need to understand why they attacked Elene's party. Go back to Baelle Heale where you will be safe.'

He was dismissing her. Her heart had hoped for much more, but she refused to beg him.

'I wanted to dream for another heartbeat that there was somewhere where we could be together.' She closed her eyes briefly and then opened them. She forced a smile. 'It is fine. I promised not to cry when we parted.'

He gave one of his smiles which was intended to melt her heart, but his eyes remained shadowed. 'Right now, our destinies lie along separate paths.'

'Are you certain?'

'Let me remember you like this, here in this

tent, not out there surrounded by everyone else. It will sustain me.' He placed something smooth and warm in her hand. 'Keep this with you. It has kept me safe since my mother gave it to me just before she died. Look at it sometimes and remember me.'

She opened her hand and saw a red-gold amber bead on a leather cord. His mother's good luck charm, the one he'd said he wore to remind him of his promise. 'You don't need this any more?'

'It is better with you.'

'You expect something bad will happen to you.' She held it out. 'Take it back. I want you safe.'

His face turned serious. 'I'd rather you kept it until we meet again.'

Until they met again. So he was planning on seeing her again. Her heart rose…then immediately sank. 'When you retrieve Palni, you mean.'

Moir gave a crooked smile and closed her fingers about the pendant. 'Something like that. Look at that and know I expect to see you again. Soon.'

'Bjartr has found his courage now. He will be an able leader in time,' she said around the lump in her throat.

A horn sounded. Moir placed a cool kiss on

her forehead. 'I have to go. Stay in this tent. Don't come out. Not if you care anything for me.'

Ansithe knew she'd stay in the tent and let him go. He had to do his duty. And he was right—his honour was something she loved about him. Without it, he would not be the man she loved. She put her hand against her stomach and hated that she was barren and would not even have a child to remember him by. She slipped the pendant over her head.

'I will wear it by my heart always.'

'Thank you for understanding.' He walked out without a backward glance.

She stood there for a long breath, wondering if she should chase after him and demand she go with him. Except he'd asked her not to. She had to respect his decision because she loved him with her whole heart.

She gave a low moan and sank to the ground, rocking back and forth. She wanted to lie down and never get up. Her entire being ached. If this was what love was like, she wanted no part of it.

'Ansithe?' Elene's worried voice sounded from outside some time later when the sun shone directly on the tent. 'They have gone and you didn't even say goodbye to them.'

'Because it wasn't goodbye. It could never be goodbye,' Ansithe whispered to the ground.

Then she stood, wiped her eyes and arranged the folds of her gown. She'd face the world because he'd want her to. She'd honour him in that way. Each evening, she'd look at the sunset, hold his pendant and think about him until he returned.

She walked out with her head held high. Even the air felt empty and bereft. 'We ride to Baelle Heale to warn Cynehild and prepare for Father's return.'

Chapter Fifteen

'I was correct in my decision to send you away, Moir,' the *jaarl* Andvarr declared, handing Moir a ring from his finger. 'You have made my son into a man. I can tell by the way he stands. I owe you a life debt.'

To Moir's astonishment, Andvarr had the gold ready when Moir returned with Nerian and the rest to the camp. He had also immediately taken charge of the prisoners. Nerian had collected the gold which now belonged to Ansithe, part of which would be used to pay her family's ransom. In a short while Moir would make everything right.

'That was not my doing,' Moir said.

'You are far too modest, Moir.' Andvarr cleared his throat. 'And as I suspected the other matter has blown over like a storm on a summer's day.'

'Other matter? You mean my quarrel with

Guthmann. We did not encounter him.' Moir's hand instinctively went for the amber bead and encountered air. A prickle of unease passed through him.

'Guthmann pledged his loyalty to me before we last parted. He no longer holds you and your mistake against me or anyone who is in this *felag*.' Andvarr made an irritated noise. 'He no longer wishes to insist on you being made a wolf's head for scarring his face. So it is a start.'

'Guthmann is a treacherous snake and not to be trusted.' Moir gritted his teeth. 'I make no apology for saving that woman's life. I warned him I would not allow him to harm her and he would not listen.'

'She was his captive. It was not your or my son's place to interfere.'

Moir clenched his fists and struggled to control his temper. It was not like that at all as Andvarr well knew. He'd been the one to request that Moir investigate the woman's whereabouts as she was the wife of an important Mercian lord. 'Andvarr, you know what happened. Why I acted. We agreed…'

'Things have changed. I require Guthmann's men. There is trouble brewing with the Saxons to the south-east. I intend to hold the lands we have conquered. Guthmann was within his rights to do what he did. The woman had strayed.'

Moir rolled his eyes. Andvarr was always looking for what would give him the most power. 'There will always be trouble brewing. Guthmann is a particularly faithless ally.'

'He is prepared to forgive you. Remember that when you next encounter each other.'

'When should I next encounter him? When I deliver the ransom gold?'

If there was an alliance between Guthmann and Andvarr, Moir knew he would be departing for Iceland sooner rather than later. After he had freed Ansithe's father and made his formal offer for her hand, then he would see if Ansithe would accompany him to Iceland.

'Guthmann has left to get married. Some Mercian lady. I can't remember her name, but he said that he was obsessed with her.'

Moir cursed. So much for trying to arrive with Ansithe's family at Baelle Heale within a few days of her return. 'Did he take his hostages with him? Or did he leave them to be exchanged?'

'Exchanged? What are in the name of Odin are you talking about?'

'Part of the gold is to go to Guthmann to release the *ealdorman* Wulfgar and his son-in-law.' Moir named the sum which was considerably less than the amount of gold Andvarr had given Nerian as the ransom for his son, Moir and the others. 'I am determined that this will happen without delay.'

'The *ealdorman* Wulfgar?' Andvarr's brow furled. 'But he is no longer a hostage.'

'Is he dead?'

Andvarr laughed. 'He is the father of Guthmann's bride-to-be. I believe it is his middle daughter.'

Moir froze. Guthmann was planning on marrying Ansithe? He had to have heard wrong. 'When did this come about?'

'He departed about a week ago, just after the rumours started spreading about your capture by a woman.'

'Did he know who captured me?' Moir's stomach twisted into knots. Guthmann was doing this for one reason and one reason only. He wanted to taunt Moir.

'He knew it was a woman, but that is all. I believe he was extremely amused by it. You, the great saviour of Ashdown, the strength in our shield wall, beaten by a mere woman.' Andvarr laughed. 'Come, why the serious face, Moir? You must see the amusing side of it.'

'You would do well not to underestimate Lady Ansithe.'

'We have much to discuss. You have lands to choose. Leave Guthmann to his bride. That is all I ask.'

Moir's heart knocked. He had thought to ensure Ansithe's safety by sending her back to Baelle Heale while he dealt with any threat that Guthmann might pose. He'd badly miscalculated. Rather than keeping her safe, he had sent her into danger. It now made perfect sense why those so-called outlaws had harried Nerian and the Lady Elene to prevent them returning to collect the Northmen. They had been trying to keep him stuck in Baelle Heale until Guthmann could arrive.

So, far from his anger at Moir vanishing, Guthmann was about to try to exact his revenge on the woman Moir loved.

However, there remained the faintest of hopes that Ansithe and her sister had not yet returned to Baelle Heale. If he left now, he might reach them before they arrived. He could keep them safe until they worked out what to do about her father and Guthmann. 'We have nothing to discuss. I have done my duty to you. Now I must do my duty towards the woman who saved my life. Give me leave to find her and take her to safety. She cannot be left to Guthmann's mercies. I—*We* all owe her our lives.'

'It is out of my hands, Moir. I forgave you and your temper once, I will not do so a second time. You will leave Guthmann alone. That is an order.'

'I cannot do that.'

Andvarr gave a pitying smile. 'There will be other women, Moir. Stay with me or leave this *felag*'s protection. How long do you think you can stand alone against Guthmann and his warriors? I am prepared to overlook this unfortunate episode, but you disappoint me greatly.'

Moir took off the ring Andvarr had given him and threw it at his former *jaarl*'s feet. His fist connected with Andvarr's jaw and sent him flying backwards. 'You cannot order me to do anything. You are no longer my *jaarl*.'

'Why is Father's banner fluttering from the roof?' Elene asked, making her horse stop.

Ansithe shielded her eyes against the sun and looked at where Elene was pointing. Their journey back to Baelle Heale had taken slightly longer than she'd anticipated as Ecgbert's horse had pulled up lame. And the horses refused to move faster than a slow walk in the heat.

The banner that normally only fluttered when her father was in residence proudly rippled in the breeze. But there was no way her father or Leofwine could be there. The ransom had not been paid. The *jaarl* Guthmann would not simply allow them to go on a promise of payment. And they had not encountered them travelling up from behind on Watling Street. 'Cynehild is up to something.'

'Could Lady Cynehild be anticipating her husband's arrival?' Ecgbert asked. 'Maybe she wants to welcome them home. Perhaps she has received word they are coming and are not far behind us.'

Ansithe turned around, but there was nothing behind them except for a dirt track. Her heart sank. She missed Moir more than she had thought she could ever could miss anyone.

She stared up at the banner, unable to rid herself of the uneasy feeling that she'd missed something totally obvious.

'I don't know.' Ansithe shifted on her horse's back. 'She might be trying to warn us.'

'Warn us about what?' Ecgbert's face turned crafty. 'My lady, if you are concerned about something, we should go and seek shelter with Lord Cedric.'

'You can be such an old woman, Ecgbert. The last person we need right now is Cedric. If we encounter any problem, I can solve it,' Ansithe retorted and urged her horse forward.

The yard was eerily silent when they went in. Not even Owain or the swineherd were about. Ansithe's stomach knotted as it did before a battle. Before she could remark on it, her father came out of the hall. His ordeal had sent his hair white and his skin resembled old parchment.

She started forward, but stopped.

At his right strode a massive Northman with wild white-blond hair and a newly healed purple scar running across his face. This must be Guthmann Bloodaxe.

Behind them stood an array of Danish warriors. Ansithe motioned for Elene and Ecgbert to keep behind her.

'Aren't you going to welcome us, daughters?' Her father held out his arms as if he expected her and Elene to run into them. 'I have finally returned from the wars.'

'Where is Cynehild?' Ansithe asked instead. 'Why isn't she here to greet us?'

Her father's eyes slid away from her. 'Your sister is in the church with Leofwine's body.'

Behind her, Elene gave a small cry.

'Leofwine is dead?' Ansithe gasped. 'You brought his body back?'

'Unfortunately, Leofwine disagreed with my orders concerning my new bride,' Guthmann said. 'He had to be made an example of.'

'Cynehild and her son have gone to pray for Leofwine's soul.' Her father gave Guthmann a nervous glance. 'It was an unfortunate misunderstanding.'

'I trust there will no further misunderstandings,' Guthmann said. Ansithe disliked the way his eyes roamed over her body as if she were a piece of meat for his enjoyment.

Her father bowed low. 'I can assure you there won't be. We all know what is at stake.'

Ansithe's mouth dropped open, unable to believe her normally proud father's obsequious behaviour towards the Danish warlord. 'Father!'

He cringed and mouthed *sorry*.

'There can be no doubting which of your daughters is the Valkyrie.' Guthmann's laughter rang out. 'How right you were to agree to my betrothal terms, Ealdorman Wulfgar.'

Ansithe fought against the rising tide of nausea. Bride and terms did not bode well for Elene. Her father could not have sold his youngest daughter to a man such as this one. Her eyes measured the distance to the horses. If they ran... She grabbed Elene's arm and took a step back towards the horses.

'Terms? What terms? Father, what is going on here?' Ansithe said, striving for a normal voice, but unable to completely disguise the faint note of panic.

Her father's right eye twitched. 'I have agreed to Guthmann's request, Ansithe, that you are to be his new wife. He has heard of your exploits and feels you are the correct woman to be his bride.'

Ansithe halted her backward progression. 'Me? You are going to marry me to this man?'

Her father waved his hand. 'I suppose I should thank you. Such is his admiration for your exploits, Guthmann released Leofwine and myself without the ransom being paid. He is even prepared to waive your dowry. I could hardly refuse under the circumstances. The ransom demand gone and my middle daughter off my hands— beyond my wildest imaginings.'

'And yet Leofwine objected and died for it.'

'It was not his place to object.' Her father's voice shook with barely suppressed rage. 'He died for nothing.'

Ansithe stared at her father, noticing little things that she had overlooked before—his pinched mouth and the way his eyes never settled on hers. Her father had arranged a marriage for her with Guthmann, the loathsome man who had held him prisoner and who had a feud with Moir. He was not worthy of her admiration, love or honour. She'd become who she was despite him, not because of him. 'If you had heard of my exploits, then you knew I already had the ransom sorted. There was no need to agree to his terms.'

'The gold will come in useful for other things.' Her father smiled. 'The estate can be restored to its former glory.'

'I see, except that the gold belongs to me and

my sisters, not you. We cannot stay here. Now
you must let us go.'

'That is impossible, my lady,' Guthmann said.
He snapped his fingers and several of his men
rushed forward, surrounding her and Elene. One
grabbed her arms while another stripped her of
her eating knife and bow.

Ansithe fought against her captor. 'Let me
go!'

'You will do what I want or you and your
people will suffer.'

Her father tugged at his tunic. 'It is a changed
world, Ansithe. I had to think of the family. We
need a powerful ally. I seriously did not expect
he would make such an honourable offer. You
are a woman to get sons on. I assured him that
was the case.'

'Father!'

'You are a woman of the world, Ansithe, not
some simpering maid. You must know this family's well-being comes before anything else,' her
father retorted.

'I refuse.'

His eyes widened. 'You can't. I am your father and you will obey me. I have accepted on
your behalf.'

'I just have.' Ansithe kicked out behind her
with her boots and connected with her captor.
He shouted, but his hold on her arms relaxed
enough for her to twist away. She glared at him.

Her father quickly turned to Guthmann. 'Forgive my daughter. I fear the travelling has tired her.'

Guthmann gave a smile which sent a frisson of fear coursing down her spine. 'I like it when women are feisty. I will give her two days to make up her mind in my favour.'

'I need to see Cynehild in the church and give her my condolences. Until I have done so, I cannot give you an answer. Elene and Ecgbert, will you join me?'

Guthmann snapped his fingers again and the pair were released. Ecgbert scampered towards the church, but Elene stood next to her and put her hand in Ansithe's. The simple gesture of solidarity brought a lump to Ansithe's throat.

'Ansithe, please, there is more than your petty personal happiness at stake,' her father called. 'I want to ensure the future of this family. You know what you did to your mother. Don't you destroy this family again.'

'After all this time, you still cannot admit the part you played in my mother's death, can you, Father?' Ansithe turned on her heel, linked arms with Elene and walked into the church.

'My father refused your request to depart and still you go. Why are you doing this, Moir?' Bjartr demanded, coming into the yard where the horses were kept. Moir had been pleased that his favourite horse remained tethered, rested and well fed.

He concentrated on putting his things in saddlebags. He had retrieved his second-best sword, savings and clothes from storage after his quarrel with Andvarr.

The sooner he left, the sooner he could save Ansithe. He did not need Bjartr or anyone delaying him. 'I don't have time for this, Bjartr. I said everything I had to say to your father.'

'He will throw you out of the *felag*. You will never get the land you wanted, the land which is rightfully yours.'

'It is not worth it if I fail someone I care about.' Moir closed his eyes. All he could see was Ansithe's face—pale and still if Guthmann had his way with her.

Moir turned back to his horse, finished tightening the saddle, fastened the bridle, then mounted.

'Step aside, Bjartr. I've no wish to harm you. I've left your father's *felag*. I owe loyalty to no man now.'

Bjartr grabbed the bridle. 'Hear me out, Moir Mimirson.'

Moir concentrated on the horse's ears. The less Bjartr knew about what he had planned, the better. The lad was likely to go running back to his father telling tales. 'Unless you wish me to knock you down, move.'

Bjartr did not. 'I refuse. You will hear what I have to say.'

'You will listen to him.' The remaining members of the *felag* dressed for travel with Nerian and his men close behind came into the pen.

Moir dismounted. He might be able to go around Bjartr, but escaping from all of them? Not possible. And he knew every breath he delayed was a breath closer to Guthmann reaching Baelle Heale and certain death for Ansithe. 'I will listen.'

Bjartr gestured to Nerian, who held up the pouch of gold. 'This needs to go to its rightful owner. The Mercian King has purchased the Danish outlaws we defeated in the forest. It must go to Lady Ansithe at Baelle Heale. I need a guide and only you will do, Moir.'

'You want me to guide you back to Baelle Heale?' Moir nodded. 'Done. And the rest of you, why are you here?'

Bjartr's face became a beacon of light. 'We stand with you, Moir. We will be your shield wall. You will not forbid us to go on this journey.'

'We are with you to the death, Moir Mimirson, our leader.' The *felag* roared and beat their swords against their shields in agreement.

Moir stared at them in astonishment, unable to speak. They wanted to go with him. All of them. They were all prepared to risk the wrath of Andvarr for him. He was not going to fight for Ansithe alone.

It took several heartbeats for Ansithe's eyes to adjust to the gloom in the church. Cynehild immediately rose from where she knelt beside the body of her husband and enfolded both Ansithe and Elene in a great hug.

'I had prayed that you would stay away,' she said quietly. 'Palni thought you might understand the reason the flag was flying.'

'We came to warn you about the outlaws we encountered,' Ansithe said, 'but I suspect now that they were Guthmann's men.'

Ansithe went over and knelt in front of the byre where Leofwine's body lay. She gripped Cynehild's hand. 'You do not know how much I regret Leofwine's passing. Words cannot express how sorry I am.'

Cynehild tightened her grip on Ansithe's hand and would not allow her to pull away. 'Hush. No more of that. Leofwine knew he was dying when they returned. They had beaten him dreadfully and living was a torment he did not wish to endure. He felt it wrong what your father was doing to you. He knew the only reason he had been able to see our baby Wulfgar or me again was because of you and what you did. I was able to hold him and tell him how much I loved him and that means far more than I can say. Do not allow his sacrifice to be in vain, Ansithe.'

Ansithe drew a deep breath. Leofwine had admired her. 'Then I honour him. I will make sure you are all safe.'

'I know you will. Even though Palni thinks you are in danger, I feel better that you are here. You will find a way to convince Father that his ideas are all wrong. That man…' Cynehild's voice broke, but she regarded her husband's face and regained control. 'That Dane will destroy this manor.'

'Is Palni still here? Or has Guthmann discovered him?'

Cynehild put her fingers to her lips. 'Father Oswald has hidden him. I can take you to him. Father Oswald said that we are to treat this as sanctuary. He believes Father will not violate it and endanger his immortal soul.'

Ansithe suspected Guthmann would be no respecter of sanctuary if it came to it, but she kept quiet and fingered Moir's pendant. Moir needed to know what had happened. Knowledge was power. And somehow this whole thing circled back to his feud with Guthmann. Palni had to know how to get word to him.

They went into the sacristy where Father Oswald kept his vestments for Mass. The large Northman lay on a pallet. Cynehild's maid and Wulfgar were there as well. Palni scrambled to his feet when Ansithe entered the room.

'Don't take this the wrong way, Lady Ansithe,' he said after Ansithe had enveloped him in a hug, 'but I had hoped never to see you here. That the banner would do the trick and you'd leave and go to Iceland with your man.'

'I'm far from infallible. I misunderstood its meaning.' Ansithe rapidly explained about what had happened. She held out the pendant. 'Do you think you might escape and take this to Moir?'

'You want him to come here?' Palni backed away from her. 'Do you know what will happen? What Guthmann must have planned for him? If Moir comes and challenges him, Guthmann will find a way to cheat so Moir loses. Moir is one of the best fighters in the entire army.'

'Would Guthmann himself fight him?'

'Only if he thought he'd win. Otherwise, he'd nominate one of his warriors to act as his champion,' Palni said. 'Please, my lady, I know I owe you my life, but do not ask me to make my best friend give up his. Not if you care for him.'

'I want you to keep him well away from here. Tell him anything, but keep him away. Like you, I believe Guthmann intends on killing him. He only became interested in me when he learned who I had captured.' Her heart panged as she said the words, but she knew they were the right ones. She refused to become the reason someone else she loved died. She had lived with that guilt long enough.

'Begging your pardon, my lady, what are you intending to do?'

Ansithe filled her lungs. She willed her voice not to break. 'I am not sure yet, but one thing I do know—Moir can't come here. Guthmann has set a trap and I am the bait. If Moir appears, Guthmann will spring it.'

Palni nodded. 'Then sending the pendant and telling him to stay away won't work. In fact, I am not sure anything will work once he suspects you are in danger.'

'What do you mean?'

'I have never known Moir to give that pendant up. We used to joke about it. He sent you back here to protect you from Guthmann. When he discovers what has passed, he will not rest until he has returned. He will already be coming for you.' He gestured towards everyone who was crowded into the small room. 'For all of us. It is something to hang on to—in a fair fight against Guthmann, he will win. Find a way, my lady, to get him that fair fight if you have any feelings for him.'

Ansithe held the pendant in her hand, trying to think. She could almost imagine the stone was warm from Moir's skin rather than from hers. She wished that he was here, holding her in his arms, believing in her ability to give him what he needed. What was it that Moir said—a good leader always uses the tool he has to hand? What tools did she have? And how best could she use them?

She looked at everyone assembled from Cyne-hild, Elene, Father Oswald and finally Ecgbert who appeared to be listening to the exchange intently. Her hand tightened about the bead and she knew what she had to do and which tool she had to use.

'Palni, Moir will be using Watling Street as it is the quickest way to get here once he discovers what has happened. And he is sure to discover the truth once he arrives at the summer gathering and the ransom is paid.'

'Yes, my lady, but didn't you listen to a word I said?'

'Give him the pendant.' Ansithe raised her voice and made certain that Ecgbert was indeed listening. 'Tell him I don't want him to come because he is far too injured from our battle with the outlaws. It would not be a fair fight until he's healed, particularly as he severely damaged his sword arm. First, he heals and then he rescues me. Until then Guthmann holds the advantage.'

Palni took the pendant. 'For you, my lady, I will do it, but you will cause his death.'

She struggled to breathe. 'Do as I request. At the very least, it means you can no longer be held as a hostage and might be able to assist Moir in his recovery.'

Palni unhappily nodded. 'Very well, my lady, but this is going to end badly.'

Elene came over to Ansithe. 'I thought…'

'Moir always made light of his injuries,' Ansithe said quickly and hoped Elene would not question her too closely. 'He won't be able to fight for weeks. I know because I saw the full extent of the wound later when we spoke in the tent. If he is to have any hope of survival, he must ensure Guthmann does not have the upper hand.'

Elene gulped. 'I hadn't realised. Let's hope he stays away until he heals fully.'

'If anyone dares whisper about my friend Palni's escape,' Father Oswald proclaimed, 'his immortal soul will be put in danger.'

Ansithe watched Ecgbert, who pretended to be suddenly interested in the chalice Father Oswald used when he visited the poor. She knew he had heard every word and that he would be unable to resist spreading the gossip to her father. She was counting on it. Every single tool she possessed needed to be used in this fight to preserve Moir's life.

She lowered her voice and murmured to Elene, 'Let us hope Moir understands my message and acts accordingly.'

Elene squeezed her hand. 'I hope he is sensible for all our sakes.'

'Someone moves towards us,' Bjartr said in a low voice to Moir. 'It won't be the Lady Valkyrie and her sister. More's the pity.'

Moir nodded, putting his hand on the pommel of his sword. 'I heard. Be on your guard. Few travel willingly in the dark.'

They'd made excellent progress since they set out from the summer gathering, only stopping briefly for a bit of hard bread and cheese. Moir reckoned they had another half-day's journey before they reached Baelle Heale and they still stood a chance of reaching Ansithe before she inadvertently blundered into Guthmann's trap.

'Moir, is that you?' Palni's voice came out of the darkness. 'I find you at last.'

Moir tensed in the saddle. 'Tell me your being here has nothing to do with Lady Ansithe.'

'She sent me.' Palni appeared out of the darkness and held out his mother's pendant. 'Her token. She bade me to give it to you. The priest assisted me in escaping.'

Moir muttered a curse. 'Then she is already at Baelle Heale.'

'And Guthmann Ulfson as well. A bad business, Moir. Her brother-in-law was murdered because he objected to Guthmann being betrothed to Lady Ansithe.'

'I am aware Guthmann is there and what he intends for my lady. I'd hoped to reach Lady Ansithe before she arrived.'

'Lady Ansithe asked that you not come because she feared you were too injured from your fight with the outlaws. If you had any feelings for her, you were to stay away.'

Moir unleashed a volley of curses, punching the air with his sword arm as he did. 'You must have told her that I would ignore her wishes. I will protect her from Guthmann with my last breath.'

Palni stroked his chin. 'From the way she was talking, she made it sound as though you were practically on your deathbed or that you had nearly lost your sword arm in the fight. She spoke in such a loud voice, I felt certain she would be heard in the hall.'

Moir went still. Ansithe was trying to send him a message. 'Who was there when she said it?'

'Her sisters, Father Oswald and that weasel-faced steward of hers.'

The weasel-faced steward who always reported everything to his master. Moir smiled. He knew exactly what she was doing. He had to make sure her scheme succeeded. 'Underestimate my lady at your peril, Palni. Ansithe knows precisely what she is doing. She is going to be a fearsome tafl player once I teach her.'

'Well, I am pleased you know what Lady Ansithe is on about for I am sure I don't.'

Moir rummaged in his saddlebag for his spare linen tunic. He started to tear it into strips. Palni looked at him as if he had gone mad.

'I need to use my undertunic to fashion bandages and a sling,' Moir explained. 'I will not fail my lady.'

Chapter Sixteen

'Thank you, Father, for saying that we can wait to celebrate my nuptials until the thirty days of mourning for Leofwine have passed,' Ansithe said the next afternoon while she sat in the main hall next to her father, picking at her pottage and trying not to be sick with fear. Thirty days had to be long enough for Moir to arrive and then she could put the next part of the scheme into action. She had to hope that Palni would find and deliver her message in time and that Moir would understand precisely what she meant.

To her surprise, her father had readily agreed to the delay. Her father was all smiles now that he believed she had gone along with his scheme.

'I do not want anyone saying that we offended anyone with the match.' Her father patted her hand. 'And you have managed to coax Cynehild and Wulfgar from the church. I worried that you might claim sanctuary. It could have caused grave difficulties. I should have known that you of all people would be sensible.'

'Father Oswald is nervous enough about the Heathen Horde without making his fears come true.'

A shout rang out that horsemen were approaching.

'Are you expecting anyone, Father?' Ansithe asked. Her stomach knotted. It was far too soon for Moir to arrive. She had to hope Palni had discovered him and delivered her message, or otherwise he'd be riding straight into the trap Guthmann had set for him.

Guthmann stood and gave a triumphant grin.

'Allow these men to come into the yard, Ealdorman Wulfgar,' Guthmann proclaimed. 'Let us see what they are on about before my men act. I am fundamentally a man of peace unless provoked.'

Ansithe balled impotent fists at the bare-faced lies Guthmann told and the way her father cravenly simpered. Her father, Guthmann and his men went out. Nodding to her sisters and Father Oswald to accompany her, Ansithe followed them.

Moir rode into the yard with Nerian of Wessex and his men, and Bjartr and the other Northmen from the *felag* that she'd captured trotting behind them. Moir's right arm was cradled in a sling.

When he dismounted, he seemed to lean heavily on his left leg. Ansithe gasped, but then she saw the amber pendant hanging about his neck.

She struggled to keep a straight face. Moir had acted on her message. Everything now depended on getting this right. Guthmann must remain in ignorance until the counter-trap had been sprung.

'To what do we owe this visitation?' Guthmann demanded, breaking all protocol that her father should speak first. Ansithe noticed that her father remained steadfastly silent.

'Nerian of Wessex, my lord.' The Wessex captain stepped forward. 'I have arrived to deliver the gold I obtained for ransoming Lady Ansithe's various captives.'

Her father held out his hands and his eyes took on a greedy gleam. 'I'm her father. You may give the gold to me.'

'Lady Ansithe is a widow and under Mercian law is therefore entitled to the gold in her own right,' Nerian replied. 'The lady captured both the Northmen under the *jaarl* Andvarr's command and the Danes whom the new Mercian King has purchased. The King has instructed me to give the gold to none but her. Mercia owes her a debt of gratitude for capturing such a fierce band of rogue warriors.'

Guthmann and her father both appeared to

have swallowed particularly sour plums. Ansithe went forward and collected the purse, which was heavier than she had anticipated.

'We are prepared,' Nerian murmured. 'Be ready. Moir has a plan.'

She gave a barely perceptible nod before retreating to where her sisters and Father Oswald stood. She rapidly handed it to Father Oswald for safekeeping in the church.

When Father Oswald retired to put the gold away, she turned to her father. 'These men should be offered refreshment, Father, before they return to court.'

'That would be kind, my lady. The men are parched from their travels,' Moir said, stepping forward.

'Why are you here, Moir Mimirson? You are Andvarr's man, little better than a dog by all accounts as I've never known you to disobey a direct order from your master,' Guthmann said with a sneer.

Moir lifted a brow. 'Nerian of Wessex required a guide. I volunteered my services. He accepted.'

'Moir Mimirson!' Her father turned red. 'This is the man who defiled my daughter if the tales my steward told me last night prove true. You must avenge this gross insult, Guthmann. My daughters are not whores.'

Guthmann blew on his nails. 'I warned And-varr before we left that any insult to my woman would be punished. And now I hear tales of you, Moir, defiling my bride-to-be after our betrothal was agreed with her father. Is this true?'

'It depends on your definition of defiling,' Moir retorted. 'I never comment on my relations with a lady, particularly not one as vibrant as the Lady Ansithe.'

Guthmann's scar on his face throbbed to a mottled purple. 'I cannot tolerate this insult to pass unnoticed or remarked on. I will not be made a cuckold.'

His voice fairly rose to a screech and he started breathing heavily. Ansithe wondered if he was going to start foaming at the mouth.

'You wish to fight me?' Moir peered intently at Guthmann. 'One on one to settle who has claim over this woman?'

Guthmann's gaze slowly drifted over Moir and appeared to take in the sling and the awkward way Moir stood.

Ansithe's heart pounded so loudly that she thought Guthmann must hear it. He had to take the bait.

Guthmann finally smiled. 'I had thought I would appoint a champion to fight on my behalf, but given the gravity of what you have done, I will undertake the task myself. I will admit to longing to see the day when I spilled your blood, Moir.'

Behind him, his men gave an ear-splitting roar.

'I accept with pleasure, Guthmann Bloodaxe. On one condition—right here and right now.'

'You were always arrogant. Know that I look forward to teaching your lady the true meaning of being bedded by a Dane.'

Moir took off his sling, awkwardly unsheathed his sword and struggled to raise it to shoulder height, much to the amusement of Guthmann's men. 'The time for talking has passed.'

Guthmann snapped his fingers and a gleaming sword was put in his hand. 'I am going to enjoy this.'

Moir forced his arm to stay still. Never had a fight or battle meant as much to him. He was fighting not only for his life, but for Ansithe and the future he hoped to share with her. 'Shall we begin?'

Guthmann made the first move, stabbing with his sword. Moir twisted at the last instant and the sword thrust missed. The circled each other and Guthmann seemed to grow in confidence, making short cutting stabs. Moir took a step backwards and stumbled to one knee. The impact made his sword fall out of his hand.

'Andvarr swore you were an excellent warrior, but I see now you were simply an overblown windbag. You are going to die today and I will take your woman until she screams. Think about that as you draw your last breath.'

'You overestimate your ability. You missed the obvious, Guthmann.' Moir rolled, grabbed his sword and forced it upwards.

Unable to stop his own downward movement, Guthmann met Moir's sword, gave a gurgle and fell, impaled. The cheers rang out.

Moir reached down and picked up Guthmann's sword. 'Does anyone wish to challenge me for the leadership of Guthmann's *felag*?'

To a man, Guthmann's men knelt and swore allegiance to their new leader. Then they rose and beat their swords against their shields, swearing to defend him and him alone to the death.

'I believe I made an error of judgement,' Ansithe's father said in a hesitant voice, tugging at his tunic and looking extremely frail all of a sudden.

'I believe you did,' Ansithe answered coolly. 'It is something you will have to ponder for the rest of your days, Father.'

Moir motioned for quiet.

'You are free from Guthmann Bloodaxe and his unwelcome attentions, Lady Ansithe. Free to do what you wish in the future. I also relinquish any claim over you. And I pledge to fight anyone who dares declare that you have been loose with your favours.' Moir crossed to her and handed her Guthmann's sword.

Ansithe took it and held it awkwardly. After all this, Moir was freeing her? Had this all been about Moir's quarrel with Guthmann, rather than his feelings toward her? A great black pit opened in her stomach. She wanted to go somewhere and hide rather than face the humiliation of Moir proclaiming nothing had ever passed between them in front of everyone. He'd done it to save her reputation, but she knew the words would ultimately destroy her. 'I take this in the spirit given,' she said quietly.

'Can we go somewhere where we won't be disturbed?' Moir asked in a low voice as more cheers rang out. 'There are things which must be said to each other, things best said without others listening. Please.'

'The apiary.' Ansithe pasted on a bright smile. 'I believe my sisters are capable of organising a feast to celebrate while I attend to this. It will not take long.'

'Take as long as you need.' Cynehild's gaze narrowed and she rolled up her sleeves. 'I am going to enjoy this. We will use the best mead, Father, and none of your nonsense about cost either.'

* * *

After the noise of the yard, the apiary's gentle hum of bees seemed incredibly peaceful. Ansithe rested her hand on a disused skep to ensure that her knees didn't give way. She wanted to run her hands down Moir's form and check that he remained uninjured.

'Appropriate spot, considering how we met.' He gave a crooked smile which made her heart skip a beat. 'I like to think the bees will approve of my actions today.'

'What do you have to say to me?' Ansithe asked before she threw her arms about his neck and demanded to know why he had declared in front of everyone that there was nothing between them.

He took off the pendant and held it out. 'I owe you a debt, a debt I can never repay. Without your help, Guthmann would remain a potent force rather than lying face down in the dirt.'

She turned towards a skep and focused on the bees going in and out. Her throat ached from unshed tears. She had been convinced that when he arrived, he would want to marry her, that he'd returned to save her. He had never made it a secret that things were going to end between them. She had made the error of falling in love with him. 'I am pleased my message worked. I had to use the tools I had to hand. That is why you gave me the pendant—to use in case Guthmann arrived. I've no further need for it.'

He froze. 'The pendant belonged to my mother. I gave it to you because I wanted you to know I would return. I planned on returning to you with honour and sound prospects as Andvarr's right-hand man, but it was not to be.'

Ansithe gulped. He had given it to her as a symbol that he would return, rather than because he had thought Guthmann might be there. 'It worked out. You saved me. You saved everyone here from him. We have no more debts to each other.'

His finger traced a line on her cheek. 'I want you to know that I will never dishonour you and that you will always have a choice.'

Her heart thumped as she glanced up into his face. His eyes were warm pools of summer blue. The hope which had faded came back in full force. Maybe he did have some feelings for her. 'I know that,' she whispered.

'Then will you be my wife, and share the rest of my life? Not because I beat Guthmann or because your father demands it, but because it is something you desire with your whole heart. You showed me what my life could be like and it will be all the richer with you being in it. I love you, Ansithe.'

'But you will require children now that you are a great warlord.'

'Don't you love me?'

'With all my heart, but someone must think practically.'

'I think I have more than successfully proved you are anything but shrivelled up.' He drew his brows together. 'I want you and you alone, not some brood mare whose only function is to give me heirs. Marry me. Be my life partner. Let our future together take care of itself. Love me.'

Ansithe lifted her hand and stroked his cheek, her warrior from the North who had come to rescue her and then had ensured she would be the one to determine her own future. Then she slipped the pendant back on. 'Willingly and with all my heart. Father Oswald volunteered to perform the ceremony this morning after he heard Ecgbert's whispering gossip about us.'

His laugh rumbled in her ear, warming her straight down to her toes. 'You were very certain of my ability to defeat Guthmann if you agreed to that.'

'Someone had to plan for the future as I know about your reluctance to.' She put her mouth next to his. 'And you must admit I was rather clever this time.'

'More than clever.' He captured her lips.

'Why didn't you ask me to marry you before you left?' she asked when she could speak again.

'I had to thought to keep you safe and to ask your father for your hand in the proper manner, once I was free from captivity and could offer you more than an uncertain future, but events overtook me.' He tightened his arms about her. 'I've left Andvarr and am now my own man. My future is ours to make what we can of it.'

Her mouth dropped open. He had left the safety of the *jaarl* Andvarr's *felag*? The man he'd sworn to obey for the rest of his life? 'Why did you leave?'

'My duty to my heart's keeper transcends everything else.' He rapidly explained about what has passed between him and Andvarr.

Ansithe forgot how to breathe. If she had had any lingering doubts about his love and devotion, his words put them to rest. He was not Andvarr's man, but hers and hers alone. 'You hit Bjartr's father. There will be no return from that.'

'Sent him right on his arse. He tried to tell me to forget you, that there would be other women for me.' His arms tightened about her. 'There will never be another woman than my Valkyrie for me. You've accomplished what I never thought possible—you have made me become a better man.'

'Your love and your belief in me has made

me into a better woman. You have made me see that I was letting other people define me rather than defining who I was myself. You made me see that there was more to life than simply existing and you are right—I am anything but shrivelled up.'

Moir moved to kiss her again, but she put her hands on his chest, holding him off.

'Why are Bjartr and the others from the *felag* here?'

'They decided to join me in this quest. They said your *felag* had not been disbanded until you declared it had. When Andvarr understood Bjartr's intention to accompany me back here, he proclaimed his son had become a man and therefore must go where Bjartr willed.' He raised her hand to his lips. 'We can go wherever you want. Constantinople. Iceland. Or even stay here in Baelle Heale if you prefer. It is your choice. I go where you go.'

To go travelling and see places she'd only ever dreamt about. Ansithe knew that with Elene and Cynehild in charge now her father's honour was diminished, Baelle Heale and its people would be safe.

'And Guthmann's men? They declared you their *jaarl* with one voice,' she asked. The time for travel would happen, one day, but first they had responsibilities to the people who had put their faith in them. 'They swore to follow you to the death.'

'What of them?' Moir asked. 'They can find other lords if you wish to travel. I want to spend my life making us happy and content, not other people.'

Making them happy. Ansithe smiled. She wanted that as well.

'Guthmann will have been awarded lands, former Mercian lands which will need to be properly managed with a lord who cares about his people more than he cares about glory. And I can think of no one better than you to do it.' She laid her head against his chest and listened to his steady heartbeat thrumming in her ear. 'Those men deserve a chance to prove they are more than raiders who simply take whatever they want. They need to prove that they can help re-build this land. You and I can ensure they have that chance.'

Moir titled her chin upwards so that she could drown in his eyes. 'Your wish is my command, my lady Valkyrie.'

Epilogue

~~~~~~~~~~~~~~~~~~~~~~~~~~~~~~~~~~

*Early autumn AD 874, outside Derby—one of
the five boroughs under Viking control after
the peace treaty*

Each day brought some new measure of happiness to Ansithe. After they reached Guthmann's
lands which Moir had been given as a wedding
gift from Andvarr, Moir had built the longhouse
into something to be proud of—something that
was not quite of the North nor fully Mercian.
The land which had been left to rot during the
various wars had quickly turned productive. Instead of being silent, the woods rang with the
sound of axes as the undergrowth was tamed and
used to build houses for Moir's men, including
Bjartr, who with his father's approval was determined to serve under Moir.

The day Ansithe had felt the baby quicken

in her womb she burst into tears. Moir had held her until the storm passed, before asking softly why she had been willing to believe the worst of herself. She had had no answer and, holding her week-old son in her arms, she still didn't.

'If that isn't the most beautiful sight in the entire world, I have no idea what is,' Moir said, stopping short when he returned unexpectedly from the fields. 'My son in the arms of my very clever wife.'

'You are biased and I love you for saying it. But you should be overseeing getting the crops in.'

'My only quarrel with you is your stubborn refusal to see how lovely you are, particularly today with Mathios in your arms.' He dropped a kiss on her lips. 'Remind me to return early often. Bjartr and the others are capable of working hard.'

Ansithe clutched Mathios tighter. 'Is something wrong?'

'Palni sent word—Cedric has confessed to supplying the outlaws and to working with Guthmann to ensure the capture of your father and Leofwine.'

Ansithe stared at Moir in astonishment. 'How did Palni uncover this?'

'Cedric tried to recruit him to undermine Cynehild. Of all people! He felt Palni would be ripe for this sort of duplicitous behaviour being from the North.'

Ansithe burst out laughing. Moir placed another kiss on the end of her nose. 'My sentiments entirely.'

'Did Palni say anything else?' she asked, lowering her voice so as not to wake their son. 'How do my father and sisters fare?'

'They were delighted to hear about Mathios and will visit soon. However, recently your father bleated noises about Cynehild and Elene finding husbands. Cynehild put him in his place. She mourns Leofwine and refuses to consider anything for either of them until she has returned his sword to their old lands. Only after that will she speak about future alliances. Palni promises to escort her and keep her from harm. They plan to visit here on their way back.'

Ansithe watched Mathios blow a milk bubble in his sleep. Cynehild certainly knew how to manage their father. 'I wish Nerian had made an offer for Elene before he returned to Wessex to settle his father's estate. We could have found him a place in our hall.'

'I admire a man who wishes to make his own way in the world. If he is the right man for her, he will return. Now it is time this young man slept.' Moir took Mathios from her and laid him in the cradle he'd carved this summer. Then he turned to Ansithe and raised her up into his arms. 'And enough about others, I need some time with my wife.'

'What are you thinking about?' she whispered at the tenderness of his expression.

He stroked the hair from her forehead. 'I once thought my destiny was never-ending war, but I was wrong. My true destiny is with you and caring for our growing family.'

'It is destiny for us both.'

* * * * *

Author Note

While it might seem incredible that bees could have been used as an effective weapon against the Vikings, Aethelflaed, the Lady of Mercians, and her supporters successfully used this technique in Chester in 891 to stop a Viking attack. I borrowed the technique because, as a beekeeper, it amused me.

We do not know much about Mercia, that slightly shadowy kingdom which centred around the British Midlands and included North London. Much of Anglo-Saxon history during this period concentrates on Wessex and its struggles rather than looking at the other kingdoms in Britain.

With regard to the Danes' conquest of East Anglia in 870—surely a momentous event—we only know precisely thirty-five words from Anglo-Saxon chronicles circa 870: 'The here rode over Mercia into East Anglia and took up winter settlement at Thetford. And that winter King Edmund fought with them and the Danes took victory and slew the King and took all the land.'

The 'here' are the Viking army and when Mercia is mentioned it is mainly in relation to Wessex.

Aethelflaed, of course, was Alfred's daughter and is quite rightly celebrated as the woman who saved Britain.

It is unclear after 871, when the King departed, why the rulers of Mercia were so carefully styled Lord or Lady of Mercia rather than King or Queen. This could be because none of the royal line remained, or for some unknown reason. Much is lost to the mists of history. Or perhaps the historians have not sufficiently pieced everything together yet.

Also, we don't really know about the relationship between the kingdoms. After Aethelflaed, her nephew Athelstan did unite England, but we don't know the actual politics or if some people preferred the Northmen to their neighbours.

We do know that in approximately 871 a peace of sorts did happen. The King of Mercia fled and was replaced by Ceolburgh for a few years. History does not recount what happened to him. After him the Mercians did not have a king or queen, but a lord. The peace treaty established the five boroughs of the Vikings—modern-day Derby, Leicester, Stamford, Lincoln and Nottingham—and the peace gave Aelfred of Wessex time to build his burghs and plan his next move.

The next time the Vikings did not find conquering as straightforward, but the Vikings had conquered West Mercia and were planning to stay. The next two hundred years—until 1066, with the Viking defeat at Stamford Bridge—the Vikings and the Anglo-Saxons vied for control of the British Isles.

Primary sources dealing with this historical period remain scarce for many reasons and those which exist are generally highly biased accounts. Archaeology often raises more questions than it answers.

As ever, I have tried to be true to the time and any historical mistakes are my own.

If you are interested in this period, may I recommend the following books?

Adams, Max, *Aelfred's Britain: War and Peace in the Viking Age* (Head of Zeus Ltd, London, 2017)

Ferguson, Robert, *The Hammer and the Cross: A New History of the Vikings* (Penguin Books, London, 2010)

Jesch, Judith, *Women in the Viking Age* (The Boydell Press, Woodbridge, Suffolk, 1991)

Magnusson, Magnus, KBE, *The Vikings* (Tempus Publishing, Stroud, Gloucestershire, 2003)

Oliver, Neil, *Vikings A History* (Orion Books, 2012)

Parker, Philip, *The Northmen's Fury: A History of the Viking World* (Jonathan Cape, London, 2014)

Rackham, Oliver, *Trees & Woodland in the British Landscape: The Complete History of Britain's Trees, Woods & Hedgerows* (Phoenix Press, London, 2001)

Williams, Gareth, Pentz, Peter and Wemhoff, Matthias, eds, *Vikings: Life and Legend* (British Museum Press, London, 2014)

Williams, Thomas, *Viking Britain: An Exploration* (William Collins, London, 2017)

COMING SOON!

We really hope you enjoyed reading this book. If you're looking for more romance, be sure to head to the shops when new books are available on

Thursday 26th December

To see which titles are coming soon, please visit

millsandboon.co.uk/nextmonth

MILLS & BOON

Coming next month

THE SECRETS OF LORD LYNFORD
Bronwyn Scott

Eliza should have left when she had the chance. She should not have lingered in the garden, tempting fate. She'd come out thinking to put some distance between herself and those dark eyes. But the garden hadn't been far enough.

He moved, subtly positioning his body to block her departure, a hand at her arm in gentle restraint, his voice soft in the darkness. 'When will I see you again?' It was 'will' with him, not 'may.' Lynford wasn't the sort of man to beg for a woman's attention. He went forward confidently, assuming the attention would be given. *Will*. The potency of that one word sent a frisson of warm heat down her spine. His dark gaze held hers, intent on an answer—*her* answer. Despite his confident assumptions, he was allowing that decision to be all hers.

'I don't think that would be wise. Business and pleasure should not mix.' She could not relent on this or she would come to regret it. An affair could ruin her and everything she'd worked for. The shareholders in the mines would no doubt love to discover a sin to hold against her.

'Not wise for whom, Mrs Blaxland?' The back of his hand traced a gentle path along the curve of her jaw. 'You are merely a patron of the school I sponsor. I don't see any apparent conflict of interest.'

'Not wise for either of us.' If she stood here and argued with him, she would lose. Sometimes the best way to win an argument was simply to leave. Eliza exercised that option now in her firmest tones, the ones she reserved for announcing decisions in the board room. 'Good night, Lord Lynford.' She was counting on him being gentleman enough to recognise a refusal and let her go this time, now that any ambiguity between them had been resolved.

Continue reading
THE SECRETS OF LORD LYNFORD
Bronwyn Scott

Available next month
www.millsandboon.co.uk

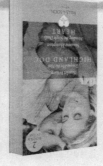

MILLS & BOON

True Love

Romance from the Heart

Celebrate true love with tender stories of
heartfelt romance, from the rush of falling
in love to the joy a new baby can bring,
and a focus on the emotional
heart of a relationship.